The woman's face floated amid the tree branches just outside her window. The barren limbs were a mass of twisted shapes that trembled and shook in a crazy dance with the wind. The face swayed there in the branches. "Hurry. Hurry," Karen called out, tensed and waiting.

The woman entered the room and stood smiling down at Karen from the foot of the bed. Her eyes were wild, dancing with a restless fire, as if, should she choose, she could see all the way past Karen to sear burning holes in the bedclothes beneath her. . . .

The woman resisted Karen's attempt to pull her closer and spoke through closed lips, the steamy sound slipping softly along Karen's ears and face: *You are mine.* Her breath and wordless words seemed to settle in chill blue crystals on Karen's cheek, stinging like the passionate kiss of a lover. *My heart has found you. . . .*

The House at Pelham Falls

Brenda Weathers

The House at Pelham Falls

Brenda Weathers

The Naiad Press Inc.
1986

Printed in the United States of America
First Edition

Cover design by the Women's Graphic Center
Typesetting by Sandi Stancil
Edited by Katherine V. Forrest

Library of Congress Cataloging-in-Publication Data

Weathers, Brenda, 1936–
The House at Pelham Falls.

I. Title.
PS3573.E147H6 1986 813'.54 86-12807
ISBN 0-930044-79-7

for my sister

Carolyn

The author wishes to thank absolutely everybody, especially Kathleen Boyle, Caitlin Sullivan, Rebecca McLeish and Victoria Lewis—and my Freshman English Teacher who flunked me in composition.

About Brenda Weathers

I was born in a small town in Texas in 1936. As a child the word I loved best, either to think, or better yet speak, was the word "she." I loved it when the radio told of a storm heading for the Texas coast as back then all hurricanes were given women's names and the combination of the female with anything of power was heady stuff.

I came out at 15 in a West Texas cotton field during a sandstorm and have been a lesbian from that windy and eventful day to this one. In 1958 I was expelled from Texas Women's University for being a dyke–arrested and questioned–then escorted to the dorm by police to retrieve my belongings. The episode, rather than sending me scurrying toward the conventions of heterosexuality instead served as the making of an activist. I was an early member of the Los Angeles Gay Liberation Front and I have devoted my time and career almost exclusively to my community every since. In 1974 I secured the largest federal grant ever given to an openly lesbian organization and founded the Alcoholism Center for Women in Los Angeles. That organization is still vital and alive twelve years later. More currently, I am a Mayoral appointee to a Seattle Task Force on Gay/Lesbian issues and was recently named as one of the Advocate 400, a listing of prominent activists from across the country.

I began writing three years ago when a friend invited me to attend her creative writing class. I recently purchased a rustic bungalow in Seattle with a view of Puget Sound and the Olympic Mountains, which I happily share with seven cats and a bulldog named Daisy.

prologue

Pelham Falls, Maine
1891

By early December, slanting drifts of snow rose to the shutters of the McCartland's austere farmhouse; a shoveled out path leading from the kitchen door cut through a bank of white the height of a man's shoulders. Down a sloping embankment in front of the house lay the sea, its lead-grey surface troubled by a stiff cold wind. On many a recent day a Nor'easter had blown waves high onto the rocks below where they crashed in great white sheets of saltwater and spume.

Blessing McCartland sat in the warm kitchen, her rocker drawn close to the fire. The room was silent except for the creak of her chair on the pine floor. She dropped a freshly peeled potato into the wooden bowl at her feet and reached for another. A smile tugged at a corner of her mouth as she circled her paring knife under the thick brown skin. It was almost time.

She rose, poured cold water from the pump into the bowl, and glanced about her. The transformation that had taken place seemed still so fragile she scarcely dared breathe when thinking of it.

* * * * *

Blessing had married Ian McCartland fifteen years earlier, though she had not wanted to. She had been twenty-seven then and fast approaching an age when she would be considered unmarriageable. While that prospect upset Blessing not in the least, it troubled her parents to no small extent. Her two brothers would, naturally, inherit the farm; one had already moved in his new bride, and the problems of having a spinster underfoot seemed to them burdensome and embarrassing. Worse, or so they reasoned, Blessing would live set apart from the ordained responsibilities of wife and mother.

She suffered no lack of eligible suitors; quite the contrary, for she was an extraordinarily pretty girl. Often in summer or at harvest time several young men at a time lounged on the wide veranda that ran the length of Blessing's house. During such occasions Blessing's mother was most happy to provide trays of lemonade or a pitcher of cool water from the well, which the young men sipped while looking shyly over the tops of their drinks. Perhaps, the looks said, they might catch Blessing's eye and spark a smile, or, more hopefully, get her aside from the others for a walk or a buggy ride during the cool of the evening.

Through it all, Blessing remained unmoved and aloof,

looking beyond them to a place no one else could see, and where no one else was included.

She was waiting. For what she couldn't name precisely, but she was certain that, once glimpsed, she would recognize and claim it as her own. While she waited she wove dreams for herself, and she painted. On Christmas her parents had given her a set of paints and she had set about rendering pictures on small pieces of stone, wood, or whatever was at hand. As she grew toward womanhood her paintings became more precise and detailed, yet retained a dreamy air, as if painted by someone who had not actually seen the flock of quail in flight or the delicate rose and violet flowers but who had conjured each exquisite stroke from a dream. She did not aspire to larger canvases, content to show the warmth and color within her in small pieces. At her father's urgings she began to exhibit at the county fair and kept a wooden box for each ribbon won. With her prize money she purchased ovals of stone and ivory, and gilded frames.

By the summer of her twenty-seventh year all the young suitors had, one by one, given a resigned shrug and married others. The veranda was empty, except for Blessing and the colorful world of her dreams. She often sat there alone, her eyes on the far distance, dreaming of riding a rented coach all the way to Boston by herself, or tasting the sweet meat of oranges in January, or the even sweeter meat of passion. When she thought these things, her eyes darkened and her lips swelled, and she knew in her belly an aching not one of the young men had inspired. She sipped her lemonade slowly, never taking her eyes from the distance, neither noticing nor caring that the veranda was empty, save for her.

The spectre of Blessing's spinsterhood continued as the subject of whispered conversations late at night or after Blessing had left the supper table and gone to the veranda.

In that same summer, Ian McCartland's wife died. Ian was only twenty years Blessing's senior, and already his face resembled an apple left too long in the sun. He was a quiet and reasonable man and soon would be in need of female company. Blessing's parents set about arranging a match. As his first marriage had produced no offspring Blessing would be doubly fortunate, for she would be able to start a family of her own. Her parents were also mindful of Ian's two hundred acre coastal farm, a beautiful spread set on a bluff overlooking the sea and with a view of a pleasant rocky cove. It had a good sturdy barn, apple orchards, and acres of potatoes and corn. If it was not Blessing's destiny to be happy in marriage, then at least she could be of the gentry.

Ian agreed readily, casting sidelong glances at the beautiful young woman as he stood, hat in hand, before her parents' hearth. Blessing said nothing. To her parents she protested loudly, but she might as well have shouted her resistance to the whitewashed balustrades of the veranda or the sea itself. Blessing's mother wept and wrung her hands, her father shouted and railed. Her brothers sat in stony silence, lips set in thin tight lines. Blessing's selfishness, her unwillingness to think of anyone but herself, became the only topic of family discussions.

There seemed no peace left. She could not spend time alone on the veranda, for as soon as she seated herself, her father or one of her brothers would come to admonish her for her selfishness and the disgrace she seemed bent on bringing to the family.

The wedding took place on a Sunday in late fall. When all the cider had been drunk, the food eaten, and the merry noises of congratulation all given, Ian drove his new bride home in his wagon. Behind her in the wagonbed were Blessing's paints, two trunks, and a black mongrel puppy, all she would need in changing one man's home for another's. As they rode slowly past flaming red maples and yellow pumpkins in rows in the fields, Blessing felt neither fear nor anticipation. She was merely changing the exterior setting in which she lived her dream-filled days. As a daughter in her parents' home she had done what was expected of her; she hoped there would be little difference in the home of Ian McCartland. Until recently her parents had not intruded on her private world and neither, she prayed, would Ian.

They rode in silence most of the way, Ian being a man who considered words a nuisance, a commodity to be used sparingly at best. He covered his nervousness by clicking his teeth at the horses and snapping the reins smartly over their broad backs.

When at last they turned into the maple-lined drive leading to the house, Blessing felt her first real happiness. The house sat in a clearing facing the sea, its clapboards newly whitewashed, a fresh coat of green paint on the shutters. It was a house of graceful bearing with simple lines but proud as an unadorned matron. One of her tasks as the new mistress, she resolved, would be to do paintings of the house in varying lights and seasons.

Blessing's life with Ian bore her neither surprise nor children and was much as she thought it would be. Year by year, they coaxed a living from the hardscrabble earth. There were always fields to be cut, fences to mend, animals to tend and butter to be made, so that the routine of chores ordered their lives, provided their conversation and, eventually, their hiding place from each other. On such occasions as was demanded of her, Blessing accommodated Ian's body into her own, but these infrequent couplings bore not the slightest resemblance to the passion she had imagined from her veranda.

Though Blessing cast her eyes less often on the far distance as the years went on, she continued painting, turning out ample numbers of her drawings of the farm or of the village in Pelham Falls or from pictures in a book of places she had never seen.

When Aimee came to live with them—just a short year ago—Blessing had all but stopped painting. Her life was now too full.

* * * * *

Blessing paced the kitchen and peered occasionally out the window to assure herself that Ian wasn't turning his wagon into the lane. It wasn't his habit to come home early, but she looked just the same. Her peerings were as much her protection as vigilance. The hour before his return for supper was precious to her. She wanted nothing to disturb it.

When Ian first informed her his niece would be coming to live with them, Blessing had been angered. Aimee's parents had died the preceding winter of influenza and while Blessing sympathized, Aimee seemed to her just another mouth to feed, an unwanted intrusion into her solitary world. Ian persisted, reasoning that Blessing could use help with the milking and housework, and in the end Blessing had agreed.

Now, and she nearly wept thinking of it, now she couldn't imagine her life without Aimee McCartland.

Again judging the time, she cocked her head toward the milkshed, listening for Aimee's footfalls. Each day, when the chores had been laid by, the women reserved this hour together, a time only for them. In winter, they sat together in the warm kitchen, but in spring or summer, they often walked by the sea, stopping now and then to examine a delicate shell and place it in an apron pocket. Blessing kept a tapestry-covered box in which she placed especially beautiful mementos of their excursions. There were several fine pink shells, thin as porcelain, so that when held to the light they appeared translucent; and a chard of darkish green glass in the shape of a crescent moon, which Aimee had given her saying the color made her think of Blessing's eyes.

Aimee came softly into the room, lifting it out of the ordinary as might a bowl of sweet smelling flowers. In Blessing's mind's eye even the faded stencil design on the walls flared to life, bright red and vivid.

"I have something for you," Aimee said. She reached into her apron pocket without taking her eyes from Blessing's face. "It was my mother's. She gave it to me as a keepsake just before she died. But I want you to have it. There's something written on the inside."

There was color high on Aimee's cheeks and a dewy film appeared around her lowered lids. "Please. Take it," she said. In the palm of her hand rested a small locket.

Blessing stared down at the gift, so small and perfect, and gingerly took it and opened the clasp. A sepia-tone daguerrotype of Aimee had been fitted into the heart-shaped locket, and opposite the picture, engraved in elegant script on the gold cover, were the words, *My Heart Will Always Find You.*

Except for the treasures gathered during their frequent walks this was the only real present that had passed between them.

Though they seldom touched except by accident or sometimes to hold hands, Blessing could not restrain her need to hold Aimee close. With the jerky, awkward motions of one not accustomed to gestures of affection she reached for Aimee and, throwing her arms around the slim woman, pulled her tight and held her. Time slipped a cog, and then another, spinning dizzyingly past the mark when an embrace between women should have ended. Blessing stood rooted and timeless, aware of the pressure of small breasts against her, a pressure made sweeter by the thin cloth which separated them.

At last, Blessing let her arms fall to her sides, relinquishing her hold on a moment in eternity. Both pairs of eyes stared at the yellow pine floor. Neither woman spoke, for neither wanted to break the bright tingling silence.

With one hand at her throat, as if to grasp the breath caught there, Blessing turned toward the table. Her long hands fluttered and finally came to rest on her small easel.

"I haven't finished your portrait," she whispered. Tomorrow was Aimee's twentieth birthday, and Blessing wanted to complete a miniature of her face as a gift for that occasion.

"Yes," Aimee said, and sat across from Blessing at the table. Blessing began to paint in the moist pink color on Aimee's cheeks. In a silence richer than all the words she knew, Blessing worked deftly, shading in the dark blonde of Aimee's hair and mixing the perfect shade of blue for the eyes. She was sure, as she worked, that her painting had never shown more grace.

* * * * *

Ian delivered his disappointing news at the supper table. Mrs. Hudson's family was expected for the holidays, he announced, and as her usual housekeeper was ill, he had promised to bring Aimee for a day of help around the house. The birthday party Blessing had planned would have to be postponed until evening.

Early next morning, Ian and Aimee, bundled in heavy coats and thick scarves, set out for town. Ian wanted an early start on the icy and treacherous roads. Blessing watched from the window, her breath a circle of fog on the pane. She continued watching until she could no longer see the wagon and, even though disappointed, felt so full of happiness she might burst from a single drop more.

The morning chores went swiftly, propelled along by Blessing's anticipation of the party later in the evening. She brought in an armload of evergreen boughs, several sprigs of holly, and a basket of pine cones from the woods. The house, she vowed, would look as festive as she felt. She allowed herself to pause only occasionally and when she did so, her thoughts turned to Aimee. These delicious moments, moments when she stopped her work and looked out to sea, were filled with Aimee, with her face, with the sound of her and her smell, like a sachet of sweet herbs.

Blessing rose from one such reverie and reached for a cranberry glass compote on top of the sideboard, her vision filled with the image of Aimee's slim throat and pale shoulders arching from the white lace of her camisole. Even as Blessing's fingers came to rest on the cool red glass, she spoke aloud the name of her feelings, saying the words to herself for the very first time. She let out her breath in a long sigh and, clasping the cranberry compote to her breast, knew she would not be deterred. All thoughts, save one, were forgotten. That which she had yearned for from her veranda, the nameless grace that descends now and again on the fortunate to make dreams manifest, was now hers. She did not stop to question the capricious nature of the bestower of such a gift, nor Aimee as its embodiment. She remembered Aimee's arms circled around her, her small hands on Blessing's back, also hesitant to release the embrace. It was enough to be thus blessed.

When the preparations were at last complete, Blessing stood back to admire her handiwork. The house did look festive, better she believed than it ever had. Except for her small paintings in gilded frames on the walls, the rooms were sparsely furnished and empty of adornment. But now, in the light from the kerosene lamps, the house sparkled, reflecting her joy. In the center of the table sat the compote, filled with holly berries and nuts, and beside it the completed portrait. Each time Blessing looked at the red glass she remembered afresh the words she had spoken, remembered them and knew that tonight, after the party was over and Ian was safely in bed, she would say the words to Aimee. A shiver of anticipation ran along her arms when she thought of it, and of holding Aimee close to her again in the evening.

By suppertime, Blessing began to grow uneasy. They should have been back before this. She stared from the window, willing the dark shape of the wagon to appear against the white fields. The first blast of wind, heralding a Nor'easter, rocked against the side of the house and Blessing watched the bare branches of the apple trees bend low before it. A heavy snow was sure to follow. Blessing kept her vigil at the window, her apprehension increasing with each howl of the wind.

When winter's dusk became night and she could no longer see the road, she turned back to the decorated room and pulled her chair close to the stove trying to replace the cold dread inside her with an image of Aimee's face. She looked first at the portrait, then at the pan of Indian pudding set on the back of the stove to cool, and then at her hands twisted around each other in her lap. When these things at last provided all the reassurance within their capacity, she rose and, throwing on a heavy woolen shawl, walked out to the barn, her head bent into the wind. Quickly, she saddled a horse and led it out into the snow-filled night.

As if in a dream, she rode slowly down the dark road, the wind whipping her hair into her mouth and her eyes as she clutched the shawl against her. With each plodding step of the horse, the certainty of what lay ahead, if not the particulars, grew in her so when she saw the wagon, tilted and askew in the road, she was only filling in the grim details.

Last summer, Ian had promised to cut down the dead maple, weakened as it was by many winters. Now it lay across the wagon, torn loose by the storm. Aimee and Ian lay pinned beneath it.

With fingers devoid of sensation, Blessing clawed at the

heavy limb, finally freeing Aimee from beneath its deadly weight. She wrapped Aimee's cold body in the shawl and cradled her head to her breast, holding her tightly as she rocked back and forth in the snow. At last, not knowing what else to do, she picked up a fallen twig and wrote in the fresh snow . . . *My Heart Will Always Find You.*

* * * * *

In the years that followed, time was not kind to Blessing McCartland, nor did she reach out of her house or from herself for anything that might have relieved her spirit. She closed the dark green shutters of her house and never reopened them, for she did not wish to look at the sea again. Her hair became white and sparse. The lines that quickly appeared in her face did so without respect to time and pattern, as if her face had crumbled from within rather than aging in creases and lines. But, from her ravaged face her eyes burned with a cold fire.

After a time neighbors stopped coming to call. They found Blessing too peculiar, an aging wraith in widow's black long after custom dictated she dress and behave so. For a few years the absence of Blessing's miniatures at the county fair was commented upon, then forgotten in the pulse of life in Pelham Falls.

With the passing of time, Blessing's black taffeta dress, which she had worn since the day of the funeral, became limp and soiled. The dress came to hang in dirty tatters around her feet and made a stiff rustling noise when she walked. When the weather turned cold, she wrapped Ian's greatcoat around her and eventually neglected to remove even that when the weather warmed again. On her hands, which no longer painted, she wore knitted gloves, her gnarled fingers protruding through the worn yarn.

Each day at the accustomed hour, Blessing pulled her

chair to the stove and slowly rocked, listening for the sound of footfalls. From the tapestry-covered box in her lap she took first one, then another of the shells and turned them over in her hands, speaking softly to Aimee as she did so.

Her only visitor was the son of the neighboring farmer who had bought up most of her land. The boy came tentatively, handing in her laudanum, then fleeing, afraid of the sight of Blessing McCartland.

Blessing's need for her medicine became stronger, and she directed the neighbor boy to bring her several of the slim brown bottles with increasing frequency. During the summer of 1902, the boy came to the kitchen door as usual, but this time Blessing wasn't waiting there to fetch the bottles from his hand. The boy moved into the room, darkened at midday, and found Blessing slumped in her rocker, a tiny locket clutched in her stiffened hand. Thinking to steal it, he pried it from her fingers and jammed it into his pocket. As he stepped out again into the sunlight, he was overcome by an intense sensation of fear, or guilt—he couldn't be sure which—and threw the locket back into the room where it wedged itself into a deep groove between the boards of the floor.

With only a few folk from surrounding farms and a few paid mourners in attendance, Blessing was buried next to her husband and niece. As the last words of the service were spoken, a stiff breeze came up, flapping the gentlemen's coattails and causing the minister to lose his place in a fluttering of pages. Those present were suddenly anxious to leave and were already turning to go as the words "Rest in peace" were intoned.

On the day following the funeral, a local merchant came and took away the furniture while a neighbor lady removed several cartons of Blessing's paintings. All that was left was the house, a silent sentinel facing the sea, its shutters closed to all that lay beyond them, stubbornly guarding the dreams of Blessing McCartland.

CHAPTER 1

The aging saltbox nestled at the edge of a stand of woods, in stark contrast to the dark gnarled forest beyond. There were green shutters at the windows and a coat of white paint had been recently applied over the worn clapboards.

Karen grabbed the folded *Boston Globe* and reread the circled ad. Older Home for Lease. Waterfront, Pelham Falls, Maine. Had she tried to imagine the home of her dreams she could scarcely have done better than the quaint house and seascape waiting for her at the end of the maple-lined drive.

An untended apple orchard grew behind the house, limbs unpruned, grass thick around twisted trunks. Many of the apples had fallen, yet the branches sagged with the weight of the remaining bright red fruit. Between the orchard and the lane were fields, separated by low stone fences, and full this time of year with brambles and tall yellow grasses.

Lean of bearing, the house faced the sea so that Karen's first view was the broad, slope-roofed angle of its side. It reminded her of a person looking out to the sea, unaware someone had come to call.

"It was built in 1799," Mrs. Gittings, the real estate agent, said reverently. She guided her sedan along the rutted lane, the tires crunching over a blanket of fallen red and gold leaves.

On Karen's right, past the flaming maples, the rock strewn coast shimmered in the afternoon sun. Mrs. Gittings drove slowly, carefully avoiding the worst potholes. As they passed a gap in the row of maples Karen was afforded a view of a sandy rock-sheltered cove. On her left, the fields gave way to a glade. Tree tops and the roof of a neighboring house dotted the ridge.

"This is all that's left of the old McCartland place," Mrs. Gittings said, gesturing at a stone fence that marked the boundary. "Most of the farm was sold off long ago. Now only about a half acre actually belongs to the house. But a lovely property, wouldn't you agree?"

Karen merely nodded, afraid words might break the spell. There was an exquisite stillness about the old house. Even the surf curling onto the shore and the song of a bird hidden in the overgrown orchard added to the dreamy quiet. Sunlight slanted against the many-paned windows, and as she turned to stare at them, the house appeared to wink at her with the bouncing motions of the car.

At last Mrs. Gittings braked to a stop in the dooryard and in one efficient gesture grabbed her clipboard and swooped from the car.

Karen followed more slowly, hesitating at the car before following the agent to the back steps. She stood a moment, her boots deep in overgrown weeds, all her senses engaged in the pleasure of discovery. The crisp fall air was pungent and she took a deep breath, filling her nostrils with the sour-sweet smell of fallen apples and the dark rich smell of the sea.

She lingered a moment more, postponing the pleasure of entering, much in the way one hesitates before opening a gift, and wishing she had a gift of her own to offer.

Mrs. Gittings smiled from the top step. She had been in this business long enough to recognize love at first sight, and had no intention of intruding.

Slowly Karen began walking, savoring the crunch of gravel under her boots and the creak of a loose board on the step. A gull sat perfectly still in the overgrown grass in the sloping front yard, its head cocked toward her. Even a welcoming committee, she thought, and reached out to lift the old-fashioned latch on the back door. It moved easily under her touch; the door creaked slightly as it gave.

Sunlight streamed through the kitchen windows and lay in pools on the burnished wainscoting and wide pine boards of the floor. Even devoid of windowsill plants, colorful cannisters and cozy touches, the room looked cheerful and warm. She noted the wooden pegs in the floor boards and grinned with relief that the wainscoting was free of the layers of chipped grimy paint so often found in houses of this vintage. The room appeared to glow with a deep luster, a patina born of age and untold applications of linseed oil.

Karen took her time, poking into cabinets and looking slowly around the room. Amid modern appliances of stainless steel and copper an old wood cookstove stood against the far wall, probably left as decoration. Even before seeing the rest of the house, she began imagining where she'd place her spice rack and willow-ware plates.

Mrs. Gittings, more than content to wait, watched Karen open cupboards and peer into the small pantry, sizing her up with a practiced eye. On any given weekend in the fall, when the weather was bright and crisp and the colors dazzling, she could be sure of showing property to hordes of people like the young woman exploring the kitchen. Faithfully they came, seeking escape, however illusionary, from the city. This one—she checked her clipboard—wanted a place to tuck herself away on sabbatical. Judging from the tuition charged by the private women's college that employed her, she could well afford the place for a year or so.

Knowing the place was as good as taken, Mrs. Gittings continued her scrutiny. She noted the absence of a wedding band, and the more she watched the young professor, the more she became convinced there wasn't likely to be one—at least not anytime soon. Karen Latham seemed much too absorbed in a clearly singular delight.

There's an interesting contradiction about her, Mrs. Gittings decided, accounting for the difficulty in assigning Karen to one of her customary niches. Fair of face and fine boned, even delicate, had she been wearing other clothes she might have appeared almost Victorian—Mrs. Gittings could see her in a high lace collar, a cameo brooch pinned at her throat. Yet there was a heartiness as well, a robustness probably accentuated by the jeans and plaid Pendleton shirt. Her hair, thick and dark blonde, was piled casually on top of her head, though several strands had come loose during her inspection of the kitchen and were now curling onto her forehead and down the back of her neck.

Karen stood in the doorway between the kitchen and parlor, a hand shoved into the pocket of her jeans. She turned into the parlor and Mrs. Gittings followed, envying the leggy gait and slightly slouched poise that made tall women seem so casually sensual. Mrs. Gittings adjusted her blue polyester blazer over an expanding girth and followed.

"How many will be living here?" she asked to verify her observations.

Karen turned slowly in the center of the room. "Just me," she replied, smiling, and moved to stand in front of the fireplace. "Just me."

In this room, as in the kitchen, the afternoon sun poured through the mullioned windows and cast tiny squares of light on the waxed pine floor. Along the length of the interior wall stood a fireplace with a generous brick hearth. The windows on the adjacent wall allowed a view of the vivid maples along the lane; the twelve-over-twelve windows in front looked out to the sea.

Karen walked to the windows, stepping across a pool of lighted squares, and stared past the sloping yard to the ocean. She lingered a moment, tracing her finger along a pane of glass, listening to the sound of waves breaking far from shore and, closer, the gentle lapping of surf meeting shore at low tide. To her surprise she felt a touch of sadness and withdrew her hand.

Remembering there was still the upstairs, she turned and in three long strides was in the entry hall. With one hand on the wooden ball, she swung around the newel post and up the narrow stairway, leaving Mrs. Gittings behind.

The bedrooms, too, had been restored with loving attention to period and detail. The bluish-grey paint on the woodwork was a color widely used a century ago. The wallpaper, a quaint design of blue ribbons and small red roses, had been carefully chosen to match.

Looking at the sea through open pine shutters, Karen thought the house looked much as it had a hundred years ago. Something more than the lustrous wainscoting, pine floors and small paned windows gave the impression time had been held back—there was something else too, a timelessness she couldn't quite name.

Two of the bedrooms had fireplaces. Karen stood in the larger of them imagining herself on a wintry morning, a cat and a cup of tea beside her, researching her notes before a blazing fire. Visions such as this, of the life she could lead here, sent her loping downstairs, her cheeks flushed.

"It's everything I could have wanted. Where do I sign?"

Mrs. Gittings pulled the lease agreement from her clipboard and led Karen toward an oak table in the kitchen. "By the way, did I mention? All the furniture is included. You'll have little moving to do."

So wrapped up in her discovery of the house, Karen had paid scant attention to furnishings. She looked around her, at fine examples of Americana pine and oak, such as the table and pie safe in the kitchen, and at other items apparently scavenged from local garage sales. A forties-style overstuffed chair and a Windsor rocker sat on either side of a cushioned sofa before the fireplace. Nothing, it seemed, had been purchased to match anything else yet it all merged into unabashed hominess. All the place really needs, Karen thought, are a few throw rugs, prints for the walls, and, of course, shelves of books.

"It's perfect. Everything is perfect." Karen extracted a pen and checkbook from her backpack.

As Karen read over the agreement, Mrs. Gittings chatted amiably. "The owner only used the place in summers when he and his family came up from Boston. Dr. Alexander planned to retire here but. . . ." Mrs. Gittings gave a slight shrug and continued, "When the market is better I'm sure they'll try and sell. But for now they'll be happy with a good tenant."

She smiled at Karen and drew up a chair. "Before the Alexanders, let me see, that would take us back twenty years or more, I believe the house sat empty for a long time. There may have been a few attempts to farm it back around the turn of the century. Actually," she chatted on, warming to her subject, "the place hasn't been a real farm since the days of the McCartlands–and the last of them died off long ago. . . ."

"Uhmmm," Karen said, still reading the agreement.

"Speaking of the McCartlands, here's an interesting bit of history. Blessing, the last of the McCartlands to live here, has developed quite a posthumous reputation."

"Really."

"Apparently she was quite the artist. Her work's shown often and she was included in a recent book on New England women artists. You might even see some of her work in our local antique shops. A few pieces do turn up from time to time."

Karen signed the agreement and pushed it across for Mrs. Gittings' signature. "Yes, I'll keep an eye out for something by her. How soon can I move in?"

"Soon as you like, I suppose. You'll need oil delivered and I'm sure you'll want a phone. If you'll let me know when you'll be up, I'd be happy to help with the arrangements."

"Well, I have some arrangements to make in Boston. . . ." Karen stiffened. The mention of home and the tangle of emotions she'd left there brought the now familiar knot of tension. Did she really have to have a phone? Yes, she supposed. If only she could block out the world for a while. . . . So much had happened lately, so much that refused to fit in the careful design she had made for her life. It was as though she had suddenly found herself lost in an unfamiliar place with no maps or street signs.

Once she had hiked into the Berkshires with a friend, carefully following the marked trails. After an hour or so the rock-lined trails gave way to several footpaths leading into the heavily forested hillside. Some led out, some led twisting and curving toward destinations neither of them knew. Her friend frantically searched her backpack but realized she had forgotten the maps. They had had to retrace their steps. Her present dilemma felt much the same, but she couldn't go back. Where were the maps? Where did the trails lead?

"I'll have to let you know." Karen stood quickly and zipped her checkbook into her pack. "Though I'm already on leave, it could take a couple of weeks. There are a few loose ends. . . ."

"Fine. Just let me know." Mrs. Gittings steered Karen toward the door.

Karen walked beside Mrs. Gittings to the car, her thoughts on the "loose ends" she had so casually mentioned. Walter, at least, would be the easiest. Their relationship had been teetering for months, saved from final collapse only by unspoken words of parting. It had been good with him for a time, or at least comfortable, yet now the whole thing seemed to have happened long ago and to someone else. There had never been wild passion, but by the time Walter entered her life, she had all but given up the notion that such a thing would ever happen to her. Romance, she had decided, was a myth. Her passion was work.

Then, during the summer, the myth was shattered, her carefully constructed world a confusion of opened doorways never sought. "Damn it, Maggi," Karen muttered under her breath. Even in the privacy of her own hearing the words sounded hollow. Karen shook her head and slid into the sedan beside Mrs. Gittings. "Thanks so much for all your help. I'll call in a few days and let you know when I'll be up."

They reached the end of the lane and Karen turned for one last admiring look at her new house. Late afternoon light slashed the shadow of a maple across the still house.

Perhaps here, in this beautiful old house hundreds of miles from home, she could hide herself away, buffer herself with a simpler life. Perhaps, she thought, I'll even try to make a quilt—or preserves. That she had no notion of how to begin such projects, or even how to sew for that matter, wasn't important. It was only important to escape to this place and, once here, fill her time and life with simplicity and isolation.

"By the way," Karen asked, as they turned onto the road "what was the name of that artist?"

"Blessing McCartland," Mrs. Gittings answered, sounding pleased at Karen's interest in local history.

CHAPTER 2

An orange and black truck lumbered away from the house, spewing bits of gravel and brownish dust in its wake. Karen stood in the doorway watching, her back to the sprawl of cartons and boxes on the kitchen floor. The twinges of loneliness she had anticipated failed to materialize—instead she was eager to turn back into her house, embrace it to her and be alone. She meant to explore every inch of her house and land, each nook and cranny, until at the end of her year there would be no measure of it that did not feel a part of her and she of it.

A flock of quail took to the air in a sudden flapping of wings, scattering into the heavy grey sky through barren tree branches. The landscape had changed dramatically since she had last looked across the fields to the sea. Gone were the brilliant colors and electric blue sky of autumn. In their place was the stark, almost sullen feeling of November, everything still and drab, waiting for the snow and the bitter cold to come.

A few perennials dotted an untended flower bed alongside the house, the only color in a pewter day. Out on the horizon, a dense fog inched slowly nearer shore.

Karen sat on the upper step, an elbow on each knee. On impulse, she reached into the bed and picked a handful of flowers—michaelmas daisies, a cluster of delicate blue forget-me-nots, deep purple asters. Even in the clutter of unpacking she wanted a bowl of flowers for the house—an offering of sorts.

Her vases were somewhere in the disarray on the kitchen floor and she searched the small pantry for a substitute. The shelves were empty, save for a few plastic lids, an interesting assortment of dead insects and several dusty Mason jars. She grabbed one of the wide-mouthed jars, washed it and placed the flowers carefully inside, then placed the flowers in the center of the table. She stepped back a few paces to admire her colorful creation, her hands raised prayer-like in front of her. "A small token of my esteem," tumbled from her throat and she smiled at the quaint phrase and because she had been here but a few hours and already was talking to herself.

After unpacking her willow-ware plates into the sideboard, she began hanging the copper-bottomed cookpots on a peg board behind the wood cookstove. She stood looking at the ancient stove, wondering how it worked. Baking bread might be fun, and she could certainly cut heating costs by using it to supplement the furnace. Figuring out how it worked was another matter. How did one proceed in the absence of knobs marked OFF and 350 degrees? The simple life had complexities of its own, she thought, and would require a few new skills. She studied the stove a moment longer, then turned to the more immediate task of unpacking. There would be time for such as this later, this and much else.

Karen moved from room to room, humming tunelessly, stopping only to make the decisions of the moment; which wall in the parlor would be best for her bookcases, where to display her collection of bright South American *Molas,* where to set up her desk.

Hours later she stepped back from the bedroom closet and closed the door gently. The contents of all the crates had been put away, her suitcases emptied into drawers and closets which now overflowed with plaid shirts, wool scarves and heavy woolen sweaters. Perhaps she had overdone it at L. L. Bean just a touch, but she could afford a few small indulgences.

She rested at the kitchen table, drumming her fingers rhythmically over the wood. It was the hour, those moments between light and dark, that she had come to call her time of suspension, a time when things of the day were past, things of the night not yet here.

It was also the dinner hour and Karen realized she'd completely forgotten about food. She rummaged the pantry, searching the canned goods and packages for something simple to prepare. Nothing really appealed and finally she put a chop in the oven. At least that would take a while to cook and perhaps by then she'd have more of an appetite. It would be nice too, she thought, to add the smell of cooking to the pleasure of seeing her things in place in the house.

She returned to the table and gazed out the window. Dusk was settling quickly, the last rays of light waning, giving over the land to the approaching night and thickening fog. Out in the orchard gnarled branches thrust a dark silhouette against the purplish evening haze.

Inspired by the sight of the darkened orchard, Karen threw on a jacket and ran out to the trees, hoping a few apples might still cling to the upper branches. How fitting for her first meal here to eat something grown on the land, something which had been here longer than she.

She wasn't disappointed and returned to the lighted house a few minutes later with several apples, cool and crisp, in the pocket of her jacket. She placed two in the oven beside the chop and sat munching the other, glancing around her house, indulging in pleasant self-satisfaction. She had done it. She was here. She sat for some moments, feeling timeless, ageless, floating in a sea of the oddly familiar.

After she had eaten, had put away the dishes, Karen returned to the parlor, by far her favorite room, still fragrant with the aroma of baking apples. She started a fire, pushed a Vivaldi concerto into the tape deck and sat at the desk she had set up in front of the windows.

Her appointment book lay open and Karen thought how useless it seemed here. Her days now would be ordered by priorities other than the parade of lines in the bulging black book, lines once organizing her life into neat half-hour segments. She swooped it from the desk and considered throwing it into the fireplace as a gesture of her independence. A pink memo slipped from between the pages and fluttered to the floor. Even before Karen bent to retrieve the scrap of paper she recognized it, and the name written there. She picked up the note and without looking at it strode quickly to the hearth where a bright fire blazed. She looked down at the memo and sat back deeply in the overstuffed chair. Maggi's face materialized, whole and beautifully projected on the backs of her closed eyelids. It was a strong face, with deep eyes that spoke of how much more she knew than she had learned from books.

The face teased her, challenged her to keep looking, to keep her eyes closed, for to open them might blot the image. Maybe it would be all right, so far away now, to let herself drift back and remember. Little by little, Karen relaxed mental fingers from their grip on her resolve and drifted back to the first time she'd seen the WHILE YOU WERE OUT slip. It had seemed so inauspicious then, that little piece of paper.

It had been terribly hot that day. She was hurrying across the quad, balancing her briefcase in one hand and a paper cup of iced tea in the other. Her light cotton shirt stuck to her back and, although she had showered only moments before, already she felt greasy and uncomfortable. Even the ivy clinging to the red brick buildings looked wilted and tired, as, she supposed, did she. Her disposition turned uncommonly sour in the short time it took to reach the campus. She attempted to revive it by wiping the cool beads of moisture on the cup across her forehead.

"I should be in the Berkshires," she grumbled, "enjoying the mountain air, not here teaching summer session." But it had been a tradeoff, one last favor before her leave. She turned into the building and paused in the cool vaulted foyer. She pinched her shirt between thumb and forefinger, fanning it back and forth, and shivered at the breeze fluttering on the damp skin of her belly. Sweat ran down her legs under the skirt; even the soles of her feet felt sweaty in the low-heeled sandals.

There were several messages in her box. She smiled at the department secretary, walked the dim corridor to the office, and sprawled in her swivel chair, propping her legs on the low window sill and pulling her skirt high on her thighs for coolness. She took a sip of tea and began sorting through the messages.

One was from the local PBS affiliate, a Maggi England. She dialed the number, annoyed with herself and with the station, and a little embarrassed. During their fund drive last month she had committed a small pledge; a reminder lay somewhere under a stack of papers on her desk at home.

As she introduced herself she vowed to be more prompt with her obligations in the future.

"Dr. Latham," a pleasant, well-modulated voice responded, "I'm so glad you called back. I know how busy you must be, but could you spare a few minutes to talk about a project we're designing? You're the first person we thought of when the subject of Andean societies was proposed."

Karen paused before answering, hastily making the switch from tardy debtor to competent professional.

"I'd really like the opportunity to talk with you in person," Maggi went on. "We're very excited about the project. The National Endowment for the Humanities has provided funding for a documentary exploring the vestiges of Incan religious practices in remote societies in the Andes. We'd love to interest you in working with us. How about lunch later in the week as an enticement?"

Karen, surprised at her lack of hesitation, heard herself say, "All right. What about the Thai restaurant just off the square? Say noon Thursday?"

Karen fanned herself with the remainder of the messages and took another swig of the iced tea. The project did sound interesting, and might even be fun. Certainly it would be a change from a routine she had to admit could stand a bit of change. Not that she'd lost her love of her chosen work, just that after five hard years she was running more on rote than a sharp creative edge. Everything in her life, now that she thought about it, seemed a little stale. She was seeing increasingly less of Walter, possibly to avoid a confrontation, and had immersed herself in a second book. But she was reminded of the old jingle about doing something more but enjoying it less. Her upcoming sabbatical should cure the ennui. But right now, a project for television might be just the thing.

The following Thursday, she entered the restaurant to find Maggi already seated at a table by the windows, a red carnation in her lapel so Karen could spot her in the crush of diners. Maggi sat with her chin resting on her clasped fingers, looking idly out the window. Something about the way she sat there, composed, her lips pursed slightly against the steeple of her fingers, gave the impression of a woman poised for reflection in the midst of a highly enjoyable adventure.

Karen walked over, extended her hand and introduced herself. Maggi's face opened in a wide grin. She half rose, took Karen's hand.

"I'm glad you agreed to meet." Maggi pushed one of the oversized purple menus across to Karen. "Order anything you like. Lunch is on the station's expense account. We stop at nothing when wooing talent." Maggi winked and signaled the waiter.

Amused and slightly flattered, Karen took the menu and nodded assent at Maggi's choice of wine. Over the top of the menu she studied her luncheon companion. She wasn't what Karen would call pretty, at least not by commercial standards. Perhaps gracefully handsome would be more apt. She laid the menu aside.

"I've been doing my homework," Maggi said. "Your first book, and the article about you and your Peruvian finds. Very interesting. Congratulations, it isn't every day one gets a write-up in *Time.*"

"Thanks."

The wine arrived and Karen took a small sip. She smiled. "It was very exciting for all of us. Such a large cairn will be a wealth of valuable information."

"Well, your published work and the publicity have certainly linked your name to the finds." Maggi raised her glass to Karen. "Here's to Karen Latham, then. You must be very good to lead such an important field inquiry."

"More a matter of being in the right place at the right time," Karen said quickly. "Now tell me about your project."

Between bites of the peanut chicken special, Maggi explained the documentary. Especially interesting to the project staff was the survival of shamanism and ritual magic in present-day villages. Karen would serve as technical consultant, as well as an on-camera narrator.

Karen listened with growing interest. This was an area of the Andean culture she found particularly interesting, although even if she hadn't, Maggi's charm and enthusiasm would have won her over. She experienced a not unpleasant lightheadedness—perhaps the air conditioning after such sweltering heat, perhaps the wine—but whatever it was, she liked it.

She said, "This project sounds interesting." She held her glass by the stem and twirled it slowly. "Lately I've had a mild case of the doldrums. I could use a little excitement. I have the time just now and," Karen grinned across at Maggi, "I'd love to join the team."

"Great!" Maggi reached across the table to pump her hand. "Welcome to television."

Karen couldn't remember when she had felt so at ease. Her openness with this virtual stranger surprised her. There was something intriguing about this Maggi England, a woman about her own age, mid-thirties, but rather more unconventional than she. Under the stylish boxy jacket, sleeves rolled to mid-arm, Maggi wore a simple T-shirt. Jutting from her tailored slacks were a pair of running shoes that had clearly seen better days. A cloche hat perched a little sideways on her short dark hair and the effect, especially with the red carnation in her lapel, was delightful.

Business details completed, they moved easily on to other subjects, each sparking genuine mutual interest. Karen would remember later that the one subject they did not discuss was men, usually the topic of greatest interest among her women friends.

She learned that Maggi had studied drama here on the east coast, then traveled west, chasing every actress's dream.

"Perhaps I wasn't cut out to be a Hollywood sex symbol," Maggi said with a grin. "I wanted to play serious parts. You know–roles showing gutsy women facing life with panache."

"Were you ever in a movie?"

Maggi screwed her face into a grimace. "Once. About a mutant jellyfish that slithered out of the sea in Southern California then set off to devour the world, beginning with a group of surfers–hardly the Hepburn image I had in mind."

Karen leaned her head back and laughed. "So you gave up acting?"

"Pretty soon after that, yes. I'm more than happy in the production end of things."

The lunch hour, as well as a good part of the afternoon, flew by before Karen noticed with surprise that the restaurant, jammed earlier, was now empty except for them. Karen hated parting from such invigorating company.

On the curb Maggi took her hand and held it a moment. "I'm looking forward to this–to working with you. We'll be seeing lots of each other over the next several weeks."

She wondered if Maggi could be reading her mind. Her thoughts too were of seeing Maggi again, of spending more time together.

Feeling oddly deserted, Karen watched Maggi pull her car away and disappear into the maze of traffic. She shoved the hand Maggi had grasped into the pocket of her full skirt and was very aware of it there, and of a strange tingling warmth.

All that evening, images of Maggi and little snippets of their conversation intruded on every page of a book she was reading for a proposed review; and while she couldn't remember for the life of her what she had ordered for lunch, she remembered quite vividly how pleasant the whole affair had been. When Maggi called the following afternoon to suggest a tour of the studio, she was only too happy to accept.

The next day she pulled her car into the station's crowded parking lot. She was several minutes early and, she realized, nervous. Heat shimmered in waves over the bluish asphalt; she quickly opened the door and started for the building, making sure her shirt was tucked neatly into her slacks and giving her hair a couple of light pats.

After announcing herself to the receptionist, she moved to a vinyl couch, picked up a magazine and began flipping the pages.

A hand fell on her shoulder. "Hi."

Startled, Karen dropped the magazine to the floor.

"Oh–hi." Karen looked at Maggi then to the floor, to the fallen magazine. "I didn't hear you come up." She stood, swooping the magazine with her, but the magazine slipped again through her fingers.

"Dammit," she breathed, trying to recover both herself and the magazine. "What's the matter with me?"

Maggi led her through the hallway and into the studio, explaining the equipment and functions of the various rooms. It was clear she loved her work, its technical side equally. She talked animatedly, explaining the workings of her trade in what Karen was coming to see as natural aplomb.

Karen listened intently, nodded often, but said little. Normally talkative and at ease in most situations, she puzzled over the curious disappearance of her poise. Yet the more she puzzled, the worse her discomfort became. She felt awkward and shy, more like an adolescent than a valued professional. Maggi appeared not to notice, or if she did gave no hint of it.

Not long after they'd arranged themselves in two chairs in front of Maggi's desk, the intercom buzzed. Maggie listened a moment, then excused herself. Karen, letting out a long breath, looked around the small room hoping to learn something of this compelling woman from the items in her office. Dissappointingly, the desk top failed to yield up any photos of Maggi's life—no smiling children, no family portraits. She looked around for something else, some clue to the persona of Maggi England.

The office was only a cubicle, with just enough room for the desk and chairs and a bookcase along the wall. There was a small Oriental-style rug, and several plants in varying stages of health. The bookcase was no more helpful than the rest of the place, containing only professional periodicals and a few volumes of poetry by unfamiliar writers. That she was inordinately curious about the personal life and habits of a business acquaintance did occur to Karen as she browsed through one of the poetry volumes, but she filed the knowledge away in the same category as her unaccustomed awkwardness.

Maggi swung back into the room and eased into the chair opposite Karen, her legs crossed at the ankles. Karen managed a few of what she hoped were intelligent questions about the process of producing a documentary. Throughout the conversation their eyes met often, and each time Karen quickly dropped her gaze or looked out the window. Even so, she studied Maggi, her gestures and manner of speech. She struck Karen as the kind of person who never enters a room without attracting attention. Not that she would call it to herself through exaggerated gestures; there would be no need for that. People would just notice.

The phone buzzed again and this time Maggi said to Karen, "Sorry, I've got to run. A little emergency in the editing room, a projector's just made a light lunch of several frames of important footage. But we might as well get you to work." She handed Karen a stack of bound pages.

Karen stuffed the papers into her bag, feeling oddly disappointed. "Thanks. I would like to get started."

At the door Maggi put a hand gently on Karen's elbow. Karen felt her there, close and warm, and could smell her mild spicy cologne.

"Sorry our visit had to be cut short." Maggi released the pressure on Karen's arm. "See you soon."

* * * * *

The video project started in earnest the next week, and just as Maggi had promised, they saw each other often though always in the company of others involved with the documentary. Nevertheless, a radiance sparked between them like so many brilliant fireflies. Even in meeting rooms crowded with people, Karen was keenly aware of Maggi, of where she sat, of what she said. Their eyes met often, sometimes in tacit agreement on a subject under discussion, sometimes for no reason at all. They took breaks together, and lunch—just the two of them in an out-of-the-way place where they could talk quietly and be alone.

The work itself was interesting and Karen became happily involved, enjoying the contribution of her knowledge to the selection of film clips and additions to the narration. But it was the lunch hours and her coffee breaks she enjoyed most.

One evening they were the last two people remaining in the studio. They sat in swivel chairs facing a bank of monitors. Karen thought Maggi had seemed a little distracted during the day and was glad for these last few minutes together. Maggi ran a hand through her hair and leaned over the table. "I won't be in for a couple of days," she said slowly. "There's some work I need to do at home."

Karen felt as if someone had just announced that she herself would be confined for the same amount of time in a bare room with nothing to do but read the phone book. "Oh?" she said, hoping her disappointment wasn't as obvious to Maggi.

"Sometimes it's hard to concentrate around here," Maggi said with a long look at Karen.

Couldn't the same be said of her? For her, even going home didn't solve the problem. Each night she arrived at her apartment exhausted but too charged to think of sleeping, having floated through the day a little off the ground, a perpetual blush on her cheeks, her hands jammed firmly into her pockets. To have taken those hands out and let them free might have meant reaching out to brush Maggi's hand, or to touch the place beside her hairline where, Karen was sure, was stored all the sweetness to be found anywhere. During these weeks she had stopped seeing Walter altogether.

Karen forced a smile. "Well, we'll just have to muddle along without you, I guess."

"I thought if you weren't busy we might have dinner tomorrow," Maggi said. There was an unusual tremor in her voice.

"I'd like that very much," Karen said quickly.

* * * * *

The following evening they arrived simultaneously at the restaurant. Karen couldn't help brushing her hand casually along Maggi's shoulder as they climbed the narrow stairway to the dining room.

The restaurant, a cavernous affair on the upper floor of a waterfront warehouse, was renowned for its generous servings and an atmosphere laced with steamed cabbage and the banter of brassy waitresses. At a small table along the wall they settled into highbacked chairs and began talking, ignoring the menus the hostess had placed on the table.

Scores of diners, some at small tables, others at long

trestles stretching the length of the room, ate lustily, to the accompaniment of clanging pans and orders shouted to the cooks. Maggi seemed as unconscious of the din as did Karen. They chatted easily, each filling in the other on events since they'd last met yesterday.

As Karen listened to Maggi, her head resting lightly on the back of the chair, a half-smile on her face, she knew a satisfaction in Maggi's company far keener than the light, almost nervous banter would reveal. Fearing a prolonged break in the conversation, she gamely held up her end of it. What might she blurt into so delicate a silence? What line might she cross if she gave even a hint of her galloping emotion?

Karen sipped her coffee slowly. She had gotten through the day somehow, dull and plodding as it seemed, counting the hours until dinner. Now here she was, a tingling along her earlobes, a flush on her cheeks, and a warm and altogether pleasant electricity running from her throat to her belly.

There were words for feelings like these, words she only half-thought and swallowed unsaid.

Maggi ceased speaking; it took Karen several seconds to realize she hadn't heard Maggi's last few words, only the pleasant hum of her voice.

When their heaping platters of brisket and vegetables arrived Karen could do little more than toy with hers, her appetite as dulled as her capacity for logic. None of this should be happening. Her feelings were as vivid and uncontrolled as they were confusing and dangerous.

Maggi seemed uninterested in food as well, Karen noticed, and ate slowly, taking frequent sips of her ice water.

After a few bites of brisket, Karen pushed her plate aside. She couldn't remember tasting any of it. "Guess I'm not all that hungry."

Maggi also pushed her plate away. "Me either." She clasped her fingers together and leaned forward. "Karen, I–"

Maggi's lips remained slightly parted, as if about to speak. She looked directly into Karen's eyes. "It's wonderful to see you."

The look on Maggi's face, the warmth and directness of the words, left no doubt about the declaration.

"Yes," Karen answered softly.

Maggi opened her hand. Karen stretched her fingertips to rest lightly on Maggi's. Karen's entire being seemed focused on that one small spot, that magic in the middle of nowhere where their fingers touched.

The waitress appeared with the check and Karen jerked her hand to her lap.

During the day, the street in front of the restaurant was host to vendors who hawked vegetables and fresh fish from colorful stands. The women walked in silence, wrapped in private thoughts, sidestepping wilted lettuce leaves and burst tomatoes gingerly, as gingerly as Karen sidestepped mention of her delight in Maggi's presence.

She remembered going to the circus for the first time. As she walked toward the tent with its pennants waving from every angle, she'd felt her heart pound for the mysteries awaiting her under the red and white awning. Without knowing exactly what they could be, these wonderful mysteries, she knew each step carried her closer to something bright and exciting. Soon she would see huge animals, spangles, feats of daring—never before dreamed of sights that would take her breath away and cause her to clap her hands together and laugh. . . .

Maggi slipped her hand into the crook of Karen's arm and Karen, yielding to age-old instincts, leaned into her. Neither spoke, the touching and the warmth of the night words enough. They walked on, turning corners at random, neither speaking nor directing their course. After what seemed too short a time they arrived at the now deserted parking lot and Karen's car. They leaned against the VW facing each other.

Karen, dreading the moment of parting, felt awkwardly adrift somewhere between custom and desire. She wanted to take Maggi in her arms, comfort herself with a more tangible bond before moving away into the steamy night. Maggi took a step forward, her face a mere breath away.

"I don't know how—" Karen faltered and stared at the pavement.

"How to say goodnight?" Maggi finished for her softly.

Still staring at the pavement, Karen nodded and felt Maggi's arms circle her, Maggi's lips brushing softly against her cheek.

Without hesitation she pulled her hands from the safety of her pockets and let them caress the unfamiliar contours of Maggi's back. When Maggi released the embrace, Karen knew her face was flushed red in the darkness. She had neither breath nor desire to speak. Karen touched Maggi's cheek and fumbled behind her for the car door.

"I feel perilously close to tears," Karen said. "And on the brink of leaving the ground—I could float home." She shifted her gaze to the chrome door handle. "But, I. . . ."

Maggi nodded and smiled in a way that let Karen know she understood, then bent to place a light caress on Karen's cheek. Karen returned the gesture and quickly slid behind the wheel.

As she drove from the parking lot, she looked into the rear view mirror and caught a glimpse of Maggi, tall and windblown, waving to her in the dim light.

The next morning she had awakened in a panic, an apprehension made more acute by her vivid recollection of the previous evening. She put on water for coffee and leaned against the counter. "My God," she said aloud. "What the hell is going on here?" The question rang hollow; for in truth, she already knew.

The Sunday paper lay open on the sofa and she made a desultory stab at the crossword puzzle, then flung it aside, too edgy to concentrate. Arms wrapped around her middle, she rose and walked to the windows. She loved the view from her apartment across the Charles River to the campus beyond. Down in that other world three stories below were tall spires and staid brick buildings. Several shells of rowers glided swiftly down the river. For the first time, instead of filling her with comfort and a sense of her place in the world, the spires and buildings frightened her and seemed, at that moment, a threat.

She wanted to phone Maggi. With all her heart she wanted to hear that clear warm voice. Once the phone had rung and she dashed for it, her throat constricted–but it had been a wrong number.

Karen stood at the phone, her hand poised over the receiver, a taste in her mouth as if she'd eaten something metal. She quickly pressed Walter's number. He answered on the first ring and that was good–one more ring and she'd have hung up. . . .

* * * * *

Something–the wind, a banging shutter–roused Karen and she pulled herself awake in the chair in front of the fireplace. She rubbed her hands over her face, then sat still for several moments. Her drowsiness slowly crumbled away leaving her wide awake but disoriented. Her first impulse on waking had been to look around the room in search of someone else, someone who had been nearby in a barely remembered dream. Fragments of the dream swam loosely around her like dropped pieces of a jigsaw puzzle; but the half-thoughts and distorted images refused to form a whole.

Earlier, the radio had forecast a heavy line of storms moving into New England from Canada. She sat quietly in front of the fireplace, the fire grown cold during her nap, and knew from the high whistling sound of the gusts and the scratch of branches on the worn clapboards that the storm had arrived. Funny, she thought, wrapping her arms around her waist, how the first moments of a storm can make one feel so vulnerable, so like reaching out for comfort in the face of nature's power.

She let her eyes fall on familiar objects in the dimly lit room and for the first time since her arrival sensed her isolation. There was no phone, and even if there was, who would she call? She had warned away family, friends, colleagues, students: "I need unbroken time for concentration on my book," she had cautioned them all. How could she now call anyone? The fire had burned low during her nap and she poked at it till flames again crackled from beneath the logs.

Even if I wanted to follow some primal urge for contact, she thought, leaning back in the cushioned chair, even if I wanted to—I couldn't.

The room was in darkness, with only a pale shaft of light from the bulb over the kitchen sink falling through the doorway, and silent but for the wind and the ticking clock on the mantle. She fought back a desire to turn on lights and instead got up and walked to the windows. Outside, the trees whipped angrily, goaded by the wind; whitecaps marked the tops of high curling waves crashing heavily onto the shore. Any minute now, torrents of water would pour from the thick rolling clouds. Patches of fog still clung to the shore and a wall of fog rose between the sea and the land a few hundred yards out. Shivering slightly and thinking how drafty the house felt, she stared out at the unfolding drama, her arms drawn tightly around her.

Dense swatches of fog rolled and curled among the trees and rocks like lost pieces torn loose from the bank at sea, parting now and again to reveal the sharp outline of an elm, the waves, or glimpses of the rocky coast. The wind whipped a patch of fog quickly away down among the rocks, and Karen's heart leapt to her throat.

Someone was standing there! Someone, a dark figure,

was standing perfectly still and looking up at the house.

Karen pulled her arms tighter and strained forward, willing herself to see through the murk to the large rock in the cove and the figure beside it. Another patch of fog obscured the rocks but she continued to stare, a damp line of perspiration forming under her shirt collar. Her heart pounded wildly as she strained forward, never letting her eyes travel from the exact spot where the figure stood. The fog parted again, the rocks clearly visible; but this time no one was there. Karen rubbed her hand over her eyes and looked again. No one.

She let her gaze wander over the unfamiliar territory along the shore and among the trees, even out the adjacent windows to the lane. Nothing. Finally, walking back to the chair on legs so numb they scarcely felt like her own, she sank down and expelled a long breath of relief. No one was there, at least not anymore. And, she chided herself gently, probably no one ever was. I'm just tired. It's been a long day. Perhaps in Boston one might see dark figures lurking about and looking into windows, but not here and not in the middle of a heavy storm.

If she had been worried about changes in her sleeping habits here, she realized she need not have. Even with the early evening nap, she was sleepy. With her glass of wine in one hand she climbed the stairs to her bedroom, carrying under her arm a selection of junk novels purchased earlier in the supermarket, the garish covers serving the publisher's intention. Her work left little time for escapist reading. The books, with their promise of departure from more scholarly tomes, were one of the first symbols of her new freedom.

Propped in bed, she selected a book, its cover done in red mylar and silver letters. *The Face in the Ivory* promised a tale about unrequited love. What could be more trite, Karen thought, and opened the book.

She awoke shortly after 2:00 a.m., sweating and disoriented. The room felt unfamiliar, and for a panicky instant she knew only that she wasn't in her Boston flat. She lay still and let her eyes scan the quiet bedroom, half expecting to see someone standing at the foot of her bed. The sensation of another presence was the last thing she remembered before waking. Through the darkness she could make out the quaint vertical lines of red roses intertwined in the wallpaper pattern, the white shutters opened at the top, the outlines of the furniture. Yet she felt vaguely detached, as if waking in someone else's room.

Outside, the storm had passed, leaving behind only a steady drip from the eaves onto the sodden ground. Dark fingers of clouds scudded across the sky, running in front of and often obscuring a pale crescent moon. Karen threw back the covers, stumbled into the bathroom and switched on the light. Her face in the mirror looked tired and puffy, as if she hadn't slept at all. Dream fragments began to surface, distinct but unconnected. Something about a woman on horseback. The vision lingered in her mind even as other images melted away just out of the range of her consciousness. Though the figure rode toward her in her dream, she hadn't been able to see the face: the head and shoulders were covered by a thick cowl-like shawl. There had been only darkness under the rough cloth and, though the rider wasn't frightening exactly, she was certainly compelling. It was the only image Karen could hold from the dream.

Still thinking of the figure, she returned to bed, again lying still in the darkened room, the covers pulled snugly under her chin. She smiled slightly, thinking that the spectre in the fog must have frightened her more than she thought. Within moments she slept.

CHAPTER 4

Karen woke but lay still under the warm cover, unwilling to give herself over to the startling chill in the room. Pale pink light streamed in through the windows, and she imagined herself waking inside an orchid, or a delicate conch. The ocean sounded farther away than it was, and bare branches of the elm and maple trees shivered in a light morning breeze. Luxuriating, letting wakefulness come slowly, she pulled the electric blanket closer under her chin and lay dozing and waking as it suited her. She had no notion of the time.

Remnants of a dream snagged in her waking moments only long enough to register before she drowsed again. The silent horseback rider had come, and this time she had seen a face. Filmy and indistinct, as though reflected in water, a dark-eyed woman smiled at her from the coarse cloth of the cowl. The woman raised a hand in greeting and motioned Karen closer, but she was moving through something too thick and heavy to reach her. . . .

She stretched her legs and turned, to a protesting ache of sore muscles, no doubt from hauling all those cartons yesterday. She had a mild beginning of a headache and was curiously tired, as if her sleep had been light or disturbed. Normally, waking in such a state brought a profound flattening of the spirit; days starting like this often held scant promise of improvement. But this was not an ordinary morning, and this no ordinary place. The day was before her, headache or no, and held out promise of time alone and time to explore her new surroundings. She'd spend hours getting to know the house and certainly take a long walk later along the beach.

With a decisive motion Karen threw back the covers, her chilled feet jigging on the cold boards of the floor. She pulled on her robe and sped for the downstairs thermostat.

Waiting for coffee water to boil she sat at the table, legs drawn under her, chin in hand, and stared groggily into the parlor. On the far wall under the window she had set up her working area, though she hadn't completed the task. Boxes of notes and cards littered the desk top and even the floor underneath. It was an irritating display, out of place and intrusive, a rude interruption in the morning spell of the house. Each time her eyes came to rest on her work, she looked away to the fireplace or out the window, preferring the dreamy spell made by sunlight on polished wood.

Right after the first cup of coffee, she promised, I'll put the desk in order. Having struck a bargain with her more compulsive self, she picked up her coffee and began a slow meander of the house, tracing her fingers along a burnished length of wainscoting or across the back of a chair. She paused often to stare out at the sea, lead grey and flat in the rain-washed morning.

Cast iron pegs cemented to the interior walls of the fireplace especially pleased her. She stood back a moment and tried to imagine how it must have looked a century ago, with a pot of baked beans simmering there. In the entry hall, small squares of glass ran the length and on both sides of the front door, the opaque greenish tint of the glass muting the sunlight. She paused there a while, tracing her finger in circles over tiny air bubbles trapped in the hand-blown glass.

She left her coffee, long since grown cold, and climbed the stairs, trailing her hands lovingly on the smooth oak bannister. Another sensation was taking form, something churning just under the sensual pleasure of the house. The feeling was vague, like something known but not quite remembered, as if she were waiting for something. Or someone.

In one of the bedrooms she discovered a small puddle of water which had seeped in through a broken window during last night's storm. The sight of the crumbling putty was disturbing, like finding a blemish on a cherished possession. She ran downstairs for her small tool box, trying to remember whether it contained putty. Later, fully dressed and carrying a small can of spackle, she drew a fine line of putty along the crack with a kitchen knife.

At first, when she heard the sound, she thought it was her imagination, or possibly a whisper of wind, but as she smoothed the putty, she noticed the tree tops were barely moving. She heard the noise again and cocked her head, the knife poised against the window. A soft rustling noise came from the kitchen; not stationary, it seemed to move from place to place. She dropped her hand from the window and rubbed it along the gooseflesh on her forearm.

The sounds were distinct though not loud, and she stood without taking breath to hear them more clearly. There were other sounds too, like a rattling of papers or perhaps soft footfalls, but these were indistinct and seemed to teeter somewhere between imagination and reality. But the rustling sounds, like fabric rubbing together, were real enough.

Karen eased quietly onto the landing, holding her breath, crouching forward to see into the parlor and beyond as soon as she cleared the stairwell.

She reached the bottom step and peered into the parlor. Seeing it empty, she forced her legs to carry her into the kitchen. In this room, like the others, bright sunlight streamed through the windows, bathing everything in morning cheerfulness. There was even the singing of a bird from a nearby tree branch. Like the parlor, the kitchen was still and empty. The quiet, the perfect order, the cheery sunlight, all combined to make her feel slightly silly. Nothing here was amiss. She stood unmoving in the doorway, the knife dangling from her hand. But there was something wrong, something different she could sense but couldn't see.

She stared at every detail and remembered a game she had loved as a child—What's Wrong With This Picture? In the game, one was challenged to find the intentional mistakes made in a drawing. She repeated the name of the game to herself as she scanned the room. Her copper pots glinted in the sunlight behind the stove, last night's dishes sat in perfect order in the wooden drainer.

Then her eyes fell on the table, and her heart jumped to her throat.

The flowers! The jar of flowers she had brought in yesterday had been moved! Instead of sitting in the exact center of the long table as before, the wide-mouthed Mason jar and its bright contents now sat far toward the end of the table, the end nearest the woodstove.

Confused more than frightened, she sat at the table and stared, willing the flowers to explain. But at least, she thought with relief, there was no intruder. She rose to reheat the coffee, reasoning that she must have moved the flowers herself when making dinner last night. Or, she thought, but with less conviction, maybe I have rats. She added traps to the list of items to buy in Pelham Falls.

The day was definitely not proceeding as planned. First there had been the minor repair, then the interlude of odd noises. Both interruptions, especially the latter, had broken her dreamy, almost trance-like appreciation of the house. When she looked out to see a blue and white truck emblazoned New England Telephone turning into the lane, she gave a resigned shrug and rose to open the door. She showed the young man where she wanted the phone and, while he worked, returned to the table and stared for a long time at the flowers.

Presently Karen looked out the window again. To her surprise she had another visitor. A shiny red jeep bumped along the lane and pulled to a stop beside the telephone truck. Karen watched, fascinated, as a tall figure unfolded from behind the canvas side-curtains and with one hand adjusted the angle of a green visor cap. It was impossible to tell whether the figure was male or female, for the deep lines and crevices of the face had long since outlived gender.

The figure, clad in khaki trousers and red-soled boots, strode confidently toward the door. Soon Karen could make out the words John Deere on the front of the cap. Karen opened the door and gazed into the square-jawed gentle face of an intensely grey-eyed woman.

"Hello," the woman said, extending a foil-wrapped package. "Name's Cavendish. Etta Cavendish. We're neighbors."

Karen reached for the package, which spilled an aroma of warm banana bread. "Hi. I'm Karen. Please, come in."

Etta strode in and stood near the table, her long gaze taking in both Karen and the kitchen. "My. You've gotten yourself nice and settled in already, I see. Good for you."

She nodded her approval, indicating short patience for layabouts.

Etta sparkled with a vitality that belied her years. Karen estimated her new neighbor at near seventy and felt she shouldn't be too surprised if Etta suggested they plan a rock climbing hike after lunch. Karen opened the foil package. "Let's have a slice. I'll get a couple of plates."

"I don't want to trouble you if you're busy. Really, I just came by to be neighborly and introduce myself."

"I'm not busy at all," Karen said quickly. "Besides, this bread is fairly begging us to indulge ourselves. Please, have a seat."

Etta pulled out a chair and shucked her parka onto the wood back. "Reckon you're not from around here then." It was more a statement than a question.

"No. Not exactly. I've come up from Boston for a year or so."

"Well then, at least you're used to the winters." Etta smiled and appeared to relax. "That solves a heap of problems."

Karen set a generous slice of bread before each of them and filled their cups with fresh coffee. It was well past noon; she had completely forgotten about lunch and was hungry. Where had the time gone?

Etta gazed warmly at Karen, one hand around her mug, the other jammed into the pocket of her trousers. "So. What brings you all the way up here? All alone in this big house?"

Karen cut into her banana bread. "I'm a teacher on leave from the university and," she added with a flip of her fork and a sour look toward her desk, "trying to finish work on a book."

"That's good." Etta nodded. "Lots of folks come to the countryside expecting things to be a lot more idyllic than they really are. Somehow they don't expect there'll be much difference in the country. But most of those don't last too long. The country has its own ways."

Karen thought she could detect just the slightest 'harrumph' at the edge of Etta's words. "Oh, but I need just exactly this sort of place for a while. A little snow and isolation aren't going to drive me away." She retrieved the last crumbs of her bread by mashing them on the bottom of her fork. She returned Etta's warm smile. "This is delicious. Won't you have another piece Mrs. Cavendish? I'm tempted."

"It's Miss Cavendish," Etta said, emphasizing the Miss.

"Oh, I'm sorry."

"Nothing to be sorry for, as I can see. But, perhaps I will have another slice of that bread." Etta smiled, her eyes crinkling at the corners, and handed her plate to Karen.

Over second helpings, Karen learned that Etta had been born and raised on the family farm; the slate roof could be seen from the kitchen windows. Etta's house sat across the fields and down the little glade, so that on first seeing it Karen had thought she was looking down on a tree-lined pond.

Etta had never married. She'd inherited the farm on the death of her parents over forty years ago. Karen's admiration for her raw-boned neighbor soared. What it must have taken to keep up the place alone. Etta's hands lay still on the table, resting lightly beside her saucer, and Karen saw in the gnarled joints and calluses vivid testimony to her lifetime of hard work. If there was a touch of the curmudgeon in her, she had no doubt earned it.

Etta stated, with a touch of sadness, that the McCartland place had often sat empty, and even the summer people hadn't been all that friendly.

Karen loved Etta's sense of time and history, a perspective allowing her to call this the McCartland place long after any McCartland had set foot here.

The telephone man strode in, tools and instruments jangling from his belt. When he saw Etta he stopped and put a hand to the bill of his cap, a vestige of a gesture from days gone by. "Miz Cavendish. Nice to see you, Ma'am."

He jerked the cap from his head and stood awkwardly for a moment. "Say, my Aunt Grace was mentioning you the other day, wondering if you might mix her up another bunch of those herbs like you made last winter." He grinned and shifted his weight. "She swears they eased her cough . . . even helped her sing better in the Christmas Pageant."

Etta turned to face him. "Course I will. Tell her to drop around anytime and I'll fix her up. And while you're at it, ask her when she's coming back to the Friday Night Musical. We miss her fiddle playing, even if she does always play a little sharp."

Etta added the last comment with a wink in Karen's direction, then turned back to her. "You wouldn't happen to play an instrument, would you? We could use some new blood. None of us are much good, I'm afraid, but we do get together every Friday, especially during winter when there's not a lot else to do. The music's passable and we enjoy the company. A couple of our musicians have dropped out for one reason or another. And as for the rest of us, it's sometimes hard to hear the pianissimo sections for the noise of our joints creaking."

At this both Etta and the young man laughed, obviously amused at the image of Etta Cavendish as anything but a bulwark against the vicissitudes of growing older.

A few minutes after the young man gathered his tools and left, Etta rose and pulled on her parka and set the green cap down firmly on her short, wiry hair. Grey-white curls poked out from the sides and back.

"Glad to have met you," Etta said.

"Me too." Karen smiled and clasped Etta's hand warmly.

Even though Karen had explained that she hadn't picked up her flute since college days, Etta wasn't dissuaded. "Come by anyway," she said. "It may not be much in the way of entertainment. But like as not you'll be wanting for company from time to time. Besides, an audience of one is better than none."

Etta reached the door and looked through the glass inset. "Radio said the first snow might fall early as the weekend." She paused with her hand on the latch. "I hope you won't think I'm being too nosey, but you've come at a very hard season. Lost of folks spend the whole year just getting ready for it. Winters can get pretty bitter up here, pretty lonely. There's a kind of strangeness that can take over . . . when the world is just one frozen white—Oh, excuse me, I'm going on too much. But do call if you need anything. And please, feel welcome on Friday."

With that, Etta was out the door and bounding for her jeep. She backed around and tossed a friendly wave before heading down the lane.

Karen knew two things as she wandered into the parlor: that Etta Cavendish was someone worth knowing, and that she herself would be in attendance next Friday night.

By nightfall she had managed to analyze only one reference separating pottery shards into separate strata. The work had been sporadic at best, broken by a long walk on the beach and other moments when she had drifted away to stare out the windows. The daydreams during those times had no particular focus, except the house and the stark November vistas around her. Often, as she had glanced around, she marveled at how much a part of the house she already felt, as if she had been years here, not a mere two days.

Karen had just finished making notations when the phone rang. The noise startled and for a moment confounded her, so harshly did it tear through the quiet. It shrilled again and she rose to answer, puzzled as to who would be calling. She had asked everyone including Walter not to contact her for a while, and as for Maggi—Karen had explained her need to get completely away and think.

"Hello," Karen spoke softly into the receiver.

Through a crackling line, static punctuating every word, Maggi's voice carried over the distance. Her words were warm and without the slightest hint of hurt or pique. "How are you making out way up there on the farm?" she inquired. Not even the malfunctions of the Bell system could ruffle her composure.

"Fine. Just fine," Karen answered. She wanted to yell across the miles, "God, you've got to see this place, Maggi!" Instead she lowered her voice to a normal pitch. "It's beautiful here. You'd love my view of the sea."

There was an awkward pause while the line crackled and buzzed. Finally Maggi spoke. "Is it all right I called? If you'd rather not talk just now I'd—"

"No. It's okay." Karen interrupted. "I'm glad." She was glad to hear Maggi's voice, glad to hear her speaking with such warmth, making a link between Karen and a world already far away. "Really, I'm fine. How about you? Are you okay, Maggi?"

"Sure, I'm fine too. We're doing final editing this week. You look great, by the way. I'm glad we decided to film that last segment at the Cape instead of in your office. The effect is marvelous." Maggi's voice softened. "The wind's in your hair, your jacket's blowing off one shoulder. Actually, you look more like a poet than a professor."

"Terrific, I'm complimented. A stint as a poet would probably do me a world of good, now that I think about it." Karen added, "Although I'm not sure I could handle all that cheap red wine."

Both women laughed easily in release of the tension just beneath their words.

"Do you need anything?" Maggi asked.

"Nothing I can think of." She paused a beat before adding, "But I'm glad you called. Maggi, I—that is," Karen paused and began again, "Please don't think I'm doing this to hurt you. You've been quite an explosion for me. But we've been all though this, haven't we? I'm sorry." Karen lowered her voice. "I don't mean to stumble around so. I just need more time to sort it all out."

"I know." Maggi paused then said gently, "I care about you, Karen. No matter how this all works out. What happened between us was a surprise to me too, you know, something I hadn't bargained for either . . . though not as big a surprise to me as to you." Maggi chuckled, and Karen grinned into the phone, the reference to Maggi's experience providing a lighter moment and also a surprising twinge of jealousy.

After she hung up Karen stood at the stove brewing a pot of tea and reflecting. The night was windless, the moon riding pale and high over the restive sea. To her, everything seemed restive and waiting, herself as well. Waiting perhaps for a veil to part and reveal a solution, waiting for a better time to really get going on the book, waiting even for the tea water to boil. Waiting.

When the tea was ready, she placed it and a taste of cheese and crackers on a tray and carried them with her into the parlor.

Above the mantle hung a mirror in an overly ornate frame, no doubt some relic of a past garage sale expedition. She hated it, and planned to replace the gaudy mirror with a colorful print as soon as she had time to prowl the local shops. As she crossed in front of the mirror, balancing the tray, her eye caught movement—a dark shadow in the mirror's reflecting surface. She snapped her head in the direction of the retreating form, almost spilling the tray. Nothing moved. Everything around her was still and silent.

Satisfied it had been a trick of her peripheral vision, something caused by eyes tired from the small writing on all those cards, she set down the tray and poked the dwindling fire.

She rubbed a hand over her brow, for a headache was again threatening, aware she did not feel at ease. Periodically she glanced over her shoulder, to the direction of the shadow, attempting to shake the notion that she was not alone in the house. She tried to relax, but twice got up and walked through the darkened rooms just to satisfy herself that she was alone.

The sense of another presence was overwhelming. Several times she caught herself looking toward the doorway, half-expecting someone to enter and join her by the fire. The rise of small hairs on the back of her neck came not from the sense of menace or danger, but from the persistent and curiously real sense of someone watching her from the shadows. The fireplace provided the only light, projecting a dervish dance on the ceiling above her. On the mantle in front of the mirror the clock ticked loudly.

With an effort of will, she forced herself to stare into the fire to hypnotize her senses with the licking flames. "This is nonsense," she breathed, though still she rested her hand on the nape of her neck.

Despite her unease, or perhaps because of it, she focused her concentration on the call from Maggi. She smiled at Maggi's reference to her as a poet, touched by the poignancy of the image. What insight, even if unwitting, into a more whimsical side of her nature, a side buried beneath the trappings of academe.

Knowing she inched toward dangerous ground, yet compelled by Maggi's mention of the Cape, Karen let herself remember the day they filmed her walking along the dunes and how she must have looked. Remembering the events leading to that time, she shivered slightly.

Maggi hadn't come to work, as promised, the day after

their dinner, nor the day after. When she did arrive, arms overflowing with books and sheaves of paper, Karen's delight was tempered with apprehension. How should they act toward each other? How would the rush of emotion, not only shared but admitted, affect their close and easy connection? It was unnerving, but not so much that Karen didn't count the hours till lunch.

When at last they spread egg salad sandwiches on the desk between them Maggi appeared more reserved than usual, her conversation less animated. Karen spoke more quietly as well, matching her tone to Maggi's. There was so much she wanted to say, but with no idea how. Her stomach fluttered, her palms lightly filmed with perspiration. What was Maggi thinking? How could they speak again of the delicate words already said?

Maggi toyed with a brown paper sack, creasing and folding it as though working a delicate origami. She cleared her throat and grinned, an almost shy smile breaking over flushed cheeks. "I've been thinking–" She carefully creased another fold into the sack. "Maybe we could take the weekend off–have a little vacation for ourselves. I have a friend who owns a cabin out on the Cape. . . ." Maggi's voice trailed off with a light, hopeful lilt.

At first Karen didn't answer. There was a rush of relief–Maggi wanted to see her. But, so much time alone. It seemed dangerous–and so sudden.

"There's only your concluding remarks yet to be filmed," Maggi said. "We could shoot the footage somewhere out on the dunes. I'm not half bad with the videocam."

Project deadlines loomed and Karen had been taught to expect the customary peeled nerves and long nights awash in bitter coffee. A short rest beforehand might be good for her. "I'll think about it," she said and tried to force down a bite of her sandwich.

The lunch hour over, they returned to separate tasks,

but all afternoon Karen felt like a car laboring uphill in the wrong gear—straining and held back. She sat in a cramped room, reviewing footage of a village performing a medicine ritual. She ran the footage several times, hoping her concentration would improve. But the question of the weekend played a much more vivid tape than the technicolor pictures on the monitor.

After several viewings, Karen pressed the stop lever and sat back in her chair. Dammit. She wanted to go. If left to her own devices, she could imagine wanting to spend every minute with Maggi—drink her up like a cup of sweet mead. She looked at her watch with a stab of panic. It was almost five. Maybe Maggi had made plans with someone else. Maybe she'd changed her mind altogether. Maybe she'd already left for home. Karen raced the maze of corridors for Maggi's office.

A little breathless she lunged into the doorway. Maggi looked up from a stack of papers, a slow smile spreading over her face. "Yes," Karen said softly, "Yes, let's go."

* * * * *

The cottage was everything Maggi had promised: a waterfront bungalow complete with knotty pine walls and a little brick fireplace. The furnishings were sparse and utilitarian, but cozy, with floral print slipcovers on the sofa and armchair.

After a preliminary exploration of their weekend home, taking separate bedrooms, they converged on the tiny kitchen. Karen, a decent cook, was struck as never before by the intimacy of preparing and eating food together. Maggi deftly cracked eggs into a bowl while Karen grated cheese. They were preparing this for one another. Each would eat, taking the offering into her body. Karen was relieved it was Maggi and not she whose task it was to break the eggs. In this mood she feared the delicate shells might shatter in her hands.

They dragged the floral-covered sofa up close to the fire and ate there, balancing plates of eggs and bagels on their knees. The flickering light from the fire cast Maggi's face in a light peach glow, her half-lidded eyes emitting no less warmth than the crackling hearth. Maggi's hand rested gently on the cushion between them, a slender brown curve floating on a delicate white peony in the fabric. Karen watched fascinated, as the thin line mooring her to resolve began to fray, loose ends twirling rapidly away from the core, leaving only a fine slim thread, it too in jeopardy of snapping.

The center will not hold, Karen breathed. She knew it, and knew, too, that from here there would be no turning back, at least not tonight. "Then, bless me to heaven. Bless us to heaven," she breathed, and trembled as she reached over to place her hand over Maggi's.

* * * * *

They lay close together at dawn. Outside a thick fog separated them from the sea and muffled the crash of the waves. Curls and filigrees of mist settled around the dunes and were woven into a loose tapestry among the tall grass. Warm skin met warm skin the length of their bodies, safe from the chill under the pile of blankets. Karen had not known until now the extent of her capacity for passion, nor that fulfillment was an expanding vessel into which increasingly more fulfillment could be poured. Each time she felt her straining boundaries could contain no more, the groaning sides expanded, hurling her further into uncharted atmospheres, a nova reborn time and time again. Maggi touched Karen's breast gently and Karen moved against her, a deep moaning in her throat.

Later, they got up and ran, chilled, to the bathroom

where they stood laughing together under the hot shower. Outside, the fog bank still rested heavily on the shore, filtering all but a weak grey light which seeped onto the dunes in small puddles. Bundled in warm jackets, they were compelled into such a morning, wordlessly bounding toward the fog and the dunes. An environment that might have been painted as melancholy or even brooding was to them magical. Tufts of fog floated lightly over Maggi's dark hair and completely obscured Karen as she bent to retrieve a small pink shell, parting seconds later to reveal her holding it for Maggi to see.

Maggi raced ahead, executing a near faultless plié while Karen applauded and whistled, then ran to catch up with her. Arm in arm, they tramped through wet grass and soft sand, passing other cottages where lights were beginning to come on. Karen wanted to compose a song and began to hum a tune of her own devising. It hadn't words but if it had she was sure they might be words like creation, or dawn, or maybe even God.

On the way back to the cottage, stomachs growling for breakfast, Maggi stopped and exclaimed, "This is it. Right here is where we should film you, strolling along the dunes and reminding us of the timeless power of the things we create and believe. God, it's great. I love it." Buoyed by the spirit of adventure and the incredible unworldliness of the moment, Karen offered no resistance. If someone had suggested she leap Niagara Falls, she was convinced she could do it with hardly a pant.

A few hours later they were back—Maggi walking backward, the camera strapped to her shoulder, Karen walking slowly toward her, talking animatedly and gesturing. Later, on film, it would appear that Dr. Latham was a woman thoroughly thrilled with her subject matter, so lively was her patter, so intense the sparkle in her eyes.

* * * * *

A sudden hissing from the fireplace, as a log broke and tumbled off the grate, snapped Karen back to the present. Surprised it was after eleven, she stretched her toes toward the fire. Maggi receded, slowly at first, her countenance melting back, replaced by the sensation from earlier. She wasn't alone. The feeling nagged at her like an uncompleted task or a piece of music whose title she could not bring to mind.

In the stillness she heard it again, the soft rustling. She held her breath in her throat and turned toward the doorway separating the parlor from the darkened kitchen. Moonlight streamed through the windows, wrapping the room in a blue-white gauze, reflecting the panes in the window on the shiny surface of the table. She half-expected to see someone crossing the shaft of light, someone going about a routine bit of business, so perfectly a part of the house did the sound seem to her. She gazed at the empty doorway, half-waiting, strangely unwilling to assign the sound to a rational cause, like scurrying rats.

The need for sleep overcame her unease and Karen trudged up the stairs, undressed, and fell wearily into bed. Like a sidewalk to one who has fainted, sleep rose immediately to meet her.

Suddenly she was swimming, her slightest movement capable of propelling her forward through a thick, viscous substance in which she could breathe and float weightless. She let herself cavort porpoise-like, diving deep in the murky warm liquid, then soaring high in a twirling arc toward a surface she could never quite reach.

Someone else was with her, swimming straight and sure toward her. As the figure neared, she could see a woman reach up and lift a shawl from her shoulders. A smile of recognition broke across a face that was dark and fine-boned, even sultry, but from whose eyes protruded a searing glimpse of pain and secrets. The woman smiled and said hello without moving her lips.

Then everything changed and they were sitting on a carriage made of wood and moving very fast, skimming the top of the water. Laughing, the wind blowing their hair, they sped giddily through a nameless dark, every sense sharpened to a brilliant point of light. The woman put her arm around Karen and said, without words, *At last.*

"Yes. At last, at last," Karen cried, though her mouth was filled with wind.

The woman reached to touch Karen's cheeks with ice cold fingers; the touch caused Karen's face to burn. White hot comets sped through her body, coming to rest in a sweet ache in her belly. She wanted to take the cold hands in hers and warm them, and did so, though the gentle massage did not take away the death-like cold. She felt wonderfully free; there was nothing to fear as she and the dark-haired woman sped along through a starless space empty of all but them. Sometimes the woman would cause their carriage to soar high into the darkness, then dive, heightening the roller coaster sensation in Karen's body.

* * * * *

In her bed, Karen slowly became aware of the warmth and the weight of her blankets. She turned to place her arm around the graceful curve of the body resting next to hers. Her hand came to rest on the cold, smooth sheet.

Confused by the emptiness where there should have been a yielding warm hip or soft breast, Karen lay still, suspended between worlds. Full wakefulness came slowly, and when it did, the normally hard edges were blurred and soft, the vivid images of the woman and the dream melting through the boundaries which should have separated them from consciousness.

Karen's face felt hot, her skin sensitive as if she had

developed a fever, and her loins ached for touching and for release. Gently, she turned and placed her hand in the warm crevice, and as quickly as release came she returned to a deep and untroubled sleep.

CHAPTER 4

Two mornings later, Karen sat resolutely at her desk, sorting through cards. Though the work was going slowly, she felt somewhat better for the trying. The day was dull and heavy, the sky thick with the curdled clouds that were a sure sign of snow. She promised herself a trip to town later after she had made some headway, a sort of gift to herself for a morning's worth of work.

The phone rang. She caught it quickly, more to stop the noise than from a desire to talk to anyone.

Walter's voice boomed out. She could almost hear the scratch of whiskers against the mouthpiece and see his full lips, ringed with hair, forming words at the other end of the line. An altogether unpleasant image, she realized, and struggled for a tone of warmth.

"I'm fine, Walter," she responded to his opening question.

"How are you getting on up there?"

"Just fine, really. I can't seem to string two good sentences together for the book but other than that I'm doing well."

There was a pause which Karen recognized as the correct moment to say she missed him, but the words wouldn't come.

Walter broke the silence. "Say, I hear you're getting snow up there soon. The first snowfall of the season is usually a pretty cozy time." He paused for a beat, and cleared his throat. "Hey, why don't I come up for the weekend?"

Karen toyed with the phone cord. "I don't know, Walter, I did come here to be alone, I'm still trying to settle in and adjust. . . ."

"C'mon, I'll only come for a day. I'll even stay somewhere else–surely there's an inn nearby. Isn't rural New England wall-to-wall bed and breakfast joints?"

"Well, Pelham Falls is hardly Bar Harbor but yes, there is the Blue Quail."

"So. How about it? I'm sort of at loose ends. The way you left–I guess I'd–I dunno, I'd like to spend a little more time together."

Karen felt her irritation grow slack, replaced by guilt-edged warmth. She owed him this much. "Okay, but please don't pressure me, Walt. I'm up here to rest, and–"

"I won't," he interrupted. "It'll be good to see you."

Karen walked to the desk and stared crossly at the piles of cards. Her concentration, what little she'd had, was broken; it seemed pointless to try to pick up the scattered threads of her work, receded now onto some stubbornly invisible spool from which she hadn't the energy to tug them. She grabbed her coat and shopping list and bounded out to her car.

By the time she reached the center of town, the sky had grown heavier and swept closer to the ground, so much so that the lower hanging clouds appeared in danger of snagging on the barren branches of sugar maples along Main Street. It would snow tonight. She could smell it in the thin, cold air.

Except for the cars parked around the square, Pelham Falls looked as if it had remained unchanged for decades. There was a commons; and the courthouse, a small well-kept building of white clapboards and black shutters, tastefully announcing its age on a brass plaque. Down the street a congregational church sat in a small grove of elms, its steeple probably having graced many a calendar page. There was a gas station, a real estate office, and a general store, suggesting that if one wanted the convenience of a K-Mart or a Safeway, one was obliged to find them closer to the highway.

The general store had fascinated Karen from her first visit. On the building facade a large sign, wooden and hand-lettered, proclaimed Pelham Falls Mercantile. Below the sign, along a boarded walk, were bright red wheelbarrows, snow shovels—and a clearance sale on garden hoses.

The warm interior welcomed her to the no-frills world of country shopping. A bouquet of aromas followed her through the aisles: machine oil, onions, woodsmoke and tobacco, and, underlying it all, the sweetish smell of the red sawdust she remembered from grade school. In one corner sat a pot-bellied stove surrounded by rough benches spread with well-read sections of the weekly paper. On the aisles stretching away from the stove were tables and shelves from which one could choose Cup-a-Soup, a new axe handle, bananas, or a checkered hunting cap.

Karen selected a plump chicken to roast for Walter's visit, and picked up several mousetraps. After starting the drive back, she remembered she'd forgotten to ask Etta about the woodstove. Surely someone as New England as Etta would be able to explain how the thing worked. She made a note to ask her later in the evening.

At eight o'clock sharp, Karen pulled to a stop in front of Etta's house, warmed by the cheery glow from her lighted windows and the sounds of tuning strings.

Everyone had arrived and Karen was enthusiastically introduced. Grace Stimson, doubtless the telephone man's Aunt Grace, extended a pudgy hand, the other clutching a violin and bow. "So nice to meet you. Heard you bought the old McCartland place." Her round face beamed from a ring of bluish finger waves.

"Well, actually, I leased it for a year." Karen shook the soft hand and smiled.

"Well, we're mightly pleased to have you. Welcome to Pelham Falls. Only next time bring your flute," Grace added with a glance toward Karen's empty hands. "And this handsome fellow is Carl Beeman." Mr. Beeman moved next to Karen, preceded by a generous paunch which he patted as he shook her hand.

Etta steered Karen toward a table in the corner and platters of homemade sugar cookies and hot spiced tea. Karen noticed for the first time the earthy, pungent odor permeating the house. Herbs were everywhere, drying in bundles, some hanging in windows, others clustered behind the woodstove; in the kitchen more piles lay in baskets on the table.

More in abundance than herbs, however, were cats—orange tabbies, slinky Siamese with wary eyes, little ones, fat ones, more cats than Karen had seen in one place before.

"Started with a couple of strays a few years back," Etta explained in response to Karen's amazed survey of the cat population. "Guess it's gotten a little out of hand. Every time there's a stray, looks like I'm the soft touch. Shoo!" Etta brushed a huge grey cat away from the cookies.

A tall, rather angular woman reached across Karen for a cookie. "Now, don't let Etta give you the impression she's hard on her animals. I'm Clara Hunt, pleased to meet you." Clara smiled and nodded in Etta's direction. "We could all tell stories about Etta and animals. Wild deer will come straight out of the woods, you know, and eat from her hand as if they were tame. It's a sight to see, I'll tell you."

Clara, who appeared to be nearing fifty, was bundled in an immense red sweater; red earrings dangled beneath her silver hair. She poured Karen tea. "Get Etta to tell you about the hunter who had the misfortune of bringing a gun onto her property." Clara's face broke into the grin of one who is in possession of inside information.

Etta merely smiled and continued handing out cups of tea and cookies.

"Well, hope we don't saw your ears off tonight," Clara said, and picked up a battered cello.

Everyone except Karen gathered around the piano. Etta slid onto the bench and sounded notes while the other musicians coaxed their strings to match. After a brief interlude, as if on unspoken cue, the musicians began a Corelli piece, the Baroque strains familiar to Karen. A white cat, pursuing a cue of its own, leapt into her lap and began purring, apparently as pleased with the music as she. Maybe next time she would bring her flute.

Karen sat in an old platform rocker threadbare along the arms and seat, and formed herself into the permanent mold cast in the lumpy stuffing. Every object in the room was well used, and most had seen better days. The linoleum floor was hospital clean but erased of its rose pattern in dark spots in front of the chair and by the door. The wallpaper had yellowed and there was a brownish stain under the cornice board from a repaired leak. In a far corner was a television set, its rabbit ears set on a white lace doily. The blond cabinet and oval screen made Karen feel that should she turn it on, she might very likely see Ed Sullivan come into focus.

Everything in the house spoke of a stubborn pride, and of a woman who would consider asking for help as not in keeping with a fiercely guarded independence. Not, Karen knew, that Etta really needed for much. Twice yearly she paid workers to harvest a potato crop and then later to pick cranberries from the bog in the glade. This small income was enough to pay for necessities like food and taxes, but few luxuries. Karen glanced over at the piano and smiled at Etta, who returned the smile while playing a decent arpeggio from Telemann on the yellowed keys.

Just behind Karen was a small alcove containing a desk and several shelves of books. A green shaded lamp on the desk illuminated a cloth bound book opened below it. As the music rose and fell behind her, she walked into the alcove, drawn as ever to any collection of books. She had always claimed she could tell as much about someone from their bookshelves as from listening to them talk and, in that mood of curiosity, began looking along the shelves for familiar titles. There were a few volumes on gardening, some on wild herbs, several books of poetry. One large section of thick cloth-bound books of various sizes and shapes was untitled; on the spines were merely dates, lettered by several different hands. One such volume lay open under the light and Karen leaned over it, gazing onto an even, neat writing. At the top of the page was carefully lettered "Pelham Falls, 1891."

Karen flipped to the front of the book. Soon she was learning whose corn relish had won at the county fair, whose barn had burned, wiping out that farmer's team of horses. Though the pages were yellowed and brittle, the hand that wrote upon them was precise and even, so that Karen could read almost all of the notations. So engrossed was she that she failed to notice that the music had ceased until Etta crossed into the alcove and laid a hand on her shoulder. "Fascinating, isn't it?" she said. "This project was begun by my great-grandmother; the women of the family have continued it ever since. I thought you might be interested in some of the old entries about your place."

"Oh yes. Yes indeed, I would," Karen said, looking into Etta's wrinkled face. "If I could take some of them home with me, I promise to take good care and return them promptly."

She tensed, fearing Etta might refuse. For some reason, these handwritten books were important.

"Of course," Etta said. "That's why I started looking through them for you. Besides, nobody ever reads them anymore but me. The folks over at the library want me to make a donation of them, and I probably will someday. After I'm gone, there'll be no one left to write in them anyway." Etta pulled several more volumes from the shelves and set them in a neat stack on the desk. "Take these with you for starters. Now, come on out and have some more tea and cookies with us," she said, taking Karen's hand.

Karen enthusiastically complimented the musicians, and helped herself to tea and a lemon cookie. "Now, what was that story someone was going to tell about the hunter?" Karen looked around the circle of faces, anxious for more lore of Pelham Falls.

"Well," Clara began, settling herself on the worn arm of a frieze-covered chair, "It was a few years back. That old reprobate, Tom Evens, considered himself a better hunter than most. He was always complaining that Etta Cavendish owned several hundred acres of the best hunting land around here and wouldn't let anyone near her place with a gun. Everyone knows how Etta feels about killing for fun. She's made no bones about it."

Clara settled more comfortably in her chair. "Well, old Tom had a cousin up from New York and wanted to show off. Show him how many big deer he could bag in a day. So, him and the cousin went out to Etta's woods early one morning, figuring there'd be plenty of deer just for the taking and by the time Etta heard the shots and found them, it'd be too late to do anything. They walked away back into the forest, back to the places where hardly any sunlight comes through at all, and hunkered down behind some brush, waiting.

"Pretty soon, a huge buck wanders up, just a few feet in front of them, and stands there, still as you please. Tom must have thought Jehovah himself set up the shoot for it was the biggest buck he'd ever seen. Slowly, he raised his rifle. The deer stood perfectly still, calm as a hen laying, and not any further away than that wall over there." Clara indicated the wall a few feet away.

"Bang! The first shot ripped through the woods. But the buck just stood there looking at him. He'd missed!

"Tom couldn't believe what he was seeing. He fired again. Then again. Still the buck just looked at him. It was like his bullets just dissolved, never came anywhere near the thick brown hide of that buck. Then, and Tom swears this is true, the buck looked straight at him with a kind of triumph, like it was saying you should have known better.

"Tom and his cousin left right then, spooked as can be, and headed straight to the tavern and told everybody Etta had put a charm on the woods and everything in them. Not a soul has been out here to try and put one over on Etta ever since. The boys down at the tavern still talk about old Tom and the buck that refused to die."

Karen looked over at Etta with far less skepticism than admiration. "That's quite a story, Etta. Did you really do that? I mean, how could you do a thing like that?"

Etta's face crinkled into a smile. "There's things as can be done in the natural world, things our books never taught us."

The room grew quiet. Clara stopped jangling her bracelets

and Mr. Beeman sank into a nearby chair. Everyone looked at Etta, including Karen, whose eyes had never left the wizened face.

"We're mostly taught reality is a flat straight line, but it isn't. It spirals and curls through layers of what's real. Once you can accept that, and find a way through the spirals, the rest is easy. And there's great power there. There's more that can't be seen than there is that can, you might say."

"Is there a name for this–uh, power? For this belief?" Karen asked, trying to subdue the scientist in her.

"Oh, I don't think so. Some like to think of it as God, but I don't. It's more like Nature. She holds us all in the palm of her hand, letting us see some things and hiding others from our natural eyesight. But you can see with more than eyes and hear with more than ears–if you want to, that is."

After a long silence, Etta finally said, "It's getting late. Let's try the Bach piece before we leave." She got up and started for the piano.

"The timing is so difficult with Bach," Grace said, falling in behind Etta and tightening her violin strings.

"Count, Grace, count," Etta said through a grin, and slid onto the bench.

Later, as Karen left, the first snow had already dusted the landscape in a thin layer of white. Large flakes drifted slowly around her as she clutched the journals and sought footing on the slippery ground. She thought of Etta and of the strange conversation, about seeing with more than eyes, and Etta's references to the power of nature. She shook her head and smiled slightly, thinking she would ask more about it one day when she had time. Right now the excitement was the stack of books beside her on the seat.

Her own house welcomed her. She had left the downstairs lights on when she left, tossing aside energy consciousness in favor of a lighted greeting, a warm hello reflecting onto the white yard.

After making a cup of tea, she went immediately upstairs to bed. The journals on the nightstand beside her, she turned the blanket setting to high and slipped a volume from the stack, propping it on her knees. Outside, the snow fell in huge wet flakes, a knobby white curtain drawn in front of the trees and sea. Feeling insulated, even cocooned, Karen pored over the aged pages, stopping only to sip tea and soon forgetting even that. She read each word carefully, imagining settings and faces of people long dead, as if watching a home movie of people she knew and cared about.

Toward the end of the journal, the one she had started while at Etta's, she found a notation which she read through several times:

In this year of sorrows, another has paid us a visitation. Poor Ian McCartland and his niece Aimee, the McCartland's housekeeper, were killed when a tree blew down across their wagon in a storm. Now Blessing's a widow, and I fear for her, for she's most inconsolable. Odd how little she seemed to care for Ian when he was alive, and yet how poorly she is bearing his death. What is to become of her heaven can only say. We will all pray for her, and that this terrible winter will pass, leaving no more sorrows behind in Pelham Falls.

There had been other notations about the McCartlands, but none so poignant as this. She had learned that the McCartlands had been present at church on Easter, and that Blessing had as usual won a prize at the fair for her small paintings. Small glimpses into the lives of the poeple who had lived here long before her.

She closed the journal and reached for another—the record of the previous year—her eyes searching for the names she now recognized. Sandwiched between an account of hostilities which had broken out between locals and French Canadians at one of the logging camps, and the proceedings of a town meeting, she read:

> *Walked to the beach today to gather mussels from the rocks. Blessing and Aimee were there in the cove. They seemed gay, and in a lively frame of mind, and walked with their hands entwined. They either did not see me or chose to pay no heed, so caught up were they in some sport of their own making. When I approached, Blessing's features grew hard and Aimee appeared impatient, both acting as if I had intruded upon a private game. I daresay this isn't the first time I've reached such inhospitable treatment, particularly from Blessing. Though we've been neighbors many years, she has turned herself more and more away from us, and, I'll venture, all since young Aimee came to reside with her. Twice I've come calling in the late afternoons, once to bring a jar of pickles, and each time have felt that my presence was not wanted. We were all so pleased when Aimee came. She seemed such a pleasant, fair thing. Now, I don't know.*

Despite herself, Karen grew sleepy. The words blurred on the page even as she tried to focus by rubbing her face and shaking her head roughly from side to side. Smoothly, sliding softly along a silken tunnel, Karen closed her eyes and let herself fall.

The woman was there immediately, motioning to her from a rock on the beach, the wave of her hand heavy and slow, like a swimmer underwater. She looked relieved, as if she had been waiting a very long time.

Karen slid along over the grains of sand, leaving no footprints, and reached out her fingertips, as if over a great distance, to touch the extended hand of the smiling figure.

A strong wind blew in from the sea and the woman reached to tuck a dark curl from her forehead, while her hair danced wildly around her. Karen heard words but the woman's mouth never stopped smiling.

Now, brushed against her ears, a word wrapped in steam, a sound borne up from the earth on an underground wind. *Now,* came again and Karen ran faster, her long skirts flattened against her legs. She reached the woman and fell into her.

Cold, oh so cold. Yet she burned at the touch, melted and reformed into soft cream moving slowly on the woman's cold-hot skin. Gliding, effortless, each sensation sharp, each cell in her body a pointed diamond, she moved with the woman toward the sea.

Karen listened to the wind and heard it say—*I have something for you.* The woman extracted an object from the pocket of her apron.

Oh, Karen wanted to see it. Never had she felt so happy. She tried to make light pierce from her eyes, but it could not part the dark mist that swirled over the woman's upturned palm. The woman brought her hand closer and Karen saw her own face, painted on an ivory white oval.

Karen reached to take it, to caress it with her fingers and press its cold smooth surface to her flaming cheek, but the woman pulled back her hand. *Not yet,* she breathed. *Not yet.*

Then Karen was lifted by arms she did not see or feel, and pressed close to the woman's body. They dove together into the air, arching down under the waves, then back again, breast to breast, thigh to thigh, no sensation less acute than the one before it. Plunging and turning they swam through air and water alike until they disintegrated into fine, golden granules that rained down over the earth from far above.

Karen awoke, frantically tugged at the blanket, pulling herself into this world and struggling for a foothold in reality. She sat up, wide-eyed, listening intently for the slight sound of movement, the sound of someone stirring in the pale dark room. There was no sound, though Karen was convinced there should be.

She sat still for long moments, relishing the luxurious sensations in her body. Outside, the snow still fell and a greyish hint of dawn seeped in at the windows. There is nothing so silent as a snow-covered morning, Karen thought before again sleeping curled in the warm bedding.

She woke again and, alarmed, looked at her watch. It was already after nine. Walter could be here any minute. Downstairs, she peered at the transformation that had taken place while she had slept. White was everywhere, lying in a thick crust on the barn roof and in perfect ridges on the outstretched branches of the trees.

Less than an hour later, Karen watched Walter's meticulously restored Volvo pull into the lane, slide a couple of times and come to a stop alongside her VW. She took a deep breath and opened the door.

He pulled her to him, bestowing an enthusiastic hug with one arm while clutching a paper bag spilling over with books in the other. He smelled like snow and Vitalis. He put the bag down, then placed both hands on her shoulders and held her out away from him, looking at her for a moment before speaking. "Gee, I was all prepared to say how rested you look." He cocked his head and looked harder. "But the truth is, you don't look so good. Are you getting enough sleep?"

Karen knew from glimpses in the mirror that circles had formed under her eyes, and she really couldn't remember whether she had washed her hair yesterday or not. "Well, actually, I could do with a little more sleep than I've been getting," she lied, unwilling to tell him that she slept quite a lot these days but was looking a little ragged from some very compelling dreams.

She took Walter's hand to lead him on a tour of the house. She had become so accustomed to quiet that the sound of his voice was irritatingly loud. His presence in the house seemed strange too, and out of place, as if he took up too much room.

"So. Did you get checked in at the Blue Quail?" she asked, partly to conceal her resentment. This definitely had not been a good idea.

"All squared away." He stood admiring the view from the bedroom window and casting an occasional glance in the direction of Karen's unmade bed.

After the tour they carried the last of Etta's banana bread into the parlor. "How about a fire?" She began gathering an armful of kindling. It was important to keep busy.

"Here. Let me do that." Walter knelt beside her.

She piled kindling on the grate. "I can do it, Walter."

As soon as the fire caught, she curled her legs under her on the settee and turned to face Walter, who rocked slowly in the chair across from her. As he talked, telling the news from Boston, she desperately searched for the warm threads of her relationship with him. She had to do something about her mood.

She tried to remember how supportive he had always been, how his experienced coaching had been so helpful to her. She thought of their long walks, of the many evenings they had spent together at her apartment or his, content to read and listen to music.

Such a perfect picture it had all seemed then. Walter, the bearded professor of languages, sitting with her in the Boston Commons. How safe, how much a part of the life she had envisioned for herself from so long ago in Downey, California. Once in a while it did occur to her that something was missing, for she felt no deep tugs of longing or passion.

But it had been heady stuff then, too idyllic to toss away; everything going according to plan.

She had known what she wanted and had set about to get it. The welder's daughter from Downey had wanted out—out of Downey and all she feared in the lives of her parents. She could have married someone there, lived in a house like all the others, gone bowling every Wednesday, taken her kids to school in a two-year-old station wagon. But she refused.

Even her parents, sensing she was capable of more, had raised her to value education, assuming she would one day leave. Sometimes she thought they had as much riding on her career as did she. They often boasted about her to friends at the Elk's Club or at Shirley's Drop on Inn, where Lawrence Welk was still on the jukebox, and where they went to drink ale and play cribbage with their cronies.

She had laid her plans carefully: the academic scholarship; the East Coast migration; the ivied playing field for exercises in intellectual curiosity. Her rise in academe had been spectacular. With careful planning she would soon be able to command the most prestigious lecture chairs and head very well-funded field expeditions. The plum was almost hers; in fact she could almost taste it.

Then Maggi England had appeared in her life and all her plans had tilted.

Walter droned on, the monologue dotted with familiar names and places, yet no longer so familiar somehow. His voice had sounded much like this on other occasions as he recounted tidbits about the lives of others: who was currently sleeping with whom; who, it was rumored, would be the next Dean of the Business School.

He had, in fact, sounded just like this the day she and Maggi returned from the Cape. She had been sitting in her office going over some old class notes when Walter came in. After pecking her on the cheek, he sat down and tilted his chair onto its back legs. "Have you heard about Dr. Prentiss?" he asked.

Karen knew Judith Prentiss only slightly, having talked with her once or twice in the cafeteria. A nice woman, Karen thought. "What about her?" She half hoped Walter wouldn't answer; in fact, she wished he weren't sitting here, trying to tell another story. Her weekend at the Cape was still fresh and, confusing as it was, beamed brightly through the maze of papers on her desk.

"She's just been asked to take an indefinite leave of absence."

"Uhmmm," Karen said without looking up. Perhaps she could discourage him with lack of interest.

"Seems she got caught having a go of it with one of her graduate students," Walter went on anyway.

"My God, Walter. What's the news in that? Doesn't everybody?"

"Right, nothing so wrong there–lots of us do it. Except this student was another woman." Walter paused for effect.

Karen struggled to catch up with his words, as the phrase 'another woman' hit her in the belly like an unexpected basketball. "What did you say?" she asked and placed a hand over the knot in her stomach.

Walter repeated the story, embellishing it this time with a few observations of his own. "I'm as liberal as the next guy," he said tugging at his beard. "I mean, some people are just that way and can't help it. They shouldn't be treated badly or anything; but they could keep it a little quieter, I think."

Karen stared at him, heat rising to her face.

"I've known some homosexuals," he went on, "men mostly. I really never thought women went for each other like that."

Karen, who had been having a great deal of trouble hearing for the ringing noise in her ears, did catch Walter's last comment. She wanted to bang her fist on the table and scream: "You're wrong, Walter!" Instead she sat quietly, feigning disinterest, and hoping her cheeks felt redder than they actually were.

Finally he had left her sitting at her desk feeling shaky and slightly nauseated. "That could be me," she said over and over. "What would I do if I couldn't do this?" She frantically sought an answer but was met only by a cold empty place in her mind.

"It shouldn't be this way. God, it shouldn't," she sobbed and dropped her forehead into her hand. Never had she so trembled on the edge of truly loving another human being. But the consequences of that loving could very well prove more than she was willing to risk.

After a few minutes, she locked her office door behind her and stepped out into the deserted corridor. There were no appointments to keep, nothing in particular she had to do. After all, she was on leave.

She walked quickly across campus toward her car. A colleague waved and she returned the greeting, not really registering any of it. In the faculty parking lot she stared, blinking back tears, at the wooden sign—DR. LATHAM—affixed to her parking slot. Instead of standing heady and expectant in love's doorway, she was instead on the brink of an abyss. Worse, there was no one she could trust to tell.

Somewhere between the parking lot and her apartment, she decided to drive somewhere for a few days—Maine, maybe—anywhere she could be alone and think . . . .

Karen looked over and realized that Walter was still talking while she had drifted away in remembrance. Curiosity compelled her to ask about Dr. Prentiss. She posed the question softly.

"Oh, there's going to be a fight about that one," Walter responded. "The A.C.L.U. is involved, and there's a Friends of Judith Prentiss Committee. She's demanding reinstatement and back wages. She says who she sleeps with is nobody's goddamn business."

"I agree," Karen said without pause and with a surge of elation. She would become a member of that Committee. Good for Judith Prentiss. . . .

Walter said he agreed too, but his face looked as if he had stepped in something disagreeable.

"It's stopped snowing," Karen said, her irritation rising again. "Why don't we take advantage and go out for lunch. Maybe a little antique browsing? I'm hungry as a wolf."

The part about wanting to get out of the house was true, but the idea of food was unappealing. The house felt, for the first time since she had been here, uncomfortable. A slight, barely perceptible sensation, like the sour beginnings of indigestion.

As they rose to leave, Walter wrapped his arm around Karen and walked with her toward the kitchen. Somewhere upstairs a door slammed resoundingly shut. Startled, Karen pulled away from him. She felt unaccountably guilty; a vague unease had settled in around her. It would be good to get out for a while.

Once outside, she started to feel better. Tension and irritability scattered away like ashes blown from a cooling fire.

They pulled to a stop at The Blue Quail. A wooden sign, swinging between white posts at the gate, depicted a huge hand-carved and painted bird. Inside, they studied the menu, a paper facsimile of the sign outside, and ordered lobster bisque.

They sat wordlessly, staring at the scene on the other side of the windows. The frozen surface of a pond picked up a glint of sun showing through the clouds to the east. When Karen did speak, it was about the book. She was surprised and relieved the words came so easily, something she was having definite trouble with at home. She felt herself relax, assisted by the bisque, which tasted as if the lobster had been plucked from the sea this morning.

After lunch they drove a few hundred feet down the road to the first of several antique shops. Inside, every square inch of surface was filled, with treasures, with junk, all of it intriguing. Picture frames of every size even hung from the ceiling, suspended on chains. A bird-like woman behind the counter smiled and returned to her magazine, leaving them to browse. Karen spied a reasonably intact oak and wicker plant stand in a far corner and knew she would buy it. Glad they had come out, she felt increasingly lighthearted and searched a huge cardboard box full of old pictures and prints for one that might be right for the mantle.

Walter had found a green satin hat with a soft pleated crown and straight round brim, probably a prop from some defunct Shakespearean repertory company. Karen smiled as he put it on. Walter placed one hand on his chest and extended the other in an oratorial gesture. "I come no more to make you laugh: things now that bear a weighty, serious brow. . . ."

Karen, touched by the prophecy in the well-delivered line, looked at him for a long moment. Watching someone leave your life was hard.

Karen remained in good spirits until around four o'clock, when she felt a compelling urge to return home, as if she remembered a pot left on the burner or a cake too long in the oven. She wanted, no, needed to return. There were more shops they had planned to visit, but Walter didn't insist and, instead, turned the car around and started back.

Once in the house, Karen's irritation rose to a crescendo. Walter didn't belong here. Hastily, fearing her resentment, she suggested they take naps. Maybe if they were apart for a little while. . . .

She showed Walter to the guest bedroom upstairs. While his face and body language indicated displeasure at demotion to guest bedroom status, he said nothing and quietly closed the door. She heard his shoes drop onto the floor and knew that he would soon be asleep. Grateful for the privacy, Karen went into her own bedroom, propped herself up in the tousled covers, opened one of the journals, and began to read.

The events and the people described on the brittle, yellow pages took shape; faces and personalities, scenes with movement and color replaced lines done in composition hand and black ink. Pelham Falls and its people, its loggers and fishermen, its farmers, presented themselves in stories both ordinary and dramatic, sad and amusing. She smiled at an anecdote about an argument over a boundary line between neighbors, one of whom turned his pigs loose in the disputed corn field by means of a torn hole in the fence. She read of the arrival of Aimee McCartland from her home in Massachusetts.

She was described as fair of face and hair and with an abundance of good health and spirits. The writer of the journal had been pleased she was coming to live with the McCartlands and hoped her presence would add a more lighthearted air, as the McCartland place, while not exactly gloomy, did seem to lack in warmth and cheer.

When Karen rose and returned to the parlor, she carried with her the gaudy stack of cheap novels and placed them in the downstairs bookcase. The journals would be reading matter enough.

In the kitchen, she rubbed the chicken with salt and a liberal amount of garlic and set it in the electric oven for supper later. She sat at the table, enjoying the illusion of being alone, but her mood, while improved, still felt precarious, like a small fester which, if pricked, would seep.

Walter came down, wearing a look of resignation. He moved over to the table where Karen had been staring into space.

"I'll be going right after supper," he said, and looked past Karen to the orchard beyond the window. "Guess this wasn't such a good idea."

Karen traced her finger over a whorl on the oak table. With her eyes still lowered, she nodded slowly.

"It's a lovely place, Karen," Walter finally spoke. "But uncomfortable. You're so distant." He paused. "So far away. I've never seen you quite like this."

Karen cleared her throat and looked at him. "I tried to tell you how I felt—about needing to be alone. There's something about this house I really need right now, Walter. The isolation—the quiet maybe. Whatever it is, though, it's all I can think of that I want for myself."

They set about making dinner in an atmosphere of enforced politeness, carefully avoiding each other's eyes. As soon as they had eaten, Walter began pulling on his coat and gloves.

Karen laid her hand on his arm. "Take care of yourself, Walter," she said softly.

He hugged her and walked quickly through the door and into the night. She watched him go with only relief. She had felt imposed upon; something far too ordinary had been allowed to come between her and her house, a house waiting expectantly for her to turn back into its warm interior, and sleep. . . .

The snow had begun again, flakes the size of pillow ticking falling in thick profusion. Karen eased over to a chair at the table, mesmerized by the snowfall. Walter's car was long gone, even the tracks filled in quickly by the fresh snow. The trees stood frozen in the windless night. The lane and the snow-covered fields were silent and still, as was the empty house around her.

There was a brief moment of feeling alone, a moment when the phrases like wanting and not having, or having and not wanting, rolled around in her mind, but they were soon dispersed by a sensation of warmth and of slipping gently toward something appealing and soft.

Karen's strength was ebbing away and she didn't care, but she wished she were in a more comfortable chair. She grew sleepy so quickly these days. She pushed herself up from the table with the flat of her hand, turned off the kitchen light, and shuffled through the door into the parlor, thinking she heard the rustling sounds again but not quite sure. Her own footsteps echoed loudly in the still house.

She started across the floor to sit in the big overstuffed chair at the fireplace and stopped. Something was out of place. It took a second in the dim light; but then she saw that one of the books she had brought down earlier had fallen from the bookcase and lay on the floor a few paces away.

She walked over to it and bent down. *The Face in the Ivory* stared back at her from the mylar cover. She looked a long moment more. How had the book gotten there? She had wedged all the books tightly between two thick volumes.

She reached for it and recoiled. The book was ice cold to her touch. Expecting the chill from the cover when her fingers touched it this time, she picked it up, examining it and turning the book over in her hands.

She was tired, so very tired, and wondered if she had the strength to make it across the floor to the chair. With a shrug she dropped the book to the floor and sank into the chair without even thinking of starting a fire. Behind her she heard the noise again and muted whispering.

Maybe it's the wind, she thought, and tried to remember whether there was a wind this evening. Her eyelids felt heavy and she closed them, still aware of the sounds, like someone walking about in the kitchen and talking, perhaps to her. She tried to listen harder but was so very sleepy, so tired.

She was slipping and falling again, falling into darkness. Behind her the whispering grew louder. It was a steamy sound, hard to make out, but the further she drifted the more distinct it became until she heard the words clearly. Someone whispered very close to her ear, *At last.*

Yes, she tried to say but couldn't because she was falling so quickly. She passed through a dark tunnel and toward a flickering orangish light, barely perceptible and still a long distance away. The voice behind her kept saying, *At last, at last.*

At the end of the tunnel the orange glow grew brighter. Soon, blinking, she saw that the glow came from two kerosene lanterns on the mantle over the fireplace. She was in the room again but now there was a fire in the hearth, the lanterns glowing brightly above it. She turned and saw that it was the same room, but the furniture was different, and the walls were hung with many small pictures. She was warm and happy, and looked expectantly around the room for the someone she knew was there.

The woman floated up beside Karen. She could feel the chill and smell a faintly musty odor. *I will come often now,* the woman breathed. *All is as it was meant to be.*

There was music, tinkling light notes as from a music box. Karen looked at the woman who smiled at her with wide teeth, her lids half-closed over the fiery green of her eyes.

A hot stab of passion pierced Karen's belly and she reached out for the woman's hand. The woman was wispy and gauze-like and, although Karen could feel the cold of her hand and the power of her presence, it seemed as if she were holding smoke.

They danced to the music and made slow love while floating in the thin air of the room, and Karen rejoiced and melted with each stinging touch. They even floated out into the kitchen where Karen thrilled at the sight of hollyberries arranged in the red glass bowl. When the lovemaking and the dancing stopped, Karen felt as if she were resting on something soft and fluffy, dreamily stretching and turning her body as the woman ran her hands over Karen's back.

Then she was struggling, being pulled back away from somewhere as if by a strong hand or a cold blast of air. There were sounds, not the music now, but other sounds. Under her fingertips she felt a knobby cloth, something scratchy and tightly woven.

The sound was the ticking of a clock, and as the blankness parted, she watched her hand move over the print in the slipcover of her overstuffed chair.

"My God," she mumbled. "My God. I've been asleep." She rubbed her hands through her hair and looked into the still room. "At least I think I was," she said softly.

Struggling to clear her head and holding onto the arm of the chair, she got up and walked unsteadily to the kitchen. The light was off, but in the darkness she could see an object on the table. She moved closer.

In the center of the table was a small sprig of greenery. She picked it up and stared, struggling for a connection between something very recent and the twig of hollyberries in her hand. In the moonlight, they looked pale and dark, the reds and greens faded to a dim grey.

CHAPTER 5

Several days after Walter left, Karen couldn't be sure how many, she stood at the kitchen window wondering when last she had eaten. Time, she was discovering, seemed very different now that she was isolated from the need of it. Delineations, like Tuesday, or noon, made little sense in her new order; it could be both or neither, for all she cared. She was regulated by a different clock; eating and sleeping her calendar pages, especially sleeping.

She roamed the house often, wandering slowly and without cause, savoring her aloneness and privacy. There was no one to note her comings and goings, no one to keep track of what she did and did not do or to criticize her poor performance on the book project.

At the front windows in the parlor she stopped and gazed

out across the white yard. It had stopped snowing though the day was grey and cold. The sea rose in thick swells below her and heaved itself, exhausted, onto the shore.

For an instant she thought she saw movement down at the cove. But she didn't see it again, and soon a large gull soared from the rocks and disappeared into the offshore fog.

Ridiculous as it seemed on such a bitterly cold day, she felt drawn to the beach and the sea, and wanted to walk there among the slippery rocks and heavy breakers. Bundled against the cold she hurried down the sloping yard, leaving a line of solitary footprints in the snow. At the shore her boots crunched into translucent strings of kelp and her nostrils filled with the fishy smell of seaweed and the faintly dusty scent of snow.

Without really planning to she headed for the cove and scampered onto the largest of the rocks, pushed back the hood of her parka and sat cross legged, staring across the dark green water.

Something was happening to her. Not only had she changed the environment of her days and nights, but her intrinsic self was changing as well. She imagined it as something like falling in love, or catching a cold. Unseen molecules were rearranging their patterns, gathering momentum, and would soon emerge to change her from who she had been only a short time before into a different someone. An image of herself from even a few weeks ago clashed against the peace she now felt sitting on the cold rock. She remembered rushing from one task to another, finishing a thing while already planning the next–lunches eaten from greasy sacks at her desk; meetings; classes; grant deadlines; all calibrated for faster and faster progress to an ever-nearing pot of gold.

Karen thought of Maggi and held an image of her in her mind. "I wish she could see this, too," she heard herself say aloud, and for a moment allowed the fantasy. She pictured Maggi's face beside hers, turned toward the sea, and like her, unmindful of the biting cold.

The pleasant picture was interrupted by a blast of wind which rocked her harshly, almost toppling her. For the first time, as she struggled for footing, she realized the cold had leached all feeling from her hands and feet.

She started down, careful not to slip, for she was slightly woozy, and noticed with a start she wasn't alone.

A figure stood in dark silhouette just down the shore, looking out at the green swells. Who besides her, she wondered, would be hardy enough, or foolish enough, to be out on a day such as this? She watched, slightly anticipatory, as the figure began walking toward her, an arm raised in greeting. It was several moments before she recognized Etta's lanky gait, then saw her face smiling from a thick wrapping of shawl and ski cap.

"Hello," Etta called, her voice muffled by the waves. "I never expected to find company on such a day." She grinned at Karen.

They hugged through many layers of clothing. Karen, having come to care for her somewhat unconventional neighbor, was puzzled at a vague disappointment in her presence.

"I love the sea this time of year," Etta said, bending to pick up a piece of man-made debris which she shoved into her pocket. "There's a stark beauty to it, don't you think?"

Karen agreed, for she did share the perception of beauty in the overlays of grey over darker grey, unrelieved by brighter colors at the other end of the spectrum.

"You look deep in thought," Etta observed. "Am I interrupting some important set of mind?"

"Oh no, not at all," she replied. "I was just caught up in the beauty of it, and thinking how different my life has become already. Do you come down here often?"

"My, yes. Sometimes I think the secret of my longevity are these constitutionals on the beach—winter or summer."

Etta laughed, and Karen thought with dismay that she should invite her to the house for a cup of hot tea. However, her need for a nap, her need to be alone in the house was taking a strong lead over her manners. She looked down at the grainy sand, awkward and displeased with herself, but heard herself say nonetheless, "I've got some things to do at the house, so if you'll excuse me. . . ."

Etta nodded and smiled and Karen turned to go, then as an afterthought added, "I'm planning a trip to town tomorrow. There's an antique store I want to browse through, and some things I need from the grocery. Why don't you come along, if you're free? We could make an afternoon of it."

"I'd love to. I'll be free about two."

"Great, I'll pick you up," Karen said, and hurried away toward the house.

Upstairs at last, she shucked her parka, dropped her heavy yellow boots to the floor with a thud and, in sock feet and jeans, tumbled heavily into bed, diving into it and some sweet mystery she couldn't name. She slept, and dreamed almost at once.

The woman's face floated amid the tree branches just outside her window. The barren limbs were a mass of twisted shapes that trembled and shook in a crazy dance with the wind. The face swayed there in the branches. "Hurry. Hurry," Karen called out, tensed and waiting.

The woman entered the room and stood smiling down at Karen from the foot of the bed. Her eyes were wild, dancing with a restless fire, as if, should she choose, she could see all the way past Karen to sear burning holes in the bedclothes beneath her.

She moved to the bed and lay down, spreading her long skirts over Karen's body and placing an icy finger on her lips. She smelled of something old, something kept a long time in the bottom of a trunk and faintly mildewed. The smell tantalized Karen and she breathed it deeply, smelling too a light lilac scent of hair pomade. Karen shivered and placed her arms about the woman's neck, surprised at how light she was to the touch, boneless and wispy as smoke.

The woman resisted Karen's attempt to pull her closer and spoke through closed lips, the steamy sound slipping softly along Karen's ears and face: *You are mine.* Her breath and wordless words seemed to settle in chill blue crystals on Karen's cheek, stinging like the passionate kiss of a lover. *My heart has found you.*

The words caused Karen's breath to stop, even though at their edge was a hint of something acidic and stern. The woman touched a finger to Karen's soft belly, freezing it in a roll of passion. Karen arched and strained toward the touch, wanting more. Then they were loving again, over and over, swirling and twisting together in a tangle of sheets and long grey skirts.

Then, as suddenly as she had come, the woman disappeared. In her sleep, Karen felt strangely bereft.

When she finally awoke, groggy and sweating, it was already dark; a light snow had painted a lacy filigree on the panes of her windows. Confused and disoriented, she stumbled downstairs, mildly hungry, clutching at the fading remnants of her dream. A faint scent of mildew clung to her hair.

In the pantry, she rummaged through the canned goods and packages of dried food but found nothing she wanted to eat. She pulled a hunk of cheese from a wedge in the fridge, poured a glass of wine and sat heavily at the table, chewing listlessly and thinking about the dream.

Planning to work awhile, she carried the cheese and wine with her into the parlor and sat at the desk. But the extraordinary sensations of the dream would not leave. Everywhere she looked she imagined she could see the woman's face; she could almost feel the dreamy presence with her in the room. Resolutely she grabbed a stack of cards and sifted through them. But her eyes blurred and the headache that had been with her since she awoke threatened to explode through her temples. For a crazy instant she couldn't understand the words written on the cards, as though she were trying to read a newspaper in a foreign language.

"It's no use," she murmured, and placed the pile of cards beside the others, as yet untouched. "Might as well go back to bed." All she craved was the warm comfort there, and the blissful sleep sure to follow.

* * * * *

The next afternoon she swung into the lane at Etta's place weary from a full night of dreams. Etta was waiting just inside the window and sprinted to the car, pulling on gloves and her green cap.

While Karen drove carefully over patches of thin ice in the road, she considered asking if Etta might have an herbal remedy in stock that would relieve her growing listlessness. She was mildly concerned that the book project was off to such a bad start and that she seemed to need more sleep than ever before. She toyed with the idea a few more miles, then thought better of it and pulled the car into the parking lot of the small shop.

The shop was set back from the road and obviously served as both home and business for the proprietor. The front wall of the faded red structure was given over to a large picture window with glass shelves sporting a colorful assortment of knickknacks, vases and ceramics. Near the front door, an old wooden wheelbarrow had been painted yellow and filled with dirt to serve as a planter, though the few mums poking out of it were brown and spindly under the crust of snow.

As the two women entered, a small brass bell and blast

of cold air announced their arrival. The shop obviously specialized in smaller antiques and objets d'art, for there wasn't a round oak table nor Hossier cabinet to be found. Instead the place was filled to overflowing with bow-front china cabinets and display cases crammed with Limoges and Royal Doulton.

A jovial woman looked up from her energetic polishing of a silver egg cup. "Why, Etta Cavendish. What a pleasant surprise." She moved from behind the counter and grasped Etta's hand.

"Lorraine." Etta grinned. "Guess it's been most of a year since I last dropped by to see you. How are things?"

"Fine. Just fine. Of course the slow season is coming up, but I was lucky enough to make the highest bid on the Chamberlain estate last week. She had some real pretty things. I should have no trouble selling them, that I can promise you."

Lorraine beamed at Etta. "Well, what charity are you putting the bite on me for today? If it's the Christmas feed, I'll donate a turkey again."

"Actually, I was going to get around to the Christmas dinner next week, Lorraine. Today I'm just here to browse and introduce my new neighbor. Lorraine, this is Karen Latham."

Lorraine extended a perfumed hand. "Well, welcome to Pelham Falls. Do you live out to the McCartland place, then?"

"Yes, I've just leased it for a year. My, you have a lovely shop." Karen smiled, her glance falling on a pair of red glass swans, bookends most likely, their necks pulled backward by invisible reins.

Lorraine's eyes followed the sweep of Karen's hand, then came to rest again on her visitor. "Say, since you're out on the McCartland place, you'd be interested in some things I got in the Chamberlain sale." She moved behind the counter, slid back the wooden panel and extracted an oblong black leather case. "Careful now. They're very old." Lorraine turned the box toward Karen on the counter.

Five oval miniatures sat propped in the velvet lining. Karen's cheeks flamed as she looked down at the small paintings.

There were four paintings of her house, one for each season; a fifth portrayed a cluster of tiny violets. On a small white card at the edge of the box she read: BLESSING McCARTLAND, 1849-1902.

Karen could feel Etta's eyes on her, searching her response. Lorraine waited discreetly for a murmur of approval. Karen reached to touch the paintings, drawn to the painted ivory as surely as if a magnet pulled her fingers.

Lorraine broke the silence. "There's another one. It's here by itself in the case." She reached in among the figurines and set the cameo on the counter.

Karen's gasp was audible.

The artist had rendered a fine, elegant portrait of a light-haired, rose-cheeked young woman, a woman who could have been Karen's twin.

"That's me," she exclaimed, and turned to Etta for confirmation of the striking resemblance.

"My, my, there is a resemblance, don't you think so, Etta?" Lorraine chimed.

"Let me see," Etta said, picking up the miniature. "Yes—yes, I should say so." Etta raised her eyebrows and looked back and forth between the painting and her new friend. Karen thought the questioning look lasted a beat too long; all that was needed was a simple yes or no. Finally Etta asked, "Do you happen to know who posed for this, Lorraine?"

"No, not off-hand. But you could probably look it up. There's a good-sized section on Mrs. McCartland's work in a book called *New England Woman Artists.* Ever have any kinfolk up this way, Miss Latham?"

It was a second before Karen realized she'd been spoken to. "Oh—no, no, I don't believe so. How much—" she stammered, "how much for the set? And this one too?" She held her likeness out toward Lorraine in a sweating hand.

"Well, they're seventy-five dollars apiece, so let me see. That would come to four hundred and fifty dollars. But since you're the new occupant of Mrs. McCartland's house, I'll make it an even four hundred."

Etta poked Karen soundly in the ribs with a bony elbow just as she was about to say "sold." In the space of time it took Karen to recover herself, Lorraine came down to three-eighty and Karen lunged to accept before Etta delivered another blow.

After Karen and Etta left the shop, Karen asked, "Would you mind if we stopped by the library? I'd like to find that book about New England artists." Karen's voice sounded light and breathless, as if she had been running.

"Of course," Etta replied. "It's our afternoon to do as we please, isn't it?"

Karen thought she detected a note of concern in Etta's voice, but shrugged it off and headed the car toward Pelham Falls.

The library was a tiny brick building that had stood for almost a century on a side street off the square. Etta waited in the car while Karen bounded up the steps. Within minutes she emerged carrying a book under her arm and wearing a look of sly delight. She felt oddly like a teenager sleuthing for a glimpse of the object of a crush. She slid into the car beside Etta and breathlessly suggested they round out the day with an early dinner at the Blue Quail, her treat. Etta accepted, on condition she buy her own dinner.

There was still the shopping left to do, and Karen pulled the car to a stop in front of the Pelham Falls Mercantile. As they walked up the steps, two farmers standing at the door lifted their hats in greeting with the deference that seemed to accompany Etta wherever she went. "Ma'am," said one. "Miz Etta," said the other, and opened the door for them. Etta strode into the store, smiling and nodding at customers and clerks who greeted her warmly in return.

They shopped quickly, using the same basket, then sat for a minute by the woodstove. A fire crackled in the stove and a dented grey teapot emitted a thin curl of steam. Etta looked at Karen tenderly, half turned toward her. "Hope you won't think I'm being too meddlesome, but you're looking kinda peaked, Karen. Are you feeling all right?"

Karen, taken aback, stammered something and turned to face the stove. "As a matter of fact, I've been meaning to ask you about a tonic, or something. I am feeling a bit listless these days." Karen prayed her tone conveyed the unimportance of her revelation. "I did buy some B vitamins today, but anything else you could suggest certainly couldn't hurt."

She continued staring at the stove and fiddling with a snap on her parka. Admitting she wasn't up to par wasn't easy, especially since she had come here to rest. Resting, however, was exactly the problem; it was all she really wanted to do. She couldn't remember ever wanting to sleep so often—and feeling so unfocused and blurred when awake.

"All right. I think I can fix up something. Let me just run over to the counter and see if Albert has some of those nice cotton tea bags."

While Etta was away, Karen flipped quickly through the book in her lap and slipped a scrap of paper into the page beginning the article on Blessing McCartland.

Etta and Karen, the first diners of the evening, were seated at a linen-covered table by the window. Karen was glad for the hour, as she guessed Etta probably ate an early supper and she herself was excited about the book and the evening ahead. She couldn't wait to return home and read about a woman, dead these hundred years, who had at one time mysteriously painted her face.

Karen was buttering a thick slab of homemade bread when a man appeared at their table. He smiled at Etta, then at Karen, and laid a beefy hand gently on Etta's thin shoulder. "I saw you come in, Miz Cavendish. I wanted to come over and say thanks. That heifer you worked on the other night—well, she got to her feet next mornin' and seems to be doing just fine."

"I'm so glad to hear it." Etta smiled. She introduced Karen, then turned back to the farmer. "Let me know if she needs anything else. I'll be happy to try and help." The man bowed slightly and moved off across the dining room.

"So," Karen asked lightly, "is this another tale of Etta and her legendary powers with animals? Tell me more, Etta. What's this all about?"

Etta made a fuss of wiping imaginary crumbs with her napkin. "Oh, I don't know so much about legendary. But I do sit with sick animals from time to time."

"Sit with?"

"Well, more like tune myself to them. I set great store by natural means of healing. Sometimes the best that can be done is to sit and touch them, sort of act as a channel."

"You mean like faith healing?" Karen stopped eating and looked directly at her dinner companion.

"You could call it that, though there's no religious meaning."

Karen smiled slightly and leaned forward. "Yes, I rather think things like that can happen. Any creature can benefit from feeling cared about. . . . But what about other things, like that story the other night? The one where you charmed the forest or whatever—hexed away those hunters?"

Etta's eyes sparkled in the light from the tall white taper. "It's not all that much of a story. Like I said, there's things we can see, and things we can't." She paused and leaned back, looking intently at Karen. "But that doesn't mean the things aren't there just the same—or they're any less powerful because they're not seen. Sometimes I think they're even more so. You might say it's a matter of acting as a link between the seen and unseen—of gathering up forces and using them to bring into being even more strength than you could without them."

"You mean, like witchcraft?" Karen was both skeptical and intrigued.

"No. Not really. But I do believe in knowing with other senses, using the powers of certain kinds of prayers, if that's what you mean. My grandmother taught me most everything I know, and," she said with a slow grin, "I've added a trick or two of my own over the years."

Etta looked away, her gaze on the light snow that had begun to fall. When she looked back at Karen, her smile seemed especially tender. "Two hundred years ago we could have been burned at the stake for this kind of talk." Etta said the words lightly, and with a conspirational wink. "Some call it God, others magic, and nowadays there's all kinds of fancy names for Nature's way. But no matter what you call it, if you want to you can make things happen, or keep them from happening, or know what will happen before it does. To me it's all just another face of nature, so I don't call it anything. What is, just is."

For a few minutes Karen concentrated on her poached scrod, trying to decide whether to talk with her dinner companion about the occurrences in her house. She knew that finding the miniatures was more than coincidence. But the last thing she wanted was for Etta, or anyone else for that matter, to see her as some kind of kook who ran around seeing apparitions. Yet, of all the people she knew, the woman across from her was probably the one person she might feel even mildly comfortable asking. Trying for a purely conversational tone, she asked, "Do you believe in ghosts, Etta? Or I guess I should say, a soul's remaining after bodily death?"

Etta looked straight at her, seeking information as much as giving it. "Yes, I do." Her eyes were prepared to take in every nuance of Karen's response. "Why do you ask?"

Karen hesitated and dabbed at her mouth with the napkin. She leaned back in her chair and looked past Etta to the anonymous diners behind her. "No reason, really. It just seemed to follow along with our conversation." She wondered if Etta could tell she was hedging.

"Do you believe in ghosts?" Etta asked gently.

Karen considered carefully before answering. "Well, I've certainly studied volumes about cultural beliefs in spirits, or ghosts—whatever one wants to call them. I've generally relegated such notions to the category of superstition. Though," she said and paused, "some reports did sound fairly credible."

Karen leaned forward, now on safer ground. "Maybe it's my academic training, but if something can't be proven or seen, then it isn't believable. So, to accept the idea of ghosts asks a difficult thing of me—that I suspend what I've labeled as belief."

"No. On the contrary." Etta spoke softly. "It asks that you suspend *dis*belief."

"Then I guess my answer would have to be, I only know that I don't know."

Dessert arrived, a creamy custard with caramel sauce. Later they exited to the same half-bows, doffed hats, and choruses of "Evening, Miz Cavendish," which Karen had come to expect in Etta's company, and which Etta herself barely seemed to notice.

It was only a little after six when Karen climbed the stairs to her bedroom. Immediately she set the stage for a proper reading of the book, placing the miniatures on top of the dresser and arranging them on a white dresser scarf edged in lace. In the center of the semi-circle of paintings she placed the portrait and set a thick white candle alongside. The light from the candle animated the fine face in the portrait. It's lovely, she thought. She looked hard at it again, still fascinated by the resemblance to her own face, then raced back downstairs for an armload of wood. Soon the narrow fireplace crackled and shimmered with flame, bathing the room in a soft amber glow.

At last, with everything in place and infinitely pleasing, Karen pulled back the bedcovers and crawled in, opening the thick blue book to the marked page.

The first page was all text, and she hurriedly flipped forward a few pages to a section containing several full-color plates of the long-dead woman's work. She flipped another page, admiring the delicate little paintings.

Then she froze, her hand in mid-air. A chill shot through her, gooseflesh rose on her arms. She stared, mesmerized, at a plate showing a faded daguerrotype of the artist. The dark, ethereal woman who came to her in dreams had a name—Blessing McCartland.

As compelling as the recognition was, it was surprisingly unsurprising, as though she had known in some secret place all along. The woman in the photograph had tied her hair back on that long ago day when the picture had been taken, while in the dreams her hair flew wild and untamed from her head. But there was no doubt she was the same woman. She had the same deep-set eyes, high cheeks, fine-boned attractiveness. She looked rather like a robust version of Virginia Woolf, Karen thought, for the eyes were shadowed with the distance-seeking melancholy so often depicted in portraits of the famous writer.

Karen ran her fingertips over the photograph and thought that the picture had probably been taken in the downstairs of this very house. The photographer had come, she imagined, in a wagon, and had set a backdrop suspended on a frame somewhere in the parlor. Then he had gently sat Blessing down, turning her this way and that, looking for just the right angle to show her deep eyes and chiseled face. By the look of her, Blessing might not have enjoyed the imposition, for the smile on her face was forced, even thin. But she had sat, smiling when the photographer squeezed the bulb on his camera, and in a blinding flash Blessing McCartland had been caught, smiling wanly and looking far off into the distance.

Karen stared for a long time at the photograph, the scene with the photographer as vivid in her mind as if she had been there. Then, reluctant, but acutely curious about the remainder of the plates, she turned the page. Five more pages of color photos reproduced Blessing's work. What leapt from every page, even without close inspection, was the sensitive beauty in each of the elegantly painted miniatures. She recognized several paintings of the beach in front of her house and the four of the house itself: the four paintings she had just purchased. So realistic were the drawings that she could almost hear the clip-clop of horses coming up the lane, hear the surf crashing loudly over the rocks. Yet each contained an element of something else, an elusive dreamlike quality that made her feel as though she were viewing a picture of something that should be real, but wasn't.

On the last of the plates, her heart again thudded against her chest. She had found what she sought: the miniature that now sat on her dresser reflecting the flickering candle . . . the portrait of her face. It was by far the loveliest painting. Inscribed beneath it were the words *Aimee McCartland.*

The fire had burned low, and the remaining light cast the room in a subdued tapestry of shadows. Karen only vaguely noticed that it had grown much colder. So, she thought, slipping down further into the covers. So, I'm dreaming, and most realistically, of a woman dead almost a century. If there is a ghost here, then it is one who walks, not in filmy apparition through the house, but vivid and life-like through my dreams.

She clasped her arms around her torso, for she had begun to shiver. The dreams were the most sensual by far of any she could remember having. In fact, they were the single most sensual experience of her life, asleep or awake . . . with the exception of Maggi. But Maggi was a different matter. . . .

What was happening to her? Just what did it mean? What could be occurring in her sleep to draw her nightly to the unworldly and seductive Blessing McCartland? Curiosity perhaps, for now she was plainly fascinated. But something more as well, something her heart knew but her mind busily attempted to censor—that she enjoyed the dreams, had even started to look forward to them. It was wonderful, powerful, compelling to let herself soar, to feel the freedom in her body as she swayed and danced with the dark woman—with Blessing.

She began to nod, her eyelids growing heavy, and soon she let the book fall to her chest. She thought she had fallen asleep, for it seemed she had slipped through an invisible net into a softer, darker world. But then she heard the voice of someone calling to her from downstairs.

Faintly at first, then growing louder, someone called *It's time.* The voice drifted up through the empty stairwell, beckoning to Karen.

Slowly she got up, except that she seemed more to rise and float than actually disengage herself from the tangle of covers. She moved out onto the landing and peered into a thick haze, as though the fog which hung out over the Atlantic had crept into the house, the grey mist swirling in the stairwell as she descended. Blade-sharp cold froze the air and made lacy white puffs of her breath, a fact she merely noted. Her bare feet touched the ribbed vinyl of the stairway treads but she felt nothing; her hand slid along the oak bannister worn smooth by a countless trailing of hands before hers.

The nearer she came to the bottom of the stairs, the thicker and more opaque the mist. She could barely see into the parlor. She walked the few steps more to the kitchen. Suddenly the mists evaporated, accompanied by a sound like that of stones rattling down an ancient well, and then she could see. Everything was cast in a pale thin light, though it was still very cold.

Blessing sat in a rocker she had pulled near the stove. Her face, unburdened and lighter than in previous meetings, brightened into a smile. Karen thought it odd the stove was aglow and radiating heat since the room was still so cold, and she wondered dimly who had started the fire; she had never learned to operate the stove. The kitchen, she saw, wasn't the same as when she had left it earlier. The curtains were gone, and in place of the wallpaper were rows of faded red flowers running in stenciled lines along the walls.

There were other differences but she couldn't bring her mind to focus on them just now. The woman was motioning to her and patting an empty chair drawn next to the rocker. *It's time.*

The woman smiled, and reached her hand toward Karen. Without hesitation Karen sat and the woman grabbed Karen's wrist in an iron-cold grasp.

Every separate molecule of her being was electrified. She felt that if she chose she could point her hand and shoot stars from her fingertips. She saw herself as a towering Christmas tree, alive with twinkling red and green lights. If she wanted, she could even levitate up from the chair and fly about the room, perhaps even hover up there by the hanging kerosene lamp. But why leave? It was so pleasant there by the fire.

Blessing traced her finger down Karen's neck from ear to collar and Karen felt the skin beneath Blessing's touch turn to ash. Then Blessing looked at her, eyes bright and blazing. Too many sorrows, too many mysteries, too much held in, they said, and threatened to unleash it all in an ice green torrent.

Let's go for our walk, the woman breathed, her voice muffled as a wave breaking far from shore.

Karen took the outstretched hand and she was outside, walking down the snowy slope toward the sea. Her feet sank deep into fresh snowfall. She struggled to keep pace with the woman who appeared to glide, leaving only the barest hint of pressure from her high boots and a trail from her long skirt in the snow.

Strange and discordant music filled the tiny holes of silence between the waves and the wind. She and the woman floated just above the spume at the water's edge, laughing and telling each other secrets without using words. The chords of music formed a song, one that she couldn't recognize but which the woman sang without words beside her ear.

The woman clasped her around the waist. Slowly, she began to dance, turning Karen gently, swaying to the unfamiliar music. There was space only for the wind between their lips and it carried the sound of their laughter away across the troubled sea.

Arms around waists, they whirled in a frenzy on the wet, fine sand, the waves licking up the prints of their feet as they passed. They spun in wide circles, giddyingly faster. Karen's belly clenched with the sweet power of passion, the woman's face fixed in a grin of fierce abandon. *Mine,* she said in steamy words. *Mine.*

They spun around and into the cove and stopped in the shelter of the large rock. Blessing reached down and plucked something from the sand and held it toward Karen. *For you.*

Karen looked down at the perfect small shell, a pink and white conch that glittered like a gemstone. Gently she took it and held it first to her ear, then to her chest, and let her heart say thank you without words. The music swelled again and they embraced, the wind swirling them toward the house. Karen felt the smooth shell slip from her fingers and wanted to cry out, but it was too late. They were already far from the beach, the music the only sound she could hear.

They entered the house and ran laughing up the stairs to the bedroom. Open-mouthed and exhilarated, Karen felt the woman all around her. They tumbled and curled and stretched together in an unstoppable dance; they were moving not to music but to the pulse of spirit gliding on spirit.

Karen felt sure she was dying, sure that the forces moving inside her would soon gather too much momentum and she would explode. When she did, it was not into darkness as she had feared but into a blinding galaxy. . . .

She awoke damp and panting, her limbs trembling, and looked around for someone who should have been there, but wasn't. She longed to return to the dream place and forego ordinary wakefulness. She tried to plunge again into oblivion, praying to continue where she had let go of the dream.

But her senses were rousing her. She could see shadows under her eyelids, feel the texture of sheets under her legs. Sleep drifted away. She lay remembering back into it, remembering the woman—Blessing—whose presence filled her even now with all the sensations of lovemaking. How like her feeling for Maggi, she thought, yet different. In her dreams, at least, she was free.

The collar of her flannel pajamas was damp with night sweat. She turned her body this way and that as full wakefulness came, wondering which world was the more real.

Throughout the morning she wandered the house, thinking of Blessing, unable to extract herself from the seductive world of her dreams. She imagined the house as Blessing might have known it, and how Blessing might have looked sitting here by the fire, or out in the kitchen preparing something to eat. It wasn't at all difficult to visualize her; Karen knew every contour of her face, could see the gliding manner of her movements. She could feel her presence here, palpable and omnipresent in the house.

Karen moved slowly, fingering objects, letting her mind and hands dwell on those parts of the house that hadn't changed much over the years, enjoying the knowledge that Blessing had at one time dusted the burnished wainscoating in the parlor, had once walked over the very same wide board floors on which she now stood. The knowledge thrilled her and made her feel more connected, closer to the dark woman who visited her in sleep.

Though it was still snowing, but very lightly, Karen felt a strong impulse to walk along the beach. Again she bundled against the damp cold and started out across the snowy slope of yard. She went but a few paces before spotting the marks in the snow. Faint indentations formed an even, straight line from the house to the shore. She stared at them for a moment remembering the dream and the walk she had taken with Blessing along the same stretch of yard to the beach. The imprints were barely visible and mostly filled with fresh snow, ready to disappear entirely given only a little more snowfall. She stepped closer and sighted along the straight and deliberate line of marks all the way down to the water. There seemed to be two trails of prints, one pressed deep into the snow, the other running along beside them, lighter and more indistinct.

She moved on, unable to explain the strange prints, but oddly pleased. At the shore she filled her lungs with the pungent cold air and turned toward the cove.

She found the rocks glazed over with a thin sheeting of ice. She was aware of the cold this time, unlike in the dream when she had been in this very spot and had felt nothing but radiating warmth and the feverish dance. She shivered and clapped her gloved hands together and tried to climb onto the rock, but the surface was far too slippery. Again she tried to gain a footing and scraped her shin as she slid down the ragged surface. The waves beat at the shore; just down the beach a gull shrieked and swooped low out over the lead-grey water.

She rubbed her hand along her jean-covered leg and wondered if she could be losing her mind. Here she was, a thirty-four-year-old woman, insistent on climbing an icy rock so that she could perch on it and survey the sea and the cove, and remember the passionate dance that had occurred there in a dream the night before. The gull swooped and cried again, the waves poured loudly onto the sand and rocks, matching the rhythm of the blood in her temple.

Maybe Etta was right: there are more things that can't be seen than things that can.

Something tumultuous was happening. She no longer wanted to be the observer, the cool academician noting the passage of people and events, but a participant, vibrant and alive, feeling every ounce of the motions in her, straining past every boundary she had so carefully constructed. The boundaries were loosening, the thin veneer of what she once considered reality cracking and peeling like something left too long near a radiator.

She gave a fleeting thought to the desk full of file cards and notes, and dismissed the twinge of guilt as if swatting a fly. She thought she heard the phone ringing but the house was too far to run to through the snow, and at this moment there was no one with whom she wished to talk.

The dream swept back into her mind, giving her fresh energy to try the rock again. This time gaining precious footing, heaving herself onto its gleaming surface, she stood, legs spread, her hair blowing in the stiff wind, and didn't bother to wipe the snow from her face as the flakes floated onto her skin and melted in tiny rivulets down her cheeks.

Blessing must have stood exactly here and seen this view countless times. Karen could picture her standing, her heavy cotton skirts pressed against her legs by the wind, hair flying, her face set firmly on the horizon, some beautiful new painting forming itself in her mind's eye. Gently Karen called her name, repeated it softly for the music it made in her heart. The waves splashed over the word Blessing as Karen repeated it toward the sea. Somewhere, high above, the gull soared and cried again, a lonely, eerie sound, and Karen listened hard into the silences for the low whispery sound of Blessing's voice. Even though she couldn't really hear an answer, she could feel her nearby and watching, waiting for her in another deeper world.

She felt giddy—silly and childlike. She wanted to do a smart little step she remembered from a grammar school dance class, but hesitated when her boots slid dangerously on the ice. She considered dancing down on the grainy, wet sand, speeding along the beach as she had in her dream, but knew somehow it wouldn't be the same. Instead, she slid off the rock and walked to a sandy strip between it and the bluff that rose sharply toward the house.

She saw the shell immediately. It was caught in the crevice of a smaller rock nearly flush with the sand. She picked it up, turning it slowly in her hand. The perfect little conch glistened, its pink and white bands bright and gleaming.

My gift, Karen thought, just like in my dream. She placed the shell in the pocket of her jacket and snapped it shut, as aware of the pressureless presence as if it had been a heavy gold piece. She turned back toward the house without dwelling on or even questioning the synchronicity of finding the shell, so like the object in her dream. It seemed meant to be, just like everything else.

She clumped heavily into the kitchen and stood for a

moment as snow melted in little puddles at her feet. Confused as to what to do next, she moved over to the woodstove to warm her hands. She removed her gloves and held her hands over the black surface admiring the nickel plate trim as she rubbed her hands together, and blew on them. After a long moment she knew her hands were getting no warmer, and realized with a jolt that the stove wasn't lit—hadn't been since she'd lived here.

How silly of me, she thought. Now why would I do that? Still cold, she moved off into the parlor and started a roaring fire, then positioned herself before it to stare at the licking flames. A dull pressure inside her head was back, and she wondered whether she should eat something. The trip to the kitchen and the process of fixing food seemed much too exhausting. Perhaps after a little nap she would make herself something nice to eat.

She pulled the little shell from her pocket and held it in her upturned palm, examining every nuance of its tone and texture in the dancing light of the fireplace. She leaned her head onto the soft back of the chair and thought she felt strong fingers massaging her aching temples.

It felt good, very good, and she relaxed into it. She was falling asleep again, drifting and falling; half-formed images of the nether world between waking and sleeping flashed quickly by and then were gone as if she were at the yawning mouth of a giant vacuum sucking her farther down, pulling her into a dark and chilly tunnel. As in all the times before, she was charged with energy, as though each cell of her body felt every sensation separately. She was delirious with it, feverish, and again there was Blessing, extending her hand.

From far away, the phone was ringing. The ringing continued and she was aware that she had moved to stand closer to the phone. She could have reached for it in one short movement, but it had been very difficult getting to the jangling instrument, as though she had moved through thick treacle. Then the ringing stopped, and she was unburdened of the decision to answer. Relieved, she turned back to Blessing who was waiting for her by the fire, smiling and showing her fine white teeth, her breast rising and falling against the white cotton top of her apron.

After an amount of time Karen could not measure, she looked out the windows and saw it was night. The night of which day, however, posed an unanswerable question. She felt she should eat something, move around. Her legs were cramped, her body stiff from cold. The fire had gone out and left behind only a cold pile of ashes on the floor of the hearth.

She moved, dreamlike, into the kitchen and switched on the light. Her eyes stung from the shock of the electric glare. She blinked and shielded them with her stiff, cold hands. She knew she must eat something. Her knees felt watery, her stomach roiled in acidic queasiness.

She rummaged in the pantry and stared blankly into the fridge, finally extracting a quart of juice and a package of cheese. These she set on the table while she made a piece of toast; then she picked slowly at the food, forcing it down her throat in tasteless small bites. It threatened to return but she held it there, pulling in her breath and waiting for the nausea to subside. She moved quickly away from the table, leaving her dishes and the crumbs from her meal scattered carelessly behind. Back upstairs, she crawled into bed, taking one of the journals with her. She thumbed through the pages, seeking only one name, pausing to read only when it caught her eye.

Another day passed, or maybe more, she couldn't be sure, but it was light again, and snowing hard. She looked down and saw that she was dressed in the same jeans and shirt she had worn almost since she came here. She looked in the mirror over the mantle and barely recognized the face that stared back at her. Deep circles had appeared under her eyes, her hair was limp and hung in oily strands. Something about her looked vacant and hollow, a look she had seen before on the faces of the very ill. Impulsively she raced to the bathroom and turned the hot water to full blast. Soon the room was steamy, and she couldn't see her face in the mirror. She peeled off her clothes and tossed them into a pile by the door, then adjusted the water and stepped in. The fine darts cleared her head, cleansed and focused her as she soaped and rubbed her body with the washcloth.

Coffee, what I need is a good cup of coffee, she thought, and looked forward to fresh clothes and the surge of caffeine.

The phone rang and this time she threw on her robe and raced downstairs to answer, picking it up on the fourth ring. "Hello."

"Hello, Karen," Etta said.

"Oh, Etta—hello," Karen said, slightly out of breath.

"I've been trying to reach you for days. I was starting to get a little worried. Are you all right?"

"Uh, yes—I'm fine." Karen struggled to hide her confusion. Had Etta said days—not hours, or a day? "I've been busy. You know, on the book. I unplugged the phone for a little peace and quiet," she lied. "Easier to concentrate, you know. Sorry I alarmed you. And how are you?"

"Are you sure you're okay?" Etta persisted.

Karen, instantly irritated, strained to keep it from showing. She liked Etta and counted her as her friend, but goddammit, she shouldn't be so nosey. It was nobody's business if she chose not to answer the phone. "Well, you know what they say about absent-minded professors, Etta," she said. "Forgot I'd unplugged the thing until this morning."

"Well, as long as you're all right. Will you be coming to the musical tomorrow night?" Etta didn't sound convinced. Her tone implied that the desire to see Karen was more to set her mind at ease than anything else.

Karen didn't answer for a moment, hastily counting back days. How could it possibly be Thursday already? "Uh—I don't know Etta. I appreciate the reminder, but I'm awfully busy. How about if we let it stand that I'll try. Okay? I'm right in the middle of something. Guess I've lost track of time."

"That's easy to do sometimes. But do try and come by if you can get away. I think having an audience even made Grace play better," Etta said lightly.

Relieved at ending on an easier note, Karen said, "I'll try. But you know how it is when time flies."

Karen giggled when she hung up the phone. Time flies. Now, that's funny. She giggled again at her little joke. Time flies; I am flying, days and nights fly—everything is flying. Blessing would be amused, and she made a note to tell her the joke the next time she saw her, which, if things went as usual, wouldn't be long.

* * * * *

And Blessing did come to her again. Karen wasn't clear whether she ever really left anymore. The boundaries of her world were growing indistinct and fuzzy. It was either day or it was night. It was either snowing or it wasn't. Such distinctions made little difference to her; everything was merging into a smooth rounded whole which required no demarcations. She was in spherical, not linear time, an altogether pleasant departure from the demands of clocks and calendars.

But Karen knew that time was somehow passing. Even if her disinterest in such events was increasing, in moments of lucidity she noted several more dirty dishes arranged on the table. Apparently she had eaten something. A few times she actually had sat at the desk and ruffled through the papers but finally had gathered them up and tossed them carelessly into a cardboard carton on the floor.

Outside, the last rays of a setting sun cast the fields with a pink and blue haze; banks of snow were slashed by dark shadows of trees in the slanting light.

The electric clock in the kitchen said 4:30. But 4:30 of what day? Did it matter? The entire notion that time could be segmented, each segment ticking off meaning, seemed to Karen more than a little absurd. "Relevancy courtesy of Timex Corporation," she chuckled into the gloom.

But there were times, too, when she landed back into the world of time with a jarring thump, as easily as she had spun out of it earlier. On such occasions she would scratch her head and look around, perplexed. "Now what did I do that for?" she muttered as she knelt in front of the box containing the notes and began resorting them. She worked at the cards for a while, listlessly putting them in correct sequence. The room seemed heavy to her and cold, and as she worked she became conscious of a faint smell of mildew.

She tired quickly of the work, even felt oddly tugged away from it. She wandered into the kitchen, and while half-heartedly straightening counters noticed she was running low on food. No matter. Some other day she could drive into town for supplies. Right now a hot shower and a change of clothes seemed appealing.

Under the stinging jets of water she scrubbed her face with a washcloth and puzzled at her loss of touch with time. It was easy to lose track of such things in the country, she reasoned. There were no appointments to keep, no buses to catch, nothing to use as a gauge but changes in the patterns and amounts of light and the changing weather.

She was in the kitchen making coffee when she saw the red jeep turn into the drive and head toward the house. It took a moment before she realized that Etta was coming to call. Etta with her knowing eyes and strong face.

She had forgotten about the musical, too. It had to be later than Friday. She hoped Etta would forgive her. After all, she had only said she'd try to attend. She felt edgy as she watched the jeep draw closer to the house.

I wonder how I look, she asked herself and dashed into the parlor to glance in the mirror. Even though she had just washed her hair, she looked awful; even she could see that. The dark circles had deepened, framing her eyes in sunken hollows. The skin of her face sagged. She was shocked at how skinny she looked; she must have lost a ton of weight. Etta knocked and Karen ran for the door, patting her still damp hair into place.

Etta carried a small package in her hand. Staring at Karen and without waiting for an invitation, Etta pushed past her into the room, keeping her face still and searching Karen's.

"I brought the tea you asked me to make for you." Etta laid the small package on the table. "And more's the better, if you ask me. You look ill, Karen. How do you feel? Tell me the truth." Etta applied pressure not with her tone but with her firm, searching eyes. She reached a hand to Karen's brow. "I think you may have a slight fever too."

Karen pulled away and protested, too quickly perhaps, for she caught Etta's eyes narrowing. She thanked Etta for the tea as the older woman extracted a small cotton bag from her package and set water on the stove to boil.

"My heavens but it's cold in here," Etta said, rubbing her hands on her arms, "where's your thermostat? I'll turn the heat up a little. If you're sick, you should be keeping a lot warmer."

Karen pointed to the wall in the parlor and Etta strode over to it. "It says sixty-eight," she said in an incredulous voice. She pulled her heavy cardigan tighter around her as she came back into the kitchen. Karen could see the slightly frayed cuffs and shiny spots on the leather elbow patches.

"Don't you have a warmer sweater?" Etta asked. "You'll catch your death running around in that skimpy outfit." She pointed to Karen's worn flannel shirt and jeans.

"Sure. I have a whole drawer full of sweaters. I'll run upstairs and get one."

"Oh no you don't, young lady. You sit here and wait for the water to boil. Rest yourself, I'll get it for you. Where do you keep them?"

"In the bottom drawer of the dresser," Karen answered and with that Etta was off, taking the stairs in quick easy strides.

When she returned a few moments later, she carried a rag sweater and look on her face that suggested she had found something upstairs decidedly not to her liking. She handed the sweater to Karen and drew a chair up beside her at the table.

"What's that on your dresser? It looks like an altar, or a shrine of some kind." Her tone was not judgmental; concern and curiosity poured out to Karen from her still, composed face.

"Damn, I forgot about that," Karen said under her breath. The miniatures, and the candles, which she remembered always to keep lit, were up there on the dresser. And Etta had seen them. Damn, she thought. Why didn't I just go and get the sweater myself? She struggled for an answer to Etta's question. "Uh . . . well I . . . actually, I just thought the paintings looked so pretty I'd display them together. The candles add kind of an artsy touch, don't you think?"

Etta sat back in her chair, her arms folded over her chest, her head cocked just slightly. Everything about her said she didn't believe Karen for an instant. She sat silently, looking like someone trying to make a decision. Then something clicked into place behind her eyes, and instead of pursuing the matter, she asked Karen when she had last eaten. When Karen responded that her stomach had been a little upset lately and she hadn't had much to eat these last few days, Etta brought her hands down on her knees, then rose in one quick movement. "Well, I'll just see what I can find around here for a little supper. Do you have any eggs?"

Watching from her chair as Etta set about scrambling eggs and making toast and tea, Karen wished she could hear whatever was going on inside Etta's head. She appeared to be thinking so loudly that Karen could almost hear her anyway. It was good to have Etta here with her though, talking and moving around in the room. The truth was, she had to admit, she had been feeling a little rough lately, and it was nice to have a friend nearby, someone who cared and responded to her warmly. Things just might be getting a little out of hand with all these dreams and her obsession with her sultry dream lover. Much as she seemed to lose track when alone, there was another world out there. A world with people in it, living people who ate food and talked with each other–and who conducted love affairs while awake. She added the last thought with a wry, downcast smile, as if the notion of what she had been doing was slightly silly, preposterous even.

Etta set a plate of eggs on the table and Karen, taking in big mouthfuls, slowly felt herself brighten. She must have been hungrier than she thought; soon she had eaten the entire meal, to Etta's nods of approval.

Etta swooped the dishes into the sink and suggested they go into the parlor and enjoy a strong cup of her herb tea. As Karen stood, the blood rushed from her head and her legs began to give way. She fell against the table, stopping herself with one hand on the hard oak edge. Etta was immediately at her side, supporting her as she stood trembling.

"Guess I do feel a little shaky," she said, and leaned into Etta as they walked into the parlor. Etta deposited her in the easy chair, then started a fire. Neither woman spoke. The fire sizzled and spat; a soft wind bent branches of trees to graze across the clapboards.

Etta sat slightly forward in her chair, an elbow on either knee, her hands holding a stick she had been using to poke at the fire. She twirled it absently and looked at Karen for a long moment.

"Karen, I have something to ask you," she said, and pushed a log back on the grate with the stick. "You may not like what I ask, but please try and answer anyway." Her face was as composed as if she were about to ask Karen if she liked hot dogs. "Is anything happening here, in this house—or to you—that you'd call unusual? Anything you find odd?" On the last word her eyebrows crept up a fraction.

Karen gaped, her cheeks blushing. "What do you mean, Etta?"

"What I mean is just what I said. We haven't known each other very long, and you may feel you can't trust me. Guess I wouldn't blame you too much if you didn't—just yet."

Etta shifted in the chair and turned to face Karen again. "To be plain about it, I'm worried about you. Something here just doesn't feel right."

There was a sudden, chill draft in the room, as though someone had opened a door and let in a gush of air from outside. Etta pulled her arms about her.

Karen remained silent, frantically searching for a response. Etta went on, "I've probably seen more in my life than most—and I do see things, Karen. Things other folks can't or won't. I see something happening to you, and it troubles me. It's more than how peaked you look, how tired you seem, though it's pretty obvious you aren't yourself. It's something more."

Karen looked down and pressed her fingertips into her forehead. She felt suddenly near to tears and vulnerable. "I suppose you're right, Etta. I have been feeling a little strange lately. Off and on I've been concerned about myself. . . ." She stopped, considering just how much she should tell. "I sleep a lot and don't have my usual energy." Her voice sounded foreign, as if she was unused to hearing it, and her mouth was dry. Maybe it would be better to listen, see what more Etta had to say before further exposing herself.

Etta tapped the stick lightly on the bricks of the hearth. "Sometimes a person can be open to things without really knowing what they are," she went on. "Things that can't be seen, but are there."

Karen stared at Etta, both dreading and anticipating what was bound to come next.

Etta's calm voice sounded far away. "Just think how it feels to walk into a room where someone is having a fight. You don't have to hear the words to know it. You can feel it. Everything leaves its mark, I guess you could say. And if you stay in the room long enough, you start to feel edgy yourself. It's like that with other things, too, only some can leave bigger and more lasting marks than others."

"I'm sure that's true, Etta. But I don't see what all that has to do with me."

"Maybe nothing. On the other hand, I've had a funny feeling about this house since I was a girl. I used to stand looking at it from the woods on my way to the beach, stare up at it from my own house. It's like something very painful happened here once and the house still holds on to that pain. Sadness, that's what I feel–lots of pent-up sadness here."

Karen drew her legs under her and took a long sip of tea. She was fascinated with Etta's information and curious to know more, but not quite willing to divulge anything about her nightly visitor.

"Karen, let me tell you something. There's things that can happen in ways that aren't good for us. They may seem innocent on the surface, but after a time they do us harm. I saw your face when you found the paintings, Blessing's paintings. And I saw that shrine up in your bedroom. Now, I can see the way you look. You're a heap different from the rosy-cheeked young teacher who came here such a short while back." Etta paused to sip her tea and then set the cup on the floor beside her.

"And I've seen other things too. Seen 'em for years here on your place. Karen, I've seen Blessing McCartland."

Karen's mouth flew open but only a muffled choking sound came out.

"Many times I've seen her, or her ghost I should say, wandering down on the beach. Sad, tearful. A black wraith somehow tied to this earth by her grief. I've seen her in the house. Sometimes when I look at this house I see a dark shadow cross in front of a window, or often as not, just standing still and looking out, eternally, for something she can't find. I'm afraid for you, Karen. I reckon you've seen her too."

Karen stared, dumbfounded. Etta was saying she had actually *seen* Blessing, watched her on her timeless wanderings along the beach. And seen her here in this house. My God. The chill intensified and the hint of mustiness swelled and Karen began to sense the same unpleasant heaviness around her as when Walter had been here. Etta pulled her cardigan closer and flicked her eyes carefully around the room. Upstairs a door slammed, its resounding thwack echoing through the empty, half-lit house. Both women jumped, startled.

Karen knew she had to respond to Etta in some way. "I hardly know what to say, Etta. This is all so extraordinary."

She felt overwhelmed by forces on every side. Behind her, in a sense, was the knowledge of her fugue life, and the anger she felt hovering in the room. Sitting beside her was a kindly woman who gazed at her with clear grey eyes, who wanted to know more, wanted to help.

In a way it all seemed preposterous. Who could have guessed a few weeks back that on some snowy evening outside an isolated village on the Maine coast, she would sit before a crackling fire and discuss ghosts with a friendly old woman she barely knew? She felt surreal, lifted out of context, a feeling that could describe her entire stay thus far.

Etta gazed steadily at her. "Karen, did you understand what I just told you?"

"Yes. I heard. . . ." Karen faltered, and cleared her throat. "As a matter of fact, there have been a few things I've had a rather difficult time explaining."

"Like what?" Etta encouraged.

"Well, like noises, rustling noises. First I thought it was rats or the wind. But I don't think so now. I hear the noises often. And sometimes I see things, shadows in the corner of my eye, or flitting away in the mirror when I look into it. Things like that," she said vaguely and waved her hand limply. Before she thought better of it, she quickly added, "And I often don't feel I'm really alone here."

Etta nodded. After a long silence she asked, her voice soft and even, "Is that all?"

"Yes. That's it. Doesn't sound like much now that I'm telling it, does it? I'm sure there's a logical explanation for everything." She had considered, but only briefly, telling Etta the rest—about the dreams. It's really no one's business, she decided. What, after all, could be more personal, more intimately one's own than one's dreams?

"Well, maybe there's a sound way to explain these things." Etta leaned back and stared into the fire. "And then there's another maybe. Maybe something—or someone—is trying to reach out to you."

"You're trying to say my house is haunted, aren't you?" Karen's voice trickled weakly from her lips, and she wished for the strength to spit out the word *nonsense.* But she knew it was true. Blessing McCartland was indeed haunting her house and her dreams, easing her into a very private world, one she had come to cherish. Karen set her lips in a tight line.

"Do be careful, Karen. What seems simple on the face of it may not be underneath. By my guess, most of the old houses around here have some form of spirit or ghost in them. Most folks just learn to live with it and no harm is done. Some folks don't even know that ghosts occupy the premises alongside the living."

Karen had said all she intended. A wall of silence loomed between them.

"How are you feeling?" Etta asked at length, and leaned to place her hand on Karen's forehead.

"Not so good, I'm afraid. I feel terribly weak. Maybe I should try and get some rest."

"Would you like it if I stayed with you? I'd be glad to, no trouble at all."

"No–no thanks, Etta. I can manage." Karen got unsteadily to her feet, feeling again the dizziness and rubbery legs, and thought maybe it would be a good idea to have Etta stay. Perhaps she had refused too hastily. She laid her hand on Etta's shoulder and wavered for a moment, smelling the musty, slightly sweet air. Finally she said, "I'll call tomorrow and let you know how I'm doing. Thanks for the company tonight, and the help. I really needed it. As for everything else–I just don't know. Nothing makes much sense right now. Perhaps when I'm feeling stronger. . . ."

"Yes," Etta said. "It's important you take care of yourself. We can talk more later. You know I'll be thinking of you so you just call if you need anything."

Karen watched the jeep disappear into the deep snowy night. Clicking off the lights as she went, she turned up the stairs for the bedroom–and sleep.

CHAPTER 6

The car wheels slid sickeningly on a patch of ice, a dirty wall of snow bore toward Karen. She remembered to turn gently into the slide and keep her foot off the brake, righting the car scant inches from the snowbank. Two bags of groceries and the mail wobbled unsteadily on the back seat as she pulled the car onto the highway and pointed it again toward the house.

It has been almost a week since Etta's visit, a week in which Karen had tried hard to establish a more normal routine. She forced herself to eat at least one small meal each day and kept track of the passage of time by marking off the days on her kitchen calendar. She avoided the frequent naps, and instead bent toward the pile of work on her desk in the afternoons. Still the work went slowly; but at least she was making the effort.

She thought often of Etta's visit and her revelations. Fragments of the conversation came during odd moments: sitting at the desk, concentrating on some piece of figurine or ceremonial necklace from her notes. She could hear Etta: "I've seen her, Karen." A slight chill hovered near her at such moments, and her hand often found its way to the nape of her neck. Yet, all in all, there seemed little cause for concern. What harm could possibly come from dreams? And as for her listlessness, that would improve with the new regimen. She tossed her head and smiled. Besides, she thought, at times like this when she was away from the house, the whole thing seemed rather absurd anyway.

She pulled the car into the snow-covered dooryard. Even before she was fully out of the door she heard the phone, its sibilant sound scraping over the faultless white. If winter had a sound, she thought, it would be a small brass bell ringing a single crisp note of music about an octave above high C. She left the groceries in the car and ran to answer, not knowing how long it had been ringing. Fully expecting a click from the other end of the line, she picked up the receiver.

"Hello," she said, sure Etta was calling to check on her.

Instead, she heard Maggi's warm voice. Karen's knees shook, whether from the exertion or the familiar voice she wasn't sure.

"Maggi. . . . What a surprise!"

"Hope I'm not interrupting you in the middle of something."

"Not at all. In fact, I've been thinking about you. I'm glad you called." The more she stayed grounded in the ordinary world, the nearer Maggi seemed.

"Oh? So the recluse bit wears thin, eh? I'm surprised . . . though pleasantly."

"Make that semi-recluse, and I am glad to hear your voice, Maggi," Karen said, surprised at herself and the warmth in her tone.

"Well, I can't say I'm sorry to hear that. In fact, you could say it makes my day. . . . Well almost, anyway. Which brings me to the reason I called, apart from the excuse of talking with you. I'm afraid I have some bad news—"

"Are you okay?" Karen broke in.

"Oh yeah, I'm fine. It's just that one of our editing machines chewed up several feet of your narration—the footage we shot in your office right at the beginning of the project. Can you believe it? I was angry enough to bite nails when I first heard about it. But, by now I'm just resigned."

"I'm sorry, Maggi. So what do we do?"

"I feel awful about asking, but can you possibly come down for a day so we can shoot the footage over? I know what a horrible imposition this is. You could stay with me. Or, uh. . . ." Maggi stammered, at a rare loss for words. "That is, we could arrange something else—"

"I can't," Karen blurted without considering the possibility. "I really can't, Maggi—I haven't been feeling all that well, and I—"

"What's the matter?" Maggi interrupted. "Are you sick?"

"Just one of those flu bugs. I really don't feel up to a trip to the city just now."

"I get kinda worried about you way up there all alone. Who would know if something happened?"

Maybe it was her delight at hearing Maggi, maybe her improved humor from the shopping excursion, but Karen blurted into the phone, "Why don't you come here instead? It's cold and stormy, but the scenery more than compensates."

There was a slight pause. "I'd love to," Maggi said quietly. "I can bring the equipment. I'd love to see you . . . and your wonderful house. That way when I think of you, which I admit is often, I can picture you in actual surroundings."

Great! Karen wanted to yell. Now that the words of invitation had left her mouth, she was flying with good spirits. "Yes. It's fine. I really would like to see you."

They agreed on the following afternoon, and after giving careful directions, Karen hung up and whirled around the parlor. How good to see Maggi, how good to have her here to talk to. Perhaps too much solitude wasn't a good thing. And it would be great fun to show off her house and the views of the sea and countryside.

Karen walked across the worn boards of the parlor. For the first time she noticed that dust had accumulated in a thin layer on the surfaces of the furniture and floated in small fuzzy balls in the corners. From the pantry she took dusting spray and a soft cloth. Then she called Etta and invited her to dinner the following evening.

She cleaned thoroughly, gaining enormous satisfaction from gleaming surfaces, order, and even the faint scent of lemon which hung in the air afterward. She took down one of the several woven baskets which decorated a wall and filled it with pine cones and berries. Finally, satisfied with her efforts, she sat down to read her mail.

Opening a magazine, she stretched her legs out in front of her and stared at the line where faded jeans met the yellowish brown of her boots. Now that she kept better track of such things, she knew it was a little after one o'clock in the afternoon.

Though the radio had again forecast a major snowfall later in the evening, a weak winter sun splayed bluish hues over ridges and valleys in the snow. She could already see a dark wall of clouds building out over the sea, then curling around and filling the north sky. A deer suddenly stepped out of the woods and stood perfectly still in the snow. It peered up at the house, almost purposefully, and Karen thought how sad it looked. But perhaps she was reflecting onto the deer the gloom she felt pressing in around her. The house seemed almost to groan with a deep sadness, deeper than words could comfort. Somewhere a branch cracked from the weight of snow and the deer bolted back into the dark woods.

As Karen sat quietly in the chair, her fingers tracing a fleur-de-lis in the design of the slipcover, her eyelids grew heavy and drowsiness began to pull her toward the soft edges of sleep. She allowed herself to sink into the weightless feeling, savoring it, knowing full well what was to follow. Then, remembering her resolve, she roused herself and sat upright, eyes wide and focused on the hearth. The drowsiness clung to her like a heavy jacket, the desire for sleep a tantalizing ache.

Like an alcoholic contemplating a leap from the wagon, she rationalized a short nap. Just a short one. The heaviness in the room and the absolute stillness bore down on her, and she could feel her eyelids begin to close from the weight. An overpowering need to sleep blotted all else from her consciousness. After a time, she gave in willingly, letting her chin fall gently onto her chest.

It seemed to take longer to descend into the world of dreams than usual, and she wandered blindly through caves and tunnels filled with smoke and thick fetid air, her feet caught by unseen sand. She wandered, alone and chilled, through the labyrinthine wastes, trying to part the thick curtain of smoke with her hands. When at last she found the figure she sought, she was no longer in the caves but suddenly back in her own bedroom, floating just above the carefully made bed, looking down on Blessing's reclining figure. She descended, floating down until she hovered just above her, the billowing tail of her shirt grazing Blessing's heaving middle.

Something was wrong, she thought in a panic. Something

is wrong with her. She felt the same arrows of passion, felt her body come alive and swell with an ache that made her breath catch in her throat. How beautiful she looks, Karen thought as she hovered just above her, watching. Beautiful—but sad, so very sad. Blessing's sobs reached her, a wretched sound rising up from a void, a place Karen feared she could not see or touch. There was no sound, not the wind, nor the steaming words, nor the eerie music that had carried them dancing along the beach. Just silence.

Karen reached out a hand to comfort her, to force into the cold still form the power of her love. Blessing pushed her hand away and turned her face, the scent of mildew and lilac increasing. Blessing's breath blew blue crystals into the air.

"What's wrong?" Karen pleaded, her voice sounding distant and far away. "What's wrong?" Her mind raced to discover something she had done, something to account for all this sadness. She let herself fall down beside the sobbing woman, curling up next to her, and running an arm around her waist. She was confused. She wanted to feel the passion again, the sensual choreography they danced together. But not this, not this withdrawal and pain. She rubbed her hand along the seam of Blessing's dress, feeling again the wispy, insubstantial nature of her body. She moved her face closer to the dark curling hair, filling her senses with the musty smell and breathing again into Blessing's ear, "What's wrong? Please. Talk to me."

Blessing shrieked, a piercing sound that shrilled through Karen's every nerve. And shrieked again before collapsing into soft gasps and sobs. Karen looked around her and wanted to run through the caves again, run away from this too bright agony; but she couldn't find the caves, couldn't find her way out.

It is my fault, she breathed silently, sucking her breath in long pulls and letting it slowly out along Blessing's still face.

Slowly she stroked Blessing, trying to console her nameless pain. Her hand, as it moved, crusted over with the bluish crystals until it became too heavy, and she rested it in the mass of dark hair, stroking and whispering. "Tell me—please, tell me."

Air spewed from Blessing's mouth, the steamy air that sometimes carried her words. Karen listened closely, parting the sounds to discover what meaning lay there. "Tell me," she heard herself say again. "Tell me what is wrong."

Indistinctly at first, then more clearly, she heard words forming in the whispery sounds, words mixed with sobs, expressions of an inexpressible sadness, *I have no body,* Blessing mourned.

Confused, Karen struggled to press warmth and substance into the hazy outlines of the woman beside her, to hold her close and silence the awful sobbing. But the harder she tried, the more filmy and weightless both she and Blessing became, until at last Blessing melted away—gone—leaving Karen to scratch and pull at folds of blankets under her fingers.

She awakened clutching to her chest a fist of bedclothes, a salty tear running down her cheek and into her mouth. Inconsolable melancholy hovered nearby. A residue of sadness thickened the air.

And there were sounds. Sobbing sounds coming from everywhere at once. Real sounds, not whispery, dreamed ones. Karen released her grip on the cold blankets and turned to locate the source. The room stood empty. Nowhere did a shadow or flash of movement give hint of a crying presence. As Karen sat listening, the sobs diminished and receded, and finally ceased, as if drawn away by a thin, unseen string, leaving behind only silence and a deathly still.

Karen threw her legs over the side of the bed and noticed she was still dressed—it couldn't be night already. She remembered that she had fallen asleep downstairs in her chair by the hearth. She rubbed away sleep. How had she gotten up here? Had such as this ever happened to her before? Outside it was dark, not from night, but from the approaching heavy clouds of the storm.

Downstairs, Karen started a fire and sat hunched as far down into her chair as she could manage. She felt unaccountably depressed and fought back tears as she stared, unseeing, into the spitting fire. Usually when she awoke she was tired, but buoyant with feelings of love and the residue of passion. This time sadness pressed into a hard knot in her chest. The very air in the room seemed ready to crack and fall from the weight of it.

She had done something wrong, but what? How could she have brought on the frustrating, nightmarish quality that had infused the dream, that still now rimmed her eyes with tears? Sleet peppered the window panes and she turned to see a whirling, fast falling curtain of snow spilling in profusion.

God, I hope Maggi's all right. I hope she will make it here tomorrow. The thought brought more tears and an increase in the soundless sorrow around her. She felt herself falling into that exhausted, trancelike state that had characterized all her recent days. Not the pelting sleet nor the crackle of the fire nor the upbeat jazz recordings she had put on the player could restore her moorage to the here and now. A call to Etta would help lift the pall, but she hadn't the energy to cross to the phone.

Finally, she climbed the stairs to bed, each step creaking loudly in the narrow passage, more so for the additional heaviness that had taken hold of her.

Deep, unconscious sleep did not come. Throughout the night she tossed and twisted, unable to relax her body into a position of comfort. She turned onto her side and mashed the pillow into a ball under her head, lying still for only a moment before the tension in her limbs forced her again to move. She was plagued by a vague itching which she tried to ignore, but which would eventually require a furtive scratch, each time pulling her back from the brink of sleep. Twice during the night she got up, once to drink a cup of warm milk, and once to investigate a moaning sound which she eventually attributed to the wind as the storm tore through the night.

* * * * *

Morning didn't so much dawn as transform the black of night to a weak grey that seeped in through the windows. She lay still and watched the changing patterns of light texture the room, not sure that she had slept at all. And when she had drifted close to a light, fitful sleep, it seemed that she had glided too close to a dangerous cataract where moaning, rushing water fell to a bottomless depth.

By early afternoon, she walked more often to the windows, expectantly scanning the road for the sight of Maggi's blue Subaru which was thankfully equipped with four-wheel drive. The morning had dragged past in maddeningly slow motion; once she even called the operator for the correct time, sure her clocks were wrong. She invented activities for herself: a half-hour workout to an aerobics record during which she puffed and winced and vowed to keep in better shape in the future; redusting the parlor; and trying, without much success, to read. The inside of her eyelids felt like sandpaper and she was tired, hungover from the sleepless night. A nap was out of the question and when the urge to sleep became intense she jumped up and prowled the house for something else to do.

The storm had lessened in intensity, but large flakes of snow still fell before a stiff icy wind. The sky hung low and heavy, and by the look of it, more snow could be expected as the day wore on. Karen stood at the window again, looking for the dark blue car roof to appear around the last bend.

She realized her palms were sweating and wiped them on the legs of her clean jeans, then turned to rearrange a sprig of berries on the basket of pine cones. Not only had she spruced up the house for Maggi's visit but she had done the same to herself, spending a full hour in the bathroom in preparation, carefully washing her hair and adding a creme rinse in an effort to overcome its lifelessness. She dressed in soft jeans and a brushed wool sweater of vivid red with a procession of little reindeer around the yoke. Her clothes seemed festive enough, the red of the sweater even cast a more healthy pink to her face; but the face that looked back from the mirror was gaunt and drawn, and for an instant she didn't think she looked at all like herself. Maggi would be sure to notice. But she had told her she had been ill. Perhaps Maggi would leave it at that and not pry too deeply.

Karen crossed the kitchen for what seemed the thousandth time and stopped at the table. She placed her hands on the basket of cones and berries, turning them slightly, readjusting needlessly. "Damn!" she spat aloud. "Just relax."

Finally, bereft of any project which could further occupy her, she plopped into a high-backed chair with a fresh cup of tea to watch and wait. As with all things watched, the act served only to delay the anticipated event. Three o'clock came and went, as did three-thirty and finally four. The clock over the stove had become her persecutor, a visual reminder of both her impatience and her growing alarm.

Be calm, she told herself. Maggi had said afternoon and that could be anytime between noon and five or six this evening. Just at the point Karen stood to phone the Highway Patrol, Maggi's car turned into the lane.

Relief, and a rush of nervousness, poured through her as she ran toward the door and flung it open. In stocking feet, for she had forgotten her shoes, she raced through the snow, and before Maggi was fully out of the car, grabbed her. They both slipped and slid, almost toppling over. Laughing and talking all at once, they struggled for footing in the ice and snow.

"You made it! I'm so glad you made it. I was getting worried." Karen laughed and hugged Maggi all the harder. They spun round and round in an energetic embrace, neither really looking into the face of the other for more than a brief second before clasping again in a massive hug.

Bright red patches appeared on their cheeks and puffs of vapor from their breath rose in the air between them. They held each other by the shoulders and each looked for a long moment into the face of the other. Maggi's face radiated the grin of one who has come a long way on hope, not knowing until journey's end whether hope would be realized. No part of her face was left out of participation in the smile. Her large eyes sparkled. "Oh, Karen. It's good to see you." Karen saw an almost imperceptible shadow flit across her face. An eyebrow raised, then lowered as quickly, and Maggi's face was again composed. Arm in arm they trudged back through the snow to the house. Maggi laughed and pointed at Karen's shoeless feet. "My lord, you've been out here all this time in your stocking feet. Why didn't you say something!"

"I didn't feel a thing." Karen laughed and tightened her arm around Maggi as they walked the last few steps to the door.

Once inside the warm kitchen, Karen walked toward the stove. "I was just having a cup of tea. Would you like some?"

"Sure." Maggi stripped off her gloves. "My God, this is a wonderful house. How did you luck onto such a beauty, you rascal? I can see now why you've been so protective of your time here. Believe me, if I had this house, I wouldn't leave either. Wow." Maggie twirled around, looking at the shining wainscoting, the yellow boards of the floor, peering into the parlor to the huge stone fireplace and the small paned windows that opened onto the sea.

Karen smiled and nodded as if she herself had built the

house, or at least had been responsible for its care over the years. Or, and the thought gave her a start, as if she were basking in the once-removed compliments to a dear and close friend. Maggi, anxious to see the other rooms, walked to the parlor for a closer look at the sea. From her position at the stove brewing tea, Karen could hear her exclamations.

"It's gorgeous," Maggi said. "It even smells like an old house."

Karen sloshed hot water onto the cabinet from the teapot. She, of course, had noticed it too, the now familiar odor. The smell had increased since she had come back into the house with Maggi. Quickly she mopped up the spill and, hands shaking slightly, carried two cups of tea into the parlor.

"I imagine they all smell like this after a while," Karen said. She handed Maggi a cup and they moved together to the windows and stood facing the sea, their shoulders touching. Karen didn't drink, sure that her shaking hands would clatter the cup and saucer too loudly.

They stared at the sea in silence, Karen wondering if she could show more—more of her delight that Maggi was really here sharing the view she had looked at so many times alone. Well, not absolutely alone, she reminded herself. "See that cove down there, just to the left?" Karen pointed suddenly, "I go there a lot. It's a wonderful place to . . . uh. . . ." She wished she hadn't started this. Some things just weren't meant to be shared—"uh . . . to stroll along and think."

"Ummm," Maggi responded, apparently oblivious to Karen's discomfort, mesmerized by the beauty of the snow and the trees and the dark green sea. She turned to look at Karen and placed an arm over her shoulder. "So. You haven't been well. It shows all over you. What's been wrong?"

She winced. She had wanted to look good. "Just a little bug of some kind. One of the ornery ones that doesn't let go." She patted her hair. "I'm much better though. I'm sure

I'll be fine in a few more days. Mostly I'm still a little weak." The subject of her physical condition had reached its toleration limit. "How was your trip?" she asked abruptly. "The roads must have been a mess."

"I didn't have any problems, except for blowing snow, sub-freezing temps and black ice." Maggi smiled and held Karen closer. "Just below Bangor I actually had to pull over and wait for a sanding truck to arrive. There was a long downhill grade—absolute treachery. I must have been awfully determined to see you." Karen didn't resist the hug and leaned into it as they stood looking out at the sea.

After a few moments Maggi whispered, "That's a great fireplace. Let's have a fire."

She released Karen, bounded over to the hearth and began laying the kindling. Karen watched, taking pleasure in the sight of Maggi's lean back arched gracefully at the fireplace.

"I'll start dinner," Karen said. "We're having company. Hope you don't mind. I have this perfectly charming neighbor. I invited her to join us. I think you'll like her." She began paring small red potatoes to bake along with the roast she had defrosted earlier. Etta had promised to bring the rest of the meal.

Maggi, finished with the fire, lounged in the doorway. "So. Tell me more about your neighbor."

Karen dropped a handful of potato peelings into the trash bag, and then tried her best to describe Etta Cavendish.

Maggi leaned against the counter and looked across at the grey rooftop just visible in the gathering dusk. "She sounds fascinating. There are lots of women like that in rural places," she said thoughtfully. "Especially New England. I've always thought a collection of stories about them would be a great documentary."

"Glad my instinct was correct." Karen smiled at Maggi.

"I'd love to meet her."

Karen's shoulder grazed Maggi's as she turned to put the roast in the oven. The same thrill ran through her as on other chance touchings. Nothing had changed. She felt the same tenderness and passion; the unruly feelings obviously had not read the script. They were supposed to weaken and die, leave just as surely as she had left Boston to escape them. "Let's go enjoy your fire," she said and took Maggi's hand.

Karen pulled a rocker next to her chair by the fireplace. Silently watching the flames lick and curl around the oak logs, they sat together, Karen looking at Maggi only when Maggi couldn't see her. And she could feel Maggi's eyes on her in the same manner, could feel their warm, questioning gaze. They sat like this for several minutes, the air replete with unsaid words, floating questions, and an awkwardness that caused Maggi to rock herself in the chair with a touch too much energy. Karen chewed a sliver of cracked skin on her bottom lip.

Now that the first blush of excitement was waning, Karen settled into an uneasy truce between Maggi's presence and the aura of sadness that hung about the room. Even Maggi had noticed the musty smell, as strong as if the woman in her dreams were standing right at her elbow. The clock ticked loudly; outside the waves rolled onto the rocks in the whispered tones of low tide.

"Well," Maggi announced, bringing the flats of her palms down on her thighs. "Why don't we talk about where to set up the camera and lights? I think over there in front of the windows. There's a nice soft backlighting, and the view of the snowy slope and the sea make a very scenic backdrop. . . . What do you think?"

Oh, my God! The video, Karen thought. In all the excitement of seeing Maggi she had all but forgotten the real purpose for the visit. At this moment she severely doubted her ability to pull it off. Words came so hard for her these days; the entire breadth of the subject had become a jellied confusion.

"Karen. Are you okay?"

"Oh . . . yes. I was just thinking," Karen stammered. "Uh . . . yes, I think the window would be a fine place."

"I'll get the equipment."

Maggi set up the lights and camera, then positioned Karen in a chair drawn beneath the windows. She adjusted the lights, bending close to Karen, checking the light meter.

Karen adjusted the cuffs of her sweater then ran her palms along her thighs, sick with fear. She knew this subject better than anything else in the world, maybe better than anybody, for that matter. But the words wouldn't come. She could remember nothing.

"Okay. Quiet on the set." Maggi grinned and swung her arm in an expansive gesture. "We're ready for you Miss Latham."

"Just a minute, Maggi." Karen jumped up. "There's something I want to check in my notes before we begin." Frantically she flipped through the cards on her desk, looking for familiar words and phrases, anything to spark her and get her going. Familiar words, names of gods and ceremonies leapt from the yellow cards.

She moved back to the chair and the glaring lights. "Okay. Let's go." Surely she could do a minute and a half on this subject without even thinking.

Karen sat with hands folded limply in her lap and faced the camera. She spoke, her voice thin and flat, "Pantheism, of course, marks most ancient civilizations, a belief in more than one god, one divine order. In the Andes of Peru thousands of years ago, such a belief guided the Incan peoples and explained for them the otherwise inexplicable. . . ." She looked down and stammered, "Excuse me, Maggi. I forgot my next thought. I just went blank. Could we try that again?"

"Sure. No problem. Just try and relax." Maggi pressed her eyes to the lens. "Start whenever you like."

Once again Karen began, and once again faltered before the tape had run but a few seconds.

Oh God! I can't do it, she thought, despair bringing hot tears to the rims of her eyes. She lightly tested her cheek with one finger to make sure no moisture showed, she tried once more to explain for the rolling camera the subject she remembered she knew so well.

She failed. Tears of panic and frustration and just plain embarrassment flowed down her cheeks.

Maggi moved quickly from behind the camera and threw her arms around Karen's heaving shoulders. "Oh, sweetie, it's okay." She hugged her tightly and rubbed her hand tenderly over her back. "Maybe this just isn't the right time. We can try again tomorrow when you're more rested Hey, everybody flubs it once in a while—you should see all the tape that ends up on the cutting room floor."

She let her body rest against Maggi's strength but couldn't staunch the flow of tears. A salty wet spot soaked through Maggi's checkered flannel shirt. Concern showed prominently on Maggi's fine face. Clearly, this was something she hadn't expected, this distraught woman weeping on her shoulder. The Karen she knew was vibrant and alive, sure of herself, a woman who exuded an aura of determination and quick intelligence.

"Why don't you rest awhile? I can look after dinner. You look like you could use a nap. I'm beginning to think you've been more ill than you've let on." Maggie squeezed her and brushed a strand of hair from Karen's face.

Karen fled instinctively from the suggestion of sleep. "No," she said, almost too emphatically. "No, I'll just sit here with you by the fire. I don't feel like taking a nap. Please, come and sit by me."

Slowly Karen composed herself, enjoying the gentle pressure of Maggi's hand in hers. It was so good to have her here. If only the listlessness and the sadness would dissipate. . . .

"Did I mention that Walter was up for a short visit?" Karen asked, her eyes focused on the hearth.

"No, I don't believe you did," Maggi answered.

Karen wondered if the slight tremor she felt in Maggi's hand at the mention of Walter was real or imagined. "We won't be seeing each other anymore." Her announcement came out in flat tones, devoid of a sense of loss. She half-turned toward Maggi as she spoke.

Maggi's eyes widened, and though her face remained composed, a flicker of something more passed behind them. "What happened?" she asked, her voice betraying not the slightest rise in tone.

"It's not the same anymore. I think in some ways I've simply outgrown him. And lately I've come to think there should be more, much more, between people."

Maggi cautiously picked up her cue. "You mean, since all this happened between us?"

"As a matter of fact, yes." Karen stood and walked quickly to the windows, drawing her arms tightly around her before speaking. "At least I've seen what else is possible; how much more it can mean when the feelings are really strong. . . ." Karen rubbed her fingertips deep into her forehead. "As you know, I have a hard time with it on a practical level, but at least I know how it feels to . . . ah, glimpse the whole loaf."

As soon as the words left her mouth she regretted them. It wasn't right to lead Maggi on, for she hadn't a clue as to how she might order her life so that Maggi could be part of it. Besides, even as the words were spoken, she heard the whispery footfalls and felt the air grow colder.

Karen turned to see if Maggi had noticed the sounds and the chilly draft. Apparently she hadn't, for her face, bathed in the flickering light from the fire, was soft and untroubled.

"There's still so much I'm trying to sort out," Karen went on. "I probably shouldn't have brought up the whole business. I'm sorry, Maggi. Can we change the subject for now?" Karen started across the room toward the kitchen. "Etta should be here any minute."

Maggi intercepted Karen at the kitchen door. She placed her hands of Karen's shoulders. "I think you know how I feel about you. But I won't pressure you into something you won't be happy with. I know this must be very hard." Maggi pulled Karen to her for the briefest moment. "C'mon. Let's check the roast."

But Karen slid her arms around Maggi's waist. "Hold me for just a minute, Maggi. I'm so confused . . . and frightened."

They held each other, Karen's head pressed tightly against Maggi's shoulder. Behind her in the parlor Karen heard the rustling noises and then the sound of Etta's jeep pulling into the lane.

The noise stopped abruptly as Etta bounded through the door.

"Hi everybody," she greeted.

Maggi, grinning widely, turned to meet Etta Cavendish, reaching out for the huge bowl of salad Etta offered. Without any hesitation they began to chat like old friends.

Karen finally stood a little to the side and watched as they worked in perfect synchronization to finish last-minute details and lay the meal on the table.

"You just sit there in your chair and rest yourself. We can handle this," Etta admonished when Karen tried to help. "You still look a little peaked to me. Don't you think so, Maggi?" Maggi nodded agreement. "Looks like your friend knows her way around a kitchen pretty well," Etta went on. "I think together we can handle this." She winked and nodded at Maggi and they resumed the hum of activity.

Karen watched them working. Maggi took a panful of homemade rolls from the oven and Etta expertly sliced the meat. Karen knew as she watched that she probably cared more for these two women, both of whom she had known for only a few months, than just about anyone else she knew. She was moved by the thought, and at the curious changes everywhere in her life.

Karen picked at her food and chewed slowly. It was delicious; the roast had a perfect pink-red center and browned edges, and Etta's yeast rolls could have melted in her mouth. Even so, she wasn't particularly hungry and had to force herself to eat.

Maggi told stories of her days in Hollywood, of what it was like to be a starlet and simultaneously a counter girl at Dunkin' Donuts. A burdensome contradiction, as she put it. She had done one television commercial, demonstrating for millions that the sponsor's brand of deodorant had kept her polo shirt daintily dry and unstained.

"Has everybody finished?" Etta asked. "I'll pour us some coffee, then why don't we go into the parlor."

When Etta came into the room and saw all the equipment for filming, she stopped short. "For heaven's sake, what's all this?"

"Didn't Karen tell you?" She explained about the PBS project and the previous filmings and the misfortune that had befallen the tape. Etta wanted to know everything about it—the lights, the camera—and Maggi enthusiastically demonstrated. Karen enjoyed watching them and smiled as Etta panned the camera around on the tripod. She actually looked as if she knew what she was doing.

She herself was definitely feeling better, and safe here in the company of her friends. Since Etta had come, she had heard only the usual noises of dinner and talk, no footsteps resounding somewhere in the house. The heavy weight that had pressed on her for days seemed lifted.

"Am I interrupting your project tonight?" Etta asked. Don't let me hold you up if you were planning to work."

Maggi said, "We were planning to shoot the sequence tomorrow when Karen is feeling a little more rested."

Karen looked at Etta, and at Maggi. She did feel better now, much better as a matter of fact. She could almost feel the strength of the other two women flow into and restore her. Maybe she could do it now. "You know, there's nothing like good food and good company. I feel much better than I did this afternoon. Let's try it again. That way we can have the whole day tomorrow to play."

Maggi readjusted the lights and Etta moved to a front row seat by the fireplace. Karen walked into the glare, adjusting her shirt collar under the red sweater, forcibly concentrating only on the words she wanted to utter. She could feel Etta's warm eyes on her, and she returned Maggi's encouraging smile with a wan but sincere smile of her own. If there's ever to be a time when this comes out right, she thought, then this has to be it. She clenched her hand over the swarm of butterflies in her stomach.

"Anytime you're ready," Maggi said from behind the camera.

Karen looked once more at Etta, then turned straight into the camera and began. By dint of a miracle she neither understood nor paused to question, the words flowed. Thoughts that had earlier been mere wisps and fragments merged together in incisive, peppery comments. The camera rolled steadily and Karen spoke without pause or hesitation, often emphasizing her comments with gestures and facial language.

When it was over, she let her shoulders fall and slumped in the chair. She saw Maggi's beaming thumbs-up sign and a tear of sheer relief slipped down her cheek. Maggi grabbed her and spun her around while Etta applauded from the sidelines.

At the hearth they talked quietly for a time, the soft conversation of friends on a winter night. Someone mentioned Christmas and all observed that the holiday would be here before long, sooner in fact than any of the three claimed they would be ready.

"What are your plans?" Etta asked, looking at both of them, but especially at Karen. Both responded with shrugs and upturned palms.

"Not anything yet, I guess," Karen said and leaned over to poke at the fire.

"Me either," Maggi chorused. "But then, I usually make my plans late. Something always turns up."

"We have quite a celebration each year here in Pelham Falls," Etta remarked. "Everybody turns out for it. Some folks spend half the year just getting ready for the Christmas Pageant. And it's worth it, I can tell you, it's quite a lovely thing." Etta smiled at the two younger women. "Maybe you could both plan to attend."

Maggi looked at Karen, obviously waiting for her to respond first.

"Yes, I think I'd like that very much, Karen said, looking at Maggi and smiling.

"Frankly, it sounds better than anything that might be going on in Beantown," Maggi added. "I'd love to come. Christmas in rural New England sounds perfect. What kind of pageant is it?"

Etta broke into a grin and described the reenactment through the streets of Pelham Falls of Mary and Joseph on a donkey, a choir of angels on the balcony of the grange hall, and the townspeople following along behind until the procession reached Mr. Cutter's barn, where everyone joined in caroling.

"I don't hold much with churches," Etta went on, "but it is nice to be in the company of well meaning people celebrating a tradition. I think you'll find it most enjoyable."

When the matter of the kitchen full of unwashed dishes came up, both Etta and Maggi prevailed upon Karen to stay seated by the fire and rest. Without much resistance, Karen agreed. She was starting to feel very tired, blaming it on the energy she had used up in the taping.

She could hear them in there, the clank of dried silverware placed in the slotted drawer, the sound of the fridge closing, the hum of their voices. The wave of fatigue had flattened her and she made no move to help, content to sit in her soft chair and listen to their reassuring noises. The sounds and sentences began to change into disjointed fragments, a word here, a sketchy phrase there, as she drifted perilously close to deep sleep. In the kitchen she could hear Etta's strong voice. . . .

CHAPTER 7

Etta said to Maggi, "Karen's been after me to teach her to use that woodstove. I think she'd like to try and bake someting in it. Just to be able to say she'd done it. But we just haven't gotten around to it yet."

"That would be fun," Maggi said. "It's something I'd get a kick out of too. In fact, maybe we could bake up some bread tomorrow," she added as she hung her damp towel over the sink to dry.

"I don't think she's up to learning tonight. She looks done in and ready for rest. Maybe next time."

"No problem at all. I'm an old hand at woodstoves. I stayed at a friend's cabin in the Berkshires once. The only source of heat, the only way to cook dinner, was an ancient wood stove. Under those circumstances, let me assure you,

I learned fast. I can teach her."

"I'm sure she'd like that, Maggi. And speaking of Karen, and I hope you won't think I'm being an old busybody, I'm a little concerned about her. As you can see, she isn't herself." Etta leaned against the counter, encouraging Maggi to do the same and not return just yet to Karen, who was dozing in the parlor.

Maggi nodded, thinking wryly that one anxiety had eased only to be replaced by another. Weeks ago she'd had no choice, as she saw it, except to give Karen the time she needed, the distance, unconditionally. She'd surrendered to her fear once, and called Karen, only to have that fear deepen. And yesterday she'd been forced to call again—and this time the fear had lifted. But her relief, her joy in being with Karen was tempered now by this new anxiety. She said to Etta, "Frankly, it was the first thing I noticed when I got here. She seems more than just physically ill. I've never seen her so—vague and distracted. What do you think?"

"Hard to say. But whatever it is, a strong dose of a good friend could only help. I'm glad you're here, Maggi, and that you'll be back for Christmas. Meantime, stay in touch with her, won't you? She's terribly isolated."

Etta eased an arm around Maggi's shoulders and together they walked into the room where Karen sat dozing. Maggi looked at the still figure in the chair and was pierced by how frail and tired she appeared, even when asleep. Neither the glow from the fire nor the bright sweater could mask the sallow, washed-out tone of her face.

"Let's get her up to bed," Etta said, moving over to Karen.

The sounds had awakened her and she sat up, mumbling apologies and wiping at her eyes. "How long was I asleep?"

"Not all that long," Maggi answered. "Let's get you upstairs."

She extended her hand. Karen took it and slowly rose to

follow her. Etta said her good nights and, promising to call the next day, departed into the snowy night.

Upstairs, Karen sank heavily onto the bed as Maggi held back the covers and helped her out of her shoes and clothes. When she was settled, Maggi pulled the blankets up snug under her chin and reached down to touch Karen's brow. Karen caught her hand and held it tightly. "Maggi, please stay with me. Just till I fall asleep."

Maggi, fully dressed, slid into bed and nestled alongside, putting her arm tenderly around Karen. "It's okay," she crooned softly. "Rest now."

Long after Karen had fallen asleep, Maggi stayed beside her—alternately soothing the thrashing, moaning woman and staring at the mysterious arrangement on Karen's dresser. A book, propped up on the top, was opened to a page showing a faded daguerrotype. Beside the book was a small painting. Off to one side were several more small paintings. On the dresser a tall white taper burned in the foreground. The painting placed squarely in front of the book intrigued her the most. It could have been Karen's face rendered there on the creamy ivory. What a strange sensation, she thought, lying there next to Karen and looking across the room into a face painted ages ago, so uncannily like that of the woman beside her.

By the amount of wax dripped onto the saucer holding the candle, Maggi judged the flame had been kept burning there for some time. As she studied the pictures, an occasional chill coursed along her forearms and she felt caught in something alien, something she didn't quite understand. She held Karen and continued to stare, until after a time she became almost mesmerized by the paintings. It was as if they came to reflect more light than that loaned by the flickering candle, and even appeared to move and dance with the jerky motions of a silent movie. A surreal and eerie movie to be sure, Maggi felt, and hugged Karen closer against her.

As Karen continued to toss and moan, Maggi wondered whether she'd be more comfortable if left in the bed alone. The shrine-like arrangement on the dresser agitated her, but try as she might, she couldn't explain her unease. Careful to get up without waking Karen, Maggi blew out the candle and tiptoed into the bedroom across the hall. Toward morning, she fell into a light sleep.

* * * * *

Karen had long since descended into a world of her own. A world that was exceedingly dark this time and filled with voids and deep crevices into which she peered but saw nothing. She was lost—lost in a chill cave of tortuous, twisted corridors and looming walls. She jumped on the ground, its sponginess propelling her high into the bluish smoke, her eyes straining to see above it. No matter how high she jumped, she was unable to rise above the dense clouds. It was as though the cave possessed no overhead walls and her very next blind step might send her careening through countless unseen caverns which stretched beyond the fog into infinity. She called out but only a hollow echo responded. The musty odor hung in the air and she tried to follow it, but it led her down narrow tunnels and into dark byways and soon dissipated, leaving her pondering which direction to try next.

A booming, pounding sound began to follow her through the cave, reverberating and careening wildly off the shrouded walls. Her legs ached and she sat on a stone to rub them and again called the name. She held her breath so as to hear even a whispered response, and realized the pounding was her own furiously beating heart.

Water dripped slowly somewhere. She strained into the silence but heard no sound. She was tired now, and frightened, and wanted to go back. But back to where? And which way would lead her there?

Then, without turning, she knew she wasn't alone, knew that Blessing had come. She could feel the cold pressure of a hand on her shoulder. The blue crystals blew past her cheek and she heard in them Blessing's words. *You must not leave me.* The cold fingers dug deeply into her shoulder.

"Oh, I won't, I won't. I'm so glad you've come. I've been so lost!" Karen turned to fling herself against the woman, but she extended her wispy arms to prevent it.

Remember your promise, the figure hissed. *My heart will always find you.*

Ice cold fingers bit again into Karen's arm. *We will always be together,* she hissed again. *Not death this time, not the time measured by all the clocks in eternity can stop my love. My love has carried me, and will now carry us both into a deathless world where we have only to be together.*

Blessing's hungry eyes blazed; they could easily have melted the grotesque ice shapes that hung from the cavern walls. Karen had never see her thus, so urgent, so aloof, her driven eyes waiting answer.

"Yes." Karen heard the sound come from deep in her throat and push out her mouth in a moan. "Yes. Always."

At last then, Blessing pulled Karen to her cold chest and embraced her tightly. At that moment Karen knew she might die from simple relief. Blessing reached to dry a tear on Karen's cheek but her icy touch froze the drop into a glittering crystal. Karen gladly took her hand as they started out of the cold empty cave.

They flew to an airless, lofty place where they made love without touching, where their bodies clung and writhed but never merged, never quite met, where Karen's body was wrapped in a blanket of hot stars. She saw that Blessing, too, was consumed and the sight drove Karen higher, each separate moment now a fresh contraction and release. Burning translucent white, they drifted and soared, tumbled and climbed until, exhausted, they drifted down toward earth and the small austere farmhouse that sat facing the sea.

* * * * *

There were sounds. Banging sounds. Harsh, rude sounds that pulled Karen toward them although she did not want to go. Slowly, she stumbled through heavy fog toward the noise, irritated. The closer she came to the outer edges of the fog, the louder the clanking noises became. At last she broke through the edge.

She was lying in her own bed amid rumpled covers. The noise came from downstairs. The sounds were familiar and she lay still for a moment attempting to place them. A pot. The sound of a pot being placed on the stove and then another sound, that of the oven door closing. It took several more seconds for her to remember that Maggi was here, that those sounds were hers, she was downstairs making something to eat. Karen sat up groggily and tried to push her dream away and secure herself to a bright, snowless morning accompanied by the smell of coffee and breakfast.

She threw on her robe and slippers and came down to stand blinking at the door of the cheery kitchen. Maggi turned and greeted her with a bouncy "Hi," then handed her a cup of freshly made coffee. "Breakfast is almost on the table. Here, sit down." Maggi pulled out a chair and tousled Karen's hair as she obediently sat and sipped loudly at the coffee.

"What time is it?" Karen asked.

"Almost eleven-thirty, sleepyhead. You were really racked out up there. Thought you'd never wake up." Maggi smiled and planted a quick kiss on the top of her head, "How are you feeling, or is it too soon to tell?"

"Let me get a few more gulps of this coffee down before

I try and answer." She flashed a thin smile at Maggi and dove again for the mug.

Maggi laid a splendid breakfast in front of them: a fluffy omelette, thick English muffins, a dash of blueberry conserve. Karen tried hard to keep down the food and even harder to keep the dream submerged. It was stilled but waiting for her in another place.

"Hey, I have an idea," Maggi said. "Let's bake some bread in your woodstove today. Etta told me you wanted to try it, and, as luck would have it, I'm just the one to show you how." Maggi scraped plates into the sink and turned toward Karen, still hunched at the table. "How about it? Do you have all the fixings?"

Karen was grateful for the suggestion. Her need for diversion was intense and growing by the instant. If there were too many gaps between conversations or lags in the simple act of eating, she felt drawn back to the flying sensuality of her other world, or worse, the lonely, hollow cave.

As Maggi came back to the table and sat next to her, Karen thought: But, it's only a dream, isn't it? and emphasized the notion by placing a hand over Maggi's. "I'm sorry if I'm still feeling a little punk this morning. What I need is a shower." Then almost as an afterthought she added, "I really am glad you're here, Maggi."

Karen gave her hand a little squeeze before rising and starting for the stairs. "I think a little bread baking would be a wonderful project today. I won't be a minute." She managed a small smile toward Maggi as she left the room. The part about needing a shower was more than true. She could smell herself, smell the residue of passion and the distinctive scent of her musty lover.

Upstairs in the scalding shower she scrubbed at the lingering smell exuding from her skin and hair, willing the hot needles of water to plant her firmly in the waking world—a world where Maggi waited downstairs. Sweet, good Maggi, checking the flues and ballasts of the stove, offering her warmth and care, and even home-baked bread.

When she came down, Maggi was ready to begin the lesson. She said, "I've checked everything—as far as I can tell, it all works."

Karen moved to stand beside her, and Maggi began pointing out the various parts of the stove. "The trick is to keep the fire burning at a constant rate so whatever you're baking will cook evenly."

Maggi demonstrated the proper way of banking the fire as Karen peered over her shoulder, acutely aware that the shower hadn't erased the persistent acrid smell. Unrest seemed to hang as a thick blanket around her and her attempts to press it away were using every bit of strength she possessed. She could all but hear the whispery voice in her ear. *There shall be no others.*

She leaned against Maggi, as much for support as for a closer view of the proceedings.

"I think we're about ready for the moment of truth. Where are your matches?"

Karen handed them to her, then sat down at the table, watching and holding her trembling hands still in her lap. The smell was overpowering, but if Maggi noticed she gave no evidence of it as she struck a match on the side of the cardboard box. She extended the flaming match into the firebox, igniting the scraps of paper and small twigs under the wood.

"After it gets going, it'll still take awhile before the oven is hot enough to bake." Maggi blew onto the kindling and stood.

Karen sat in a frozen instant of terror as a powerful, explosive sound rocked the room. Giant tongues of flame shot from the stove in all directions. Dense, choking smoke filled the room, columns of flame shot from the round holes on the top and along the stovepipe to the ceiling.

Through the smoke Karen saw Maggi, her hair afire. She lunged toward her. She threw a dishtowel over Maggi's head and dragged her to the door and safety.

"Are you all right?" Karen yelled over the roaring sound of the powerful draft. "Oh my God, Maggi. Are you okay?"

"I'm okay. Get some water," Maggi gasped.

Coughing, shielding their faces, they ran back into the smoky room and toward the sink to draw water into pans. They stopped, stood rooted to the spot. The fire had died out as suddenly as it had begun. A few curls of smoke drifted lazily around the stove, but the fire was definitely out.

Cautiously, Maggi walked to the stove and kicked open the door to the firebox. Inside the few sticks of wood she had placed there were barely charred; a piece or two of kindling still rested intact beneath them.

"What the hell?" Maggi whispered, her voice muted by the tremors of a close call. She stared, open mouthed, at the stove and up the pipe to the smoke-blackened ceiling. "There's no way that could have happened. I checked everything. Besides, there wasn't even enough wood in there for a fire that big."

She sat shakily at the table and for the first time Karen could see she was injured. Just below the hairline and extending halfway down her cheek her skin was tinged red. As Karen moved close, she could smell singed hair and see burnt, wiry sprigs of it protruding from the side of Maggi's head.

Desperately, Karen tried to remember what to do. "Ice," she said aloud and ran to the fridge. She emptied cubes into a bowl and began patting them against Maggi's face. "God, I'm sorry. Oh Maggi. How bad does it hurt?"

"It hurts a little. But I'm okay. It's just a surface burn. No worse than a bad sunburn—I got out of the way fast when those flames shot up. Good thing I was already standing up.

I just can't understand it. How could that have happened?"

"I don't know," Karen said quickly, and stopped herself before adding, I was afraid something like this might happen.

It must have been an accident. A freak accident, for sure, but an accident. Just because they couldn't explain it didn't mean it wasn't accidental. Oh please, God, let it be an accident.

She drew Maggi to her and cradled the good side of her face against her chest. She thought she could hear the rustling noises again and instinctively laid a hand over Maggi's exposed ear. And was it possible that she had heard those sounds just before the flames shot up, from somewhere over by the stove? She shook her head hard. No, it was impossible. She hadn't heard it, she couldn't have.

There were few alternatives but to try to go on with the day. Their visit would end tomorrow morning when Maggi returned to Boston and the faraway world Karen now only barely remembered. Even as she cradled Maggi and gently stroked her neck and shoulders, she could feel the bridges between her world and that one crashing down around her. But now, in the tenuous and fragile present, she had Maggi with her, and before her a day in which she must try to hold for a few more hours to the teetering rails of this bridge.

* * * * *

The day was resplendent. Brilliant sun shone from a cloudless sky onto the pristine white of fresh snow. Not the slightest breeze bothered the trees which stood like frozen sentinels in the bright hush. Maggi had brought her camera and Karen knew of a beautiful drive along the coast, as well as a couple of quaint covered bridges that would make excellent photographs.

Soon they were bouncing along the coast road in Maggi's car, neatly avoiding some potholes and landing squarely in the midst of others. The farther they drove from the house, the more Karen felt herself relax. The knots of tension that had plagued her shoulders and belly smoothed and melted, and for the first time in days, her headache was gone. Often Maggi stopped the car and got out to photograph a view that captured her, and it was only then that Karen could see the scalded face and singed hair. In the car she could see an uninjured Maggie and, often as she looked at her, felt a quickening pulse.

They turned off the coast road and onto a smaller one that led to the covered bridge. The road was narrow and slippery and they hadn't traveled far before realizing that to continue would be dangerous. They left the car in a wide place in the road and continued the less than a quarter mile on foot. The cold air stung and numbed her face, yet it felt good to Karen, cleansing and healing, as if the clarity of the air itself could scrape away the sludge of her discomfort. Here, on the curving, isolated road, it would be all right to talk, to let down walls made of the unspoken.

She placed her arm through Maggi's and even the bulky down stuffing of the parkas couldn't muffle the warm pleasure of so simple a gesture. They walked on in silence for a time, their boots squeaking into the snow. They walked in step and close together, Karen content, for the moment, to be doing exactly this. The air smelled of pine forests and faintly of woodsmoke, and in front of their mouths it gave way to streams of white vapor.

They came round a bend to the bridge, its weathered grey boards spanning a frozen river. They marveled at the structure, at how many winters it had stood there, weighted by snow and ice but without sag or tone of tiredness. In spring the snow would melt and the river flow again, letting the wood-pegged joists and hand-hewn timbers warm in the sun.

Maggi shot pictures from every angle, even climbing down onto slippery rocks near the wooden pilings to get a shot of its massive underside. She took Karen's hand, and they walked through the bridge, bright sunlight splashing into either end while leaving the middle in dusk. Their footsteps resounded on the wooden planks and echoed off the dark, weathered walls. They entered the pool of light at the end of the bridge and blinked at the glare.

Maggi cleared her throat, "Uh, Karen. Could we talk about what happened? I mean with the stove. I just can't get over it, the thing was so—so uncanny. It all happened so fast, and I can't see how it happened at all. It's spooky, Karen. Has anything like that ever happened before?"

She pulled her hand away from Maggi's grasp and jammed it into her pocket. "No, of course not. Like I said, I've never even used it—"

"I don't mean just the stove. I mean anything at all—that you've found unusual, or couldn't explain."

They stopped walking. Maggi turned Karen to face her. Karen felt the clean sting of the cold, felt a slight breeze ruffle her hair and looked out across the pure endless white in the direction of her house. It seemed very far away. Maggi looked steadily at her and held her gaze, compelling Karen to return the look. A slight shudder ran through Karen's body as she spoke. "I don't know much about things like this but yes, there have been some things I'd call odd."

"Like what?"

"Like noises. . . . At first I thought they were rats . . ." Karen stopped abruptly, and looked away.

"C'mon, Karen," Maggi prodded gently. "Tell me. What kind of noises?"

Karen repeated the story she had told Etta not so long before, leaving out all reference to Blessing and the dreams.

As she talked, she half turned from Maggi and looked often at the ground, as if the angle of her body might lend obliqueness to the words she spoke.

"That's about it, Maggi," she finished, "there's not a whole lot to tell. Actually, I seldom notice anymore." Karen shrugged. "Guess I've more or less gotten used to the idea that strange things happen around me in the house. Implausible," she added, "and usually benign." She put her arm through Maggi's and smiled, urging them to move on along the quiet road.

Maggi moved easily into step beside her. After a few seconds she asked, "Karen, do you know what a poltergeist is?"

"Sure." Karen tossed her head lightly. "I've been known to indulge in a little genre fiction. Mostly though, I'm familiar with the term as a cross-cultural phenomenon. It means a mischievous spirit, or even a harmful one, that can hurl things through the air, make objects vanish—"

"Or cause a stove to flare up beyond any reasonable expectation of the amount of wood inside—"

"Oh for heaven's sake, Maggi. Surely you can't be serious."

"Okay, okay, I know it sounds weird, but just suppose there is a ghost or whatever in your house. Maybe you could be in danger. I mean, I really believe in things like that, the things that go bump in the night, so to speak."

"Well, what if there is? I mean, what could I possibly do about it? After all, I'm all right, aren't I?" It was a question Karen wished she hadn't posed, though Maggi let it pass, obviously sensing this an improper moment to confront her.

"Just be careful, okay? Funny noises and things that pass in the corners of our eyes may be harmless, even interesting. Sometimes there's a perfectly plausible explanation." Maggi looked closely at Karen. "I'm concerned, Karen. I know how much you love your house, and anyone can see why. It's lovely. But frankly, I feel a little edgy there."

"Don't you think the situation between us could have something to do with that?" Karen retorted, her tone brisk. "I'm getting cold—could we start back to the car?"

They walked faster and without touching. "There's something I wanted to ask you," Maggi said, looking at Karen and jamming her hands deep into her pockets.

"What?" Her tone was brittle even to her own ears.

"Well, last night, up in your bedroom, I couldn't help noticing those little paintings on your dresser. One of them looks exactly like you, Karen. And there was the arrangement itself. I got the strongest feeling that it was set up like an altar, or a shrine of some kind. Who are those women?"

"Oh, that." Karen would have bolted like a rabbit, but everywhere were endless snow-covered fields, dense woods. Down to the left, a stranger's house with smoke curling up from the chimney. She forced lightness into her tone and stretched her lips into a thin smile. "Aren't they pretty? I found them in an antique store the other day. Etta was with me. Both women lived in the house. Quite a coincidence, don't you think?" She rattled on, "The darker one was an artist. I bought several of her beautiful miniatures as well. I'll show them to you when we get back."

"Who are they? What are their names?" Maggi asked.

"Well, the one that resembles me was Aimee McCartland, a relative who came to live on the farm when her parents died. And the other is . . ." Karen took a drink of air, pulling it into her lungs in one large draw. "The other one is named Blessing McCartland—or, that is, was named Blessing McCartland. She's the one who was the artist," she added quickly to cover her possible blunder. "Some of her paintings were shown recently in Boston. Maybe you've heard of her."

"No. Can't say I have." They reached the car, and Maggi

quickly unlocked both doors.

Alongside the coast road, stuck in among a stand of evergreens, stood a diner made from an old railroad car, its purpose announced in the most utilitarian of neon signs: EAT. A few cabins were set in the woods behind the diner.

"What do you say?"

"I'm game," Karen responded.

Inside, a row of booths ran the length of the car and on the adjacent wall refrigerated cases held small cans of grapefruit juice and an assortment of pies. At one end a massive, gaudy Wurlitzer poured out music of the forties. Maggi slid into a booth, the seat sporting a duct tape patch. A man in white T-shirt and apron appeared. They ordered glasses of wine and the Blue Plate Special.

Karen toyed absently with the salt shaker and watched Maggi, wishing she could bridge the schism that had opened between them during the afternoon. The wine arrived and they toasted each other, locking into a long glance over the tops of their glasses.

Whatever dark, brooding mood had overtaken her earlier in the day began to slip away in direct proportion to the music, the warming of the wine, and above all, Maggi herself. Maggi was real—a flesh and blood woman sitting there across from her. And her feelings about Maggi were real too—flesh and blood feelings unlike any she had known before. She could hide from the feelings, protect herself for a time, but sooner or later she would find herself without armor, vulnerable again and open. She had no disguise, no impenetrable walls she could hide behind. The connection with Maggi was as vivid and powerful as ever. Some moments she felt she could actually see it shimmering in the air between them . . . moments like this one. Love didn't vanish simply because it proved inconvenient, or because its fire burned too frightfully deep, or even because one refused to think about it. It simply was, existed with a life of its own. People made decisions every day about whether to act on such feelings, but no decision was required on whether the feelings existed.

Maggi got up to play the jukebox. Karen watched her with a lover's appreciation, admiring the firm curve of Maggi's jean-covered buttocks and longing to touch the sweep of her shoulder through the soft flannel of the shirt. But she wanted more in this moment than physical pleasure. She yearned to know whether Maggi believed in God, what her parents were like, how she and Maggi might share the paper on a Sunday morning, what were Maggi's unspoken, private fears. She wanted to know the threads which, woven together, were Maggi England. And knowing that, to lose herself in moments pressed close to her. Be swallowed up by her mouth. . . .

Moonlight Serenade provided the backdrop, and without speaking, they reached across the formica and touched hands.

"Maggi, I do care about you . . . a lot." Karen faltered at first, then found bravery in the look on Maggi's face and the pleasure of touching hands. "I've come closer to knowing what real love is with you than with anybody. Ever. I want you to know that, Maggi. If we can't know anything else right now, then please, at least know this."

"I do know, Karen. I've known almost from the start. Things like this, what's happened between us . . . well, you just know." Maggi gave her dark hair a light ruffle and smiled. "Sometimes I try to put myself in your shoes by imagining what it would be like to wake up one morning and find myself in love with a man."

She winked at Karen. "It's kinda like sauerkraut. All my life, as far back as I can remember, I never liked the stuff. So, I make the reasonable assumption that I won't suddenly develop a taste for it." Maggi spread her hands palm up between them and smiled widely. "We make assumptions like that all the time, based on preferences. Based on my preferences, it's reasonable to assume I'll go to my grave without tasting sauerkraut again. Same where emotions are concerned. I've always just preferred the company of women. As a result, I've probably been required to wear far fewer layers of subterfuge and facade. Besides—" Maggi winked and cocked her head. "We're far more interesting people, don't you think? Women, I mean. And gentler with each other."

"Yes. I do think that's true." Karen took a small sip of wine. "When I look back over my life it seems that I've always felt more comfortable, more myself—safer around other women." Karen looked down at the table, then back at Maggi. "I like knowing that—and how I feel about you. And us. It's just—at the moment I can't seem to find the way to weave this logical extension of my feelings into my daily life."

Karen shook her head sadly and looked past Maggi to the Wurlitzer. "I've worked hard, Maggi, very hard to get where I am. I've sacrificed—pushed myself. The hell of it is that my success is in one of the most provincial professions anywhere. Interesting isn't it, that the public thinks of the world of universities as liberal and free thinking. A bastion of all things visionary and creative."

Karen's thin smile curled the edges of her mouth down instead of upward. "The truth is—the bottom line—is that I couldn't bear to lose my job. It's all coming my way now, Maggi. Soon I'll be able to pick and choose among the best lecture chairs, snap up well-funded research expeditions, even become one of those rare scientists whose name is recognized by people outside their field of endeavor. Not that that in itself means a great deal, but you must see what I'm talking about. Everything was going according to plan. Then . . ." Karen paused and increased the pressure on Maggi's hand, squeezing it and holding it in a firm grasp. "Then you showed up."

As she talked, she was surprised by her clarity, her surety in telling Maggi more about herself. The wearisome tiredness that had become so much a part of her had been lifted away.

She felt almost elated. Telling Maggi her fears, letting her see the more rigid, even posturing, side of her nature, was good; a healthy purge of secrets. Why hadn't she done this sooner? She could tell by Maggi's face that the revelations had done nothing to reduce her warmth. In fact, if anything, the warmth had grown.

"There is one question, though," she went on. "You said earlier that you were required to wear far fewer facades because you had chosen to live your preferences. It seems like just the opposite, that you'd have to hide so much of yourself."

"Not really. Lots of people at work know who I am. But there are times and places where I do keep it to myself. It's a trade off, I guess. In my personal life, with myself and the people I care about, where it really counts, I prefer to be honest and real."

Karen sat perfectly still and thought about Judith Prentiss. A teacher and a woman who, presumably, did try to keep it to herself, but when that became no longer possible, had chosen to be openly honest and real. To not surrender to others' disapproval and fade away, but to fight for her right to have both love *and* career. Her *right* to be honest and real. . . .

Karen turned her attention back to Maggi.

The food appeared and sat untouched while they talked, letting each other see aspects of self as yet unrevealed. Eventually they picked at bits of the food, unappetizingly cold, then pushed the plates to the far end of the table.

Maggi grasped Karen's hands in both of her own. "I love you, Karen."

"I love you too, Maggi."

They sat in silence, looking at each other, and occasionally at their hands, still clasped on the table.

Karen knew she had not told it all, that there was a part of her life she couldn't tell, wouldn't ever tell anyone. The life she lived in her house: the dreams, the woman. All of it must remain only hers. Whatever was happening to her there was happening in an exclusive non-reality, a world where she seemed out of control and not entirely certain she would exercise control even if she could. And, whatever it was, it was hers alone. A private reality that was not reality at all—merely dreams.

Karen knew, too, that she wanted to make love with Maggi again. An urgency greater than the drive of passion spun her toward thoughts of the little cabins strung out in the woods behind the diner. It had to be here, now; not later at the house.

"Maggi," she said softly, "I want to be closer to you. I want to feel you close to me. Can we make love and not feel that it—"

"Means we're married?" Maggi interrupted. "Or cements us together at the waist?"

"Something like that. I'm still fitting things together in my head, please understand. . . . Oh, I want so much to touch you."

Wordlessly, Maggi slid from the booth and returned to the table carrying a key. "We can at least try."

* * * * *

If the first lovemaking at the cabin on the Cape had surprised Karen, the second proved an extension of a measure Karen had judged inextendable. There could be no more room for the sweeping passion, yet there was. And this time another element swelled, a tenderness born of the heart's wish to rush open to another and, once opened, to rejoice that the gift of oneself was returned equally. In such moments as these, the lovers didn't require boundless passion as an expression of what was best spoken by a gentle caress, or a hand stroking cheek while eyes locked together.

"Oh," Karen spoke, her lips sliding along the curve of Maggi's throat, and all she could say of love was carried on that one word, repeated once as she moved her mouth to the velvet skin of Maggi's breast.

Rocking, moaning softly, locked in a deep kiss she stroked bare shoulders and soft thighs, as though caressing the aura of love rising out of them. Each time release neared they denied it, breaking the rhythm or pulling apart, trembling in exquisite tension. Karen felt tears fill her eyes, the last gift to be offered by a heart so filled and stunned. Tension built toward release again, and could not be stopped. In a world without sound, Karen came, shattering and trembling, like a glass skyscraper tumbling down.

At last she lay in that most satisfied of exhaustions, still and quiet beside Maggi. She knew even the slightest movement of hip against thigh, or shoulder grazing shoulder was capable of beginning the fiery dance again.

Later, giddy with pleasure, Karen half-giggled, "We don't even have toothbrushes."

"Do you care?"

"Not in the slightest." Karen moved her leg so that it rested against the full length of Maggi's.

No more was required and the loving began again, this time slower, each languid touch and gesture relished as a separate being, a complete act of love in itself. Each time release neared, she moved away from it, exquisite tension played out on a high voltage wire. They careened again toward each other and the exploding colors of the flash point.

Toward morning they slept briefly, curled tightly against one another. Later, they ate breakfast in the little diner. Lovers still cocooned in the magic they had made, they had little use for the intrusion of words.

The mood continued throughout most of the trip back, but as they drew nearer the outskirts of Pelham Falls Karen grew restless. She twisted her hands in her lap and turned often to stare out the windows. She pulled into herself with each mile they drove, and with each passing mile grew more agitated.

Though the morning was bright, dark clouds were massing on the horizon.

"I hate to leave," Maggi said finally.

They had reached the village and were headed along the stretch of road to the farm. Karen averted her eyes and didn't respond. There was a strained silence between them, but she could think of nothing to say. She had to get back to the house. Then, everything would be all right.

"I didn't mean that the way you think, Karen. I'm worried about you."

"I'll be fine," Karen said quickly. "Besides, look at the sky. There's nasty weather brewing. You'll have to make a run for it soon."

They approached the turnoff to the house. Etta's red jeep was parked at the kitchen doorway; the engine was running and swirls of vapor covered the rear. She waved heartily as they approached the house and bounded over to the car.

"Dropped by to bring you a sample of some of my teas before you left, Maggi, and to check up on our girl. I was just leaving when I saw you pull into the drive."

"Etta. What a great surprise! I wasn't expecting to see you again this trip."

Karen got out of the car. "C'mon, let's all warm up with some coffee."

As they started for the door, Etta said with surprise, "Your face! What on earth happened to you?"

"A little accident with the stove yesterday morning. Maybe I'm not quite the expert I touted myself to be." Maggi's tone was light, as if to ward off further inquiry. "Nothing to worry about. I'm fine now."

"Here, let me have a look at it," Etta said as they came

into the kitchen. "Have you put anything on it?" Gently she tilted Maggi's head toward the light and looked closely at her. "How in the world did it happen? Did you check the flue and the damper?"

Karen moved to intervene, "Oh yes, she checked everyting. But something, gas or soot, must have gathered in the stovepipe. Anyway, it's over now, let's go into the parlor and sit down." She wished everybody would leave, Maggi included. Leave and let her have some rest. . . . She was tired, suddenly so very tired. . . . She wanted nothing more than a short nap, a chance to lie down and be alone.

Maggi began packing up her equipment, working efficiently, taking down lights and packing the delicate camera with ease, all the while telling Etta about the covered bridge and the beautiful shots she had gotten along the coast road.

"When were you planning to leave?" Etta asked. "Looks like we've got some weather coming down."

"Soon as I finish packing this stuff and maybe have a bite of lunch," Maggi replied.

"Stay for lunch too, Etta. There's plenty left for sandwiches," Karen said. "But I'd like to lie down for a minute before we eat. I'm feeling a little tired again."

"Sure, go ahead. Etta and I can make lunch and call you when it's ready."

Karen walked wearily up the stairs, aware of each step as it demanded response from her aching legs. At the top of the landing she paused, her hand on the knob of her bedroom door. Perhaps it was guilt at leaving her friends again to prepare food for her, or perhaps a momentary fear that made her hesitate.

She opened the door, and knew instantly something was wrong. Even before her senses collected themselves, she knew something had gone terribly wrong in here. The room looked vandalized. The candle, which she had so carefully kept burning on the dresser, was smashed and broken, lying in little wads of broken tallow. Even the delicate saucer that had held it was shattered into minute fragments on the dresser top. And the painting of Aimee was gone!

Karen's hand flew to her throat as she stared in horror at the mess on the dresser. What lay there was clearly the residue of anger, a violent, pounding anger. Frantically she looked about the room to see what else might have come under attack. She had not yet taken a full step into the room.

The barren dresser looked somehow mocking, glaring at her in mysterious retribution. Downstairs, she could hear Maggi and Etta talking, the sounds muffled and far away. Softly she shut the door behind her, closing out the world from this place and from whatever had happened here. Gingerly, taking small steps and searching about the room, she walked further into its hushed and still center. Only when she reached the middle did she see the portrait of Aimee.

It lay on the floor under the windows, broken in half, as though hurled against the wall with enormous strength. The break had split the portrait in two horizontal pieces, the fracture line breaking along Aimee's mouth.

Karen knelt, picked up the pieces and held them together in her palm so that they would again form a whole. Feeling as if her own face had broken, Karen placed her hand instinctively over her mouth. It can be fixed, she murmured, and wiped at a tear that had run onto her upper lip. The painting could be fixed. But where was the book? The picture of Blessing?

She stood up and looked warily around the room half-afraid of what she might see, but desperate to locate the picture. She looked down at the bed which was perfectly made, for it had not been slept in last night. There, on the pillow propped up on the unmussed surface, was the book, opened to the delicate daguerreotype of Blessing's dark face. The somber, sultry eyes blazed up at her.

In a sweeping motion, Karen snatched the book from the bed and held it in a trembling hand at her side. She dared not look at it, into that accusing face. For the first time since she had lived here, she was truly frightened.

She sat down on the edge of the bed and held the book pressed between the palms of her hands. She could hear herself sobbing, from fear and from utter confusion, but the sounds, like those of Etta and Maggi downstairs, seemed to be coming from a long way off. She would have to clean up the mess and mend Aimee's painting. But she would do all that later. Right now, she had only the strength to lie back on top of the covers and close her eyes.

Still clutching the book, she curled closely into herself and let herself drift. She could smell the familiar mustiness; it had been faint when she entered, but had swelled as she walked among the ruined mementoes. Now it filled her nostrils as she closed her eyes and sank deeply into the bed. She lay still and felt her body float into the blankets under her, the blankets fluffing up softly next to her skin. Then she was falling. . . .

She was in the caves again. How she hated the caves! Always, when lost in their murky depths, she felt cold and alone, and so frightened. For a moment she thought she heard laughter and talking—voices like Maggi and Etta's reaching down to her, and she tried to run toward them, toward the sounds, but couldn't. Instead the spongy ground gave way and she was falling, falling through dark space, no light, deeper and deeper, tumbling down in a bottomless shaft. The voices had been erased by the sounds of wind and rushing water.

If only I could wake up, she thought, and pinched herself—which only served to make the fall faster, increasing her panic with each moment of descent. Maybe I'm not really asleep, she wondered, but was afraid to pinch herself again. Her shirt was wet and stuck cloyingly to her skin. The smell was everywhere.

She heard the whispering sound of Blessing calling to her but could scarcely see through the darkness. Then her body changed direction, veering off into the maze of openings and arches, flying horizontally like a bird, deeper into the underworld caverns.

A single word, a reverberating steamy whisper came toward her from all directions at once. *Here.*

Trembling, she turned to look. She dove and soared, looking into the mass of tunnels and ragged gaping holes. She couldn't see her. A gust of rancid wind spun her crazily in a circle, round and round until she could no longer see the outlines of the damp walls. Her ears rang with the word *Here.*

Something dark and noisy slid through the air in front of her face and she brushed at it, clearing for an instant the dense smoke.

Then she saw her, standing on a rock across a rushing torrent of steaming water. Her skirts flapped against her legs and her hair blew in wild profusion around her head, like snakes coiling out into the smoke.

"I'm lost. Please, let's go back." Karen's voice was thin as a reed and no match for the power of the woman's tall presence nor for the unearthly fire smoldering on her face.

Not yet. The words flew out of the woman's mouth, washing over Karen like claps of thunder. Her face was steely, malignant fury showing only through the narrow slits of her mouth and eyes.

Karen's knees were weak, her heart pounded in her chest. Why were they here again? Why was she so angry?

She wanted to cross the water and touch Blessing's familiar face, fold her arms around the muslin of the dress and feel safe again, safe to feel the bounding love they shared soar to life and sweep them away from here, back to the cool wet beach and their dance.

Come here, Blessing commanded, and with hardly an effort she leapt the torrent and stood facing Karen. *You have wronged me,* she said, never relaxing the determined slit of her mouth. *You wronged our love.*

The accusation pierced Karen, confusing her. She thought back to their last time together. They had made love, over and over again until Karen had exploded into thousands of brilliant stars. Whatever could she mean? Desperately she needed to know. She tried to remember, but the rolling of time was difficult in a world where, somehow, time didn't exist at all.

And there was something else she tried to remember, something vague and filmy. A something that had happened in another time and place. She couldn't recall it, but she knew from her feeling that it could have angered Blessing. Something she had dreamed perhaps. . . .

Again Blessing's voice rent the air. *I will not be wronged again. I have waited here in these caves, walked them and waited. And I have waited on the beach and in the house, always waiting. Looking for you, waiting for you to come. You left me before, a long time ago, and I will not let you leave me again. Be true to your promise. Do you remember?*

Karen remained mute, staring at Blessing and grasping at the words she spoke, trying to learn their meaning.

Remember this. Wherever you go, I go too. I am everywhere with you. When you left, I mourned you and waited. Then you returned and I rejoiced and loved you again. Now, our love will not know time, nor death, nor any other endings. I must know you love me too. Do you love me?

"Oh, yes." Karen moved to stand closer to her and put her hand on Blessing's face. She had to make her know.

Then, you must do something. In the world of chance,

too much can go wrong. We could lose each other again. Do you want that?

"No. I never want to lose you." The very thought made shivers run along Karen's back and through her legs, weakening them such that she feared she might fall.

Then there is something we must do together, a promise we must make. We will seclude ourselves. We can know our happiness without interruption if only we promise to hide ourselves away and let no one near. No one at all. There must be no one in our house but us, where we will love beyond all boundaries, beyond all caring for anyone else, beyond all thought save those we share with each other. Will you do this with me?

Karen hesitated, trying to understand Blessing and her fervent request.

Blessing's voice grew hard, its edges sharp and cutting. *Say it,* she demanded.

"Yes. Yes, I will. There will be no others but us, always."

Blessing's face softened and she brushed a sprig of Karen's limp hair from her forehead. *Good. There are people there now, people who don't belong, and they must be made to leave. Send them away quickly and no harm will be done, and when they've gone I'll come to you, and we can soar and fly together, forever.*

Without remembering why, Karen knew Blessing meant what she had said about harm. She had seen her temper here in the caves; but the danger was something more than that. She could almost see something hot and flashing that symbolized the hurt that Blessing could make happen; but the image faded as quickly as it had come.

Their hands touched, icy and hot at once, and Karen felt the tingle from it glide up her arms, dusting them with gooseflesh. Blessing smiled at her, showing her even, white teeth, and Karen saw that the grim, hard look was gone now, replaced by a hungry fire.

Go now. The sooner you go and do what must be done, the sooner I can come again to you. Hurry.

Slowly Karen began her ascent from the cave, floating up as if pushing from the bottom of a deep, dark pool. She heard sounds tinkling in among the sounds of dripping water and the ever-present wind. The nearer she came to the surface, the more distinct the sounds became and soon she could make out Maggi's voice, talking in low tones to someone else. It was hard to pull herself upward. She was tired and going slowly, oh, so slowly toward the voices. . . .

CHAPTER 8

Maggi and Etta sat at the table drinking tea and talking. The car was loaded, the sandwiches on the table, but they had not as yet made a move to wake Karen. Etta raised her cup slowly to her lips and drank, then set the cup down in the saucer with a clatter. "Tell me again about the stove." She looked once more at the side of Maggi's face.

"It was bizarre, Etta. I've never seen a thing like that in my life. It just exploded. Fire and smoke poured out, it all happened so fast. There wasn't even a buildup of any kind. The whole thing was suddenly a mass of flame and smoke. I'm lucky I didn't get burned worse." She paused. "I have to admit I'm a little spooked. Maybe even a little more so after a talk Karen and I had yesterday after it happened—" Maggi broke off.

Etta's eyes opened wider and her face grew more intent as she leaned forward.

"Etta, I have the feeling that the stove wasn't an accident. More like something . . . I don't know—unusual things had happened here.

Etta tensed slightly, as if bracing for something she already knew. "And what did she say?"

This wasn't shaping up to be an ordinary conversation. Regardless, she had to continue. Etta was no ordinary woman either—certainly not from what she'd seen, and what she'd heard from Karen. That knowledge, plus Etta's intent look, a look without a trace of skepticism or ridicule, sent Maggi on.

"She sometimes hears footsteps, even though no one else is in the house, and other noises. . . . Sometimes a sound of rustling fabric. She's seen things, shadow-figures in the corner of her vision."

There was a pause which stretched to Maggi's exact limit of comfort.

"Yes, I know," Etta said quietly. She laid a rough knobby hand on Maggi's arm and smiled gently. "She told me."

No words or gestures could have been more welcome. Maggi blew out a long, noisy breath of relief.

"There's more, too, more I could tell you about this house and what may be going on here." Etta paused, then went on. "Not everybody can understand what I'm about to say, but I get the feeling you can, Maggi." Etta removed her hand but the soft smile remained firmly in place. She took another sip of tea.

"If you mean about the paranormal," Maggi said, "then yes, I do. I've been interested for years. I've read everything I could find. I'm a believer. Please go on."

"Ever since I was a girl," Etta began, "I've paid heed to this house. I used to stand over in those fields just across the road and look up at it. It scared me some, but still I would look over here, knowing there was more here than just boards and plaster. The place seemed broody to me, sad and empty, even when folks lived in it. In my playtimes, when I needed to make up a place that was grim and spooky, maybe a little fearsome, I'd always bring to my mind a picture of the McCartland house.

"One day, I must have been around eight or nine, I was out walking on the beach with my grandmother, we were down almost in front of this house. She stopped me and put a finger to her lips, she pointed to the rocks just ahead. I saw her—a dark-haired woman walking slowly among the rocks in the cove. She looked strange to me, filmy, like there was a gauze curtain between us. And she was dressed peculiar. I started to say something but my grandmother put her hand over my mouth to shush me. We stood there for a bit and I remember feeling I was an intruder in somebody's private sorrow. Then my grandmother turned us away, and we went on back down the beach.

"On the way home, she made it clear to me that we'd seen a spirit, the ghost of a woman dead, at that time almost twenty years. My grandmother talked to me all the way home about ghosts, and how it is some people become earth-bound after death. Usually those who die sudden, or people who for one reason or another can't let go of something from their lifetimes, something that can keep their spirit from passing on. As I walked home that day all mindful of the woman, I felt so sorry for her and for whatever it was had happened to make her so very sad."

The room had grown darker. Maggi leaned forward.

"I saw her often after that," Etta went on. "Sometimes at the beach, sometimes passing a window in her house, and always sad, so terribly sad. I believe she is still here, Maggi—and what's wrong with Karen has something to do with her presence. Her name is Blessing McCartland."

"You were with Karen when she bought those little paintings" Maggi said. "Karen told me the young, light-haired girl is Aimee."

"I don't know much about Aimee. Seems she was a relative of Blessing's by marriage and came to live on the farm when her parents passed on. My grandmother's journals took notice that Aimee and Blessing were quite close, a great source of comfort and friendship to each other. Aimee died tragically, and quite young." Etta shook her head, "It's odd how much she resembles Karen."

"Etta, I'm frightened. I haven't known Karen long, but I've never seen her like this, so drawn and fragile. What do you think is happening?"

"I'm not sure yet, Maggi. But deep in me I do know two things. One, whatever's going on here is bad for Karen, and two, she shouldn't remain here any longer. I know she loves this house, and to pry her out of here will take a bit of doing. Still, I can't help but feel it's the best thing for her. It's more than just loving the house–more like an obsession with it. Maybe you've taken notice how much better she seems when she's out, away from it."

"She'll never leave, Etta," Maggi said with a wave of her hand. "Karen is a very determined woman, and I get the feeling she's bound and determined to stay here. And yes, I did notice."

"Interesting you used the word bound, for that's just what she is. But not in the sense you meant it. Many things can happen to a person who chances on a spirit. The most common one is possession, but I don't hold much store by it, it's just the kind of junk that ends up in those papers you buy at the supermarket. The other is obsession. A person can become bound to a spirit, sometimes without even knowing it–in some way that spirit lives through a living person. Usually to carry out some powerful purpose they were pledged to in life. That seems more like what could be happening to Karen." Etta paused and lifted her eyebrows. "But I just can't figure the why of it." She gazed steadily at Maggi as she spoke. "What does Blessing McCartland want with her? Karen is bound to the house, and in some way to Blessing, but I don't know why."

"Jesus Christ," Maggi said and ran her hand vigorously through her hair. The epithet hung in the air between them while Maggi tried to take in Etta's words and make sense of them.

From upstairs they heard the sounds of Karen moving about in her bedroom. She would be down soon. They looked at each other in silence.

Maggi toyed with the blue patterned edge of the plate that held the neatly made sandwiches. "Well, at least we have to try," she said, then turned toward the door as Karen came into the room.

She looked groggily at them, first at Maggi, then at Etta, before sitting down heavily between them. "Am I interrupting something?" she asked finally.

"As a matter of fact, we were just talking about your being so out of sorts and alone here. We were thinking that maybe it would be a good idea if you went back to Boston with Maggi awhile, at least till you're feeling better."

Even Etta showed surprise at the haste with which Karen jumped from the table and busied herself at the sink. Over the sound of running water she said in a voice meant to sound firm but which extended well past it into defense, "That's absurd. I'm perfectly all right here and I'm sure in a few more days I'll feel fine again. I did come here to finish a book project. Unfortunately, this bout with the flu has put me way behind schedule. Please, let's not discuss it any further."

With that, she turned and faced the women, wearing a look that invited no opposition. She crammed her hands into the pockets of her jeans and looked down at the sandwiches.

"Let's have lunch. The storm is coming this way pretty fast. If you're going to outrun it, Maggi, you'd better not dally around much longer."

Maggi felt her heart sink. Not only had Karen flatly refused the suggestion, but she was again hostile and distant. Maggi was baffled. Karen was entitled to the time she needed to assimilate the shock of their relationship into her life. But if Emma was right about the peril in this house. . . . To continue to argue would surely mean deepening the schism between them. To let it go would immeasurably increase her own worry.

She picked up a sandwich and looked out the window. The storm was indeed coming on fast. A gust of wind careened around the side of the house, sending several small twigs scurrying along the crusted top of the snow. The temperature had been falling steadily all afternoon, she was sure, as was the barometer, heralding the arrival of heavy snowfall. But by what barometer should she gauge the falling energies in the room around her, or the rising tension?

"It wouldn't have to be my place," she said. "You could stay with a friend of mine. There'd be people close by to help you, see that you had the things you need. My place is small," she finished, with a look in Etta's direction.

"Absolutely not," Karen replied firmly. "I'm not leaving here. I'm not going to your place, Maggi, or a friend's place, or any other place. This is my home and this is where I'm staying." She paused to let the anger drain from her tone. "Look, I appreciate your concern, really I do. And I'm touched that you both cared enough to offer your help. But you're making too much of this. Really. I don't need help. I'll be fine."

Karen let herself relax and sat at the table. "I care about you both a lot, and it feels good to know I'm cared about in return. C'mon, let's finish lunch. I'm getting worried about Maggi having to drive in this weather."

Etta rose and gently began to massage Karen's shoulders. "We didn't want to be meddlesome, Karen. It's up to you, of course. Can we go halfway? If you won't go, then you and I can stay in close touch over the next few days, okay?"

"That would be lovely," Karen said without conviction, and stared at her hands in her lap.

Etta turned to Maggi. "I reckon Karen's right. Now's the time to make a run for it. I'll stay with Karen awhile and clean up the kitchen. Karen, you go on back to bed. Maggi, why don't you go with her, see she's all right. I'll just stay down here and put things away."

Maggi blessed Etta's sensitivity in arranging for a little time for them to be alone. She put her arm around Karen, gently guiding her toward the stairs.

Upstairs, Karen sat on the edge of the bed. Maggi, without taking her arm from around Karen, sat beside her. "Promise me if things get worse, you'll call—perhaps even reconsider coming down to Boston for a while." Maggi tugged playfully at Karen's shoulder. "This isn't a lurid setup to get you into my apartment for a few days." She laughed lightly. "I am concerned about you and want to help if I can. And I think you know I love you."

"Maggi," Karen said, taking Maggi's face in her hands, "I care about you more than I could possibly have imagined." She kissed Maggi lightly and then dropped her hands to her lap. "I need just a little more time to finish sorting everyting through about how I might handle all this . . . these feelings between us. And some things are falling into place. . . . Just please know I do care."

Maggi gave a gentle squeeze to Karen's shoulder. "Yes, I know," she breathed softly. "I know it and hold that knowledge very precious to me."

Karen leaned over and rested her head in the crook of Maggi's neck. "And do be careful driving back."

"I will. And I'll be in touch in a few days, to see how

you're doing." They kissed lightly and Maggi rose, leaving Karen to stretch out on the bed. Karen said tiredly, "Say goodbye to Etta for me."

"I'll call," Maggi said and squeezed Karen's outstretched hand. "Take care." She gave a parting glance to the dresser and, noticing it empty, took it as a sign that perhaps things would be all right after all. As she descended the stairs toward the clatter in the kitchen she realized what thin hope it was, but knew, too, that it would have to serve, along with her trust in Etta.

Etta was wrapping the uneaten sandwiches. Maggi said wryly, "Well, we didn't get very far with Karen, did we?"

"That's so," Etta responded. "But not too surprising. I'll talk to her again. Maybe she needs time to let everything settle into place in her mind. It's not exactly the most commonplace thing."

"Hardly," Maggi said. "I feel better knowing you're here to check on her. It just feels so strange, Etta. That we're dealing with a most extraordinary occurrence in the first place and trying to help someone who seems not to want any help at all. It's frustrating to say the least, and frightening, too. Let's exchange phone numbers—I'd feel better knowing I can call you."

They hugged as much to reassure each other as to say goodbye. Maggi bounded to her car as the first snow began tumbling in huge flakes from the leaden sky. Before she turned the car around to drive out, she gave Etta an energetic wave. Etta, standing in the doorway, waved back, her smile reflecting their newly formed bond as well as their shared dilemma.

Etta moved back into the kitchen and closed the door firmly behind her. She leaned against the door, hands still clasped on the latch. She hadn't wanted to alarm Karen's nice friend unduly, but her own concern was mounting. She would have to talk with Karen again and try to make her see that staying here was dangerous. It was a task that would require a considerable amount of thought. From what she could see, Karen was much too practical and intellectual to be swayed by anything faintly smacking of cheap sensationalism—or the urgings of an old woman who attempted to frighten her with stories of wraiths and restless ghosts.

In no hurry to leave, Etta sat at the table and tried to focus herself on the house and what she knew of it. She sat perfectly still, seeing with more than her eyes, listening into the silence with other ears.

If only she could see the connection between Blessing McCartland and the young woman asleep upstairs. What was it that had fastened Karen so firmly to the house and the ghostly presence? The frustration was not unlike reading a poem from which the last stanzas had been deleted.

While she sat, another sensation began to gather about her. The strong sense returned that her long fascination with this house and the spirit in it was no accident. Somehow, she felt that all she knew and all she could learn was being called into focus now, and as the pieces came together she would move inexorably toward a truth and a confrontation she couldn't as yet see.

So involved was she with her own thoughts that she didn't hear Karen descend the stairs and come to stand behind her chair until Karen spoke.

"You're still here," she said.

"Why, I was just sitting here thinking. Come sit with me a minute, there's something I want to say."

Karen sat down and Etta leaned close to her. "Things are happening here. I don't want to alarm you, but I must tell you they aren't the kinds of things anyone should welcome. Please pay more heed to Maggi's offer. Or, come stay with me a few days."

The blank, blinking look on Karen's face firmed and changed into a resolute mask. "We've already been through this. You and Maggi are talking like I'm in danger—"

"You are."

At the mighty slam of the back door Etta jumped, but not fast enough to avoid a shard of glass that flew from the window as it shattered into thousands of pieces on the floor. She placed a hand over the cut on her forearm to staunch the flow of blood and stared at the wreckage of the window. She had closed that door herself, and closed it tightly. There was a strong wind blowing outside, but hardly sufficient to blow the door open with such force.

Karen stood motionless, staring at the mess on the floor. The air had grown redolent with the now familiar odor. She knew she had to get Etta out of here. But to her dismay, she heard Etta say something about cleaning up the glass.

The room was growing cold from the icy wind that plunged into it through the ragged hole where the window had been. Karen swept up the broken glass.

Etta grabbed a flashlight from a shelf just inside the cellar door and started into the murky half-light. She advanced steadily along the dirt floor, careful not to bump her shins on discarded furnace parts, empty boxes, and the other litter normally found in cellars. The white of the washer and dryer shone in the twilight like teeth in a huge dark mouth, and she walked toward them, toward the portion of the cellar directly under the kitchen; she could dimly see some boards piled against the rock walls just to the side of the machines.

As she drew nearer, she could see a big section of the subflooring had sagged under the kitchen and a portion of it had fallen down altogether. She walked closer and shone the flashlight up onto the sagging wood, thinking to call Karen's attention to the repair job as soon as she got back upstairs—not that Karen appeared in much of a mood to hear about fallen subfloors.

She played the light along the ruined boards, assessing the extent of the damage, and stopped short as the glint of something metallic caught her eye. She brought the light back to the spot and saw what appeared to be a piece of chain protruding down from the space between the boards of the kitchen floor. Grabbing the object between thumb and forefinger, she slowly pried it from its hiding place.

Etta rested the locket in her palm and shone the light down on it. Words were engraved on its surface, but time and dirt had all but obliterated them. With the sleeve of her sweater she rubbed the locket's surface until she could at last make out the words inscribed there: *My Heart Will Always Find You.*

Without knowing why, she knew that somehow the memento she held in her hand would play a role in unravelling the mystery taking place upstairs. Finding the locket was just too much to assign to coincidence, even if she believed in such a thing, which she didn't. Those cameos Karen had enshrined upstairs, the locket she held in her hand, all that she knew about the McCartland house, all of it taken together must form the clues she would soon need to extricate Karen from what she now believed grew more dangerous as each day passed. That shattered glass of the door had been no accident.

Karen helped her to secure the makeshift buffer to the door, performing all these activities as if in a trance, focused only on completion of them—and Etta's departure.

Etta was speaking to her again: "Karen, try and fix your mind to the things you feel, to yourself and your body, to what you know to be true of who you are. And then see whether anything appears to be changing."

Far from understanding what Etta was saying and not even listening all that closely, Karen drummed her fingers on the table with impatience. "Everyone is making too much of this. I'm quite all right. I wish we could just drop the subject," she added testily. "Now, if you'll excuse me, Etta, I really could do with a rest. I'll walk you to your jeep."

Karen stood on the top step and watched Etta fold herself into the jeep. After promising to return soon, Etta pulled away. Karen watched from the step until the jeep disappeared behind the white wall of the last bend.

In the jeep, Etta fingered the little gold locket resting deep in the pocket of her parka. Up to now, she thought, she had been more or less passive, merely observing and passing on information. That would have to change. She took a deep breath, trying to fix her gaze more firmly on the mystery around her. Yes, that would all have to change, and very soon.

* * * * *

Long after her usual bedtime, Etta sat in the little alcove off her living room and read the cloth-bound journals she had retrieved from Karen. She had, of course, read them before, but never with such intent interest. She sat in a circle of light from the green shaded desk lamp, the only lamp burning in the house, and stroked the calico cat in her lap.

Her grandmother's penmanship curled across the yellowed pages, reminding Etta of the woman, of her stately presence, and all Etta had learned from her as she grew. Part of the reason she understood things as she did, saw them through more acute eyes than most, was due to her grandmother. Who else but this woman would have encouraged her when as a young child she had announced that she often knew what would happen before it did—or that she sometimes didn't see people as people at all, but as radiating circles of color?

On the desk before her lay the little gold locket she had found in the cellar, engraved with the words, *My Heart Will*

Always Find You. Time had crusted the tiny locket with grime; rust was gathered on the clasp. Carefully she cleaned and polished the surface, then gently pried open the hinge. Inside, only barely visible after years of neglect, was a faint but discernible portrait of Aimee McCartland. The same woman whose painting rested on Karen's dresser, alongside Blessing's picture. The same woman anyone would take for Karen's twin.

She picked up the locket again and looked at it in the light from her desk lamp. The cat purred and changed position, laying its head over the cut on Etta's arm. Etta turned the locket over in the beam of light, and gazed long at Aimee's face.

In that long ago time when Blessing and Aimee had lived in the house just over the rise, lockets were often exchanged as symbols of love. Etta projected onto the screen of her imagination all she knew of those long dead inhabitants: Blessing, her husband, Ian, and Aimee.

From what she had read of Ian, of whom no pictures survived, she saw him as an unassuming man, hard working, older than the women, angular and gaunt, his neck and hands protruding in knobs from the collars and cuffs of his clothes. Hardly a visage to inspire lockets inscribed with such endearments, nor a woman's timeless and ghostly wandering through a century of earthbound sorrow. No, it had nothing to do with him. The locket was a gift passed between Blessing and Aimee, a token of a deeply felt bond.

The more she read the journals, the more she became convinced of her conclusion. The pages contained more than a few references to the relationship between the sultry artist and Aimee, and its increasing exclusiveness. Etta read on, fondling the locket as she slowly turned the brittle pages. The mists had evaporated from at least one part of the puzzle: Blessing's restless wanderings, her empty, searching eyes, her sorrow, were what survived of her love for Aimee McCartland.

Etta carefully closed the last of the volumes and turned her gaze in the direction of the house on the hillock just above her. At night she couldn't see the house itself but could make out a light burning somewhere in an upstairs bedroom. Without really knowing why, she knew that Karen was up there, doing something at the dresser. Not with her ordinary senses but with her other vision, Etta could see the thin, gaunt figure moving her hands over the dresser top and as Etta looked, she mouthed a prayer.

The woman prowling the dark house—what was left of the bright energetic professor who had come here but a few weeks before? That woman was all but melting away before Etta's eyes. What was it, besides her uncanny resemblance to Aimee, that had sucked her into this ghostly drama? It was of Karen that Etta needed to know more.

* * * * *

It was nearing two a.m. when Etta prepared to retire for the night. It wasn't often she stayed up so late. Sometimes when she had to sit with a sick animal, and a couple of times at birthings, and once, she remembered with a wry grin, when she had drunk too much gin on the occasion of a barn raising. That one she had never repeated.

As she climbed the stairs to her bedroom, she felt, as was rarely the case, her age. Her legs hurt and her very bones felt tired. A heaviness pressed hard on her chest. As she contemplated the task before her, she knew she must gather up and store all the strength she could muster. She would eat lightly, rest often, extend her daily constitutionals for a longer period, and begin to meditate and form her special prayers. Also, she vowed as she pulled the covers up to her chin, she would call Karen first thing in the morning. . . .

* * * * *

After Etta had breakfasted and trekked to the barn where she forked hay into pens for her goats, she returned to the warm, herb-pungent house, treading her way cautiously through a thickly falling snow. She yanked off her red-soled boots, leaving them to drip on the mud porch. She dialed Karen's number and waited. The rings had that peculiar, empty sound that signal to the caller no one is home. Etta knew the phone wouldn't be answered, not if she let it ring twenty times or all afternoon. Karen either wasn't home or wasn't going to answer.

Etta tried to keep busy. She packaged herbs for one of her neighbors, made quick work of the scrubbing she had promised the kitchen floor, and later in the afternoon sat down at the piano. The beginning chords of a Berlioz Requiem floated into her mind and she began playing, but the music was too sad, too full of lament, and she changed to a piece by Mozart. She played from memory, trying to lose herself in the music. Such moments were a meditation for her, a time when the conscious mind disengaged, and behind the drawn curtain her deeper being worked quietly, undisturbed. She had once known someone who achieved the same result by spending hours focused only on the shape, pattern and color of tiny pieces of a jigsaw puzzle, and while she had never tried that herself, she thought with a half smile that under the circumstances perhaps she ought.

At round five-thirty the phone rang. Etta leapt to answer. It was Maggi. Etta's initial disappointment vanished. Maybe Maggi would have news.

"Etta, I'm calling in hopes you've heard from Karen. I've tried several times, there's never an answer. I'm getting edgy."

"I'm a touch edgy myself. Why don't I check things out and call you later?"

"That would be great, Etta. Truth is, I'm more than just edgy. I'm downright worried. Let me give you my work number. I'll be here most of the night."

* * * * *

In Boston, Maggi replaced the phone on its cradle and started out of her cramped office and down the hall toward an equally cramped viewing room. She opened the door of a cubicle crowded with monitors, playback consoles and banks of knobs, levers and buttons. The video cassette of Karen lay in front of her on the counter. She picked it up, wanting to see it again, yet recoiling. The first viewing this morning had brought tears she furtively brushed away, hiding them from the other studio personnel gathered around the monitor. Even though Karen had finally gotten the right words and even punctuated them with gestures, Maggi had seen in the unflappable eye of the camera a changed Karen, a woman not in possession of herself.

Maggi inserted the tape into the console, and on impulse, reached over for a cassette of earlier footage which she placed in an identical monitor. She forwarded the tape to the segment taken of Karen on the Cape. Then, simultaneously, she pressed the play buttons. On the right hand monitor Karen walked, or rather seemed to glide, along the beach, windblown and healthy, her animated face spilling over with life. On the left, Karen sat still, and even though she spoke well, something dark played with her features. She looked small and frightened. The juxtaposition showed the changes in Karen so dramatically that Maggi, alone in the room and without need to check herself, wept openly.

Tomorrow, she told herself, she would call a meeting of the staff and urge they use only the sound from this last tape as a voice-over, not show Karen at all. Anyone could see—including a large national audience—that a massive change had occurred in Dr. Latham sometime during the filming.

She punched rewind, grabbed for a tissue, and blew her nose loudly. One of the night security guards called from the door behind, her, "Phone call for you, Miss England."

The line crackled. Etta spoke over the din. "I talked with her, Maggi. She finally answered. She claims she was working and had the phone unplugged."

Maggi could hear the long intake of breath. "She sounded dreadful," Etta said. "I tried to talk about the Friday night musical but she acted as if she wasn't mindful at all of what I was talking about. She didn't hold much interest in having company, either."

"Etta," Maggi plunged in. "I've just been viewing the tapes we made. She looks much worse than I was willing to see when I was there. What can we do?"

"Well, maybe the only thing as can be done right now is just sit tight and keep trying to contact her. I've been giving this considerable thought, Maggi, trying to figure out what's happening. And I think I understand some of it a little more than I did. For now let's us both keep in touch, and with Karen too. I plan to go over there in a day or so, invited or not."

"I wish I were there to go with you."

"I'll call you after I've seen her. Maybe by then I can piece together more of what's going on."

"Can I do anything?" Maggi asked.

"We can both think good strong throughts about her and try to see her in a bright white light. I wish there were more, Maggi. I'll call soon as I know anything."

Maggi pulled on her coat and went home.

The next day she waited for a call, lunging for the phone each time it rang. When she tried calling Karen herself, she was met with the same empty ringing. At work she was irritable and impatient, barking at staff members and taking her lunch and coffee breaks alone. Her usual good humor waned in direct proportion to the number of hours that elapsed with no news of Karen.

At last, able to bear it no longer, she placed a call to Etta and stood disconsolate and frightened as the phone rang shrilly, unanswered. Perhaps Etta was out in the barn, or on some errand in town, she thought. But, each time she placed a call, she heard only the empty ringing.

CHAPTER 9

Etta awakened to the sure sense that this was the day. She would go to the McCartland house and see things for herself.

She drove cautiously over the short distance between her farm and Karen's house. The storm had played out, replaced by a day of unseasonably warm weather. Yesterday the temperature had climbed to the low forties during the afternoon, melting an inch or two of snow. Then last night the winds had screamed down from Canada, freezing the melted snow into a treacherous lake of hard ice.

Smoke rose from Karen's chimney as Etta turned into the lane; Karen's car was parked in its accustomed place by the kitchen door.

She honked to signal her arrival, stepped out, and

fastened her eyes on the house. Apart from the smoke slowly circling upward from the chimney there was no sign of life. From the amount of snow piled on Karen's car it hadn't been driven in days.

She gave a hearty "Hello!" before stepping up onto the back stairs and knocking loudly at the door. Her feet, accustomed as they were to ice, slipped unsteadily beneath her and she grabbed at the door jamb for support.

There was no answer—not even the sound of movement in the house. She knocked again, this time with the flat of her palm against the hard wood surface. "Karen?"

Etta waited on the steps with mounting unease. Karen had to be in there. She tried the latch but it wouldn't budge. Karen had locked herself in.

Carefully, aware of the danger in the gleaming sheen of ice, she stepped from the porch and started across the frozen snow to the windows along the front of the house.

Using her hand on the side of the house to steady herself, Etta moved to a position directly in front of the small paned windows. She bent down and peered in, cupping her hands beside her face to help focus on the dim interior. At first, as she looked around, she thought Karen couldn't be in there, so quiet and deathly still did the room appear. But she had to be. As quickly as the thought came, Etta saw her.

Karen came slowly down the stairs, eyes unfocused, lips moving as if she were talking with someone. She moved into the parlor, still talking, and seated herself by the fire. Etta rapped on the window pane and called out.

Karen appeared not to hear and stretched out her hand to the empty chair as if reaching to touch someone sitting there. She laughed a high, tinkling laugh Etta could hear through the glass.

Her worst fears confirmed, Etta leaned against the clapboards and tried to think. Somehow, and for reasons she could guess, she felt weakened simply by being here. She was not wanted. The thought angered Etta and deepened her resolve. She would enter the house and physically remove Karen now that it appeared such an act was necessary.

She remembered the thin plywood she and Karen had nailed over the door. Perhaps it would give with a good hard push. She turned back toward the kitchen door, inching her way along the slippery ground at the side of the house.

She reached the steps and mounted them. The air grew suddenly fetid. A stiff wind had arisen and carried the smell in a rushing gust toward her.

All she knew next was the sensation of falling, and of blinding pain in her side. She crashed against the hard packed snow. Blackness overwhelmed her, pulling her away from the pain and consciousness and, though she fought against it, darkness closed in around her.

* * * * *

Inside the house, Karen noticed only the reappearance of the dark woman, and smiled as she seated herself beside her at the fire. *Today is Wednesday,* the woman breathed, *and on Wednesdays we make butter. You remember, don't you?*

Actually, Karen wasn't sure she did, but she agreed most cheerfully. "Of course," she said in a voice that sounded no longer like her own.

And later we'll take our little walk, the woman went on. There had been many such walks, to their special place in the cove, and the woman had seemed unaffected by the cold, hadn't even worn a coat. Karen though, bundle as she might, felt the cold seep into her. She still couldn't shake the chill from her bones.

She and Blessing moved into the kitchen and began assembling a churn and a large crocker bowl full of warm milk.

It was odd that none of these objects could really be felt; they were more like the imaginary toys of a child. They stopped occasionally to nestle against one another, and at such times Karen cared not a whit whether the implements could actually be held in her hand. She cared only for the chance touchings and warm caresses.

* * * * *

Consciousness returned to Etta in what seemed drips and bits. It was finally the pain that brought her firmly awake. That, and the aching cold throughout her body. She tried to turn to relieve the pain in her left arm, which was pinned under her, but a blinding stab wrenched her quickly down again. She lay still a moment longer, assessing her body. She could move her legs and feet all right. It was her side and left arm that sent white hot stars into her vision when she tried to rise.

She looked up and realized that she had fallen only a few feet from the jeep, its engine still idling.

Etta Cavendish, she reminded herself, you have made many a monumental effort in your day. And you've got another one in you. Just make it to the jeep and drive into town for help.

Taking a deep breath against what she knew would be searing pain, she rolled onto her stomach, and from there to her right side. The pain brought tears to her eyes. Slowly, gritting her teeth, focused only on the bumper of the jeep, she pulled herself along the frozen ground, inch by agonizing inch. At last she could reach out and grasp the cold metal. Etta pulled herself slowly to her feet and stood, waiting for the pain and nausea to subside. She eased herself around to the door and onto the seat, grateful it was her left side that was injured. At least she could operate the gears.

At last, out on the road and headed for Pelham Falls,

Etta mouthed a clenched-lipped prayer that the threatening blackness would hold off until she reached the village or that someone might spot her in her weaving jeep. She drove slowly, taking breath in short gasps.

Etta pulled to a stop in front of the general store and allowed her head to fall back. The last image she remembered was of Joe Grime, the stock boy, bounding off the porch toward her, his lips forming the words, "Miz Cavendish!"

* * * * *

Still unable to reach Karen or Etta by phone, Maggi prowled her apartment. She walked again to the bay windows and stood looking down at a young woman bounding across the park on the heels of a laughing child. With a start, and a fresh wave of anxiety, she realized how much the anonymous woman reminded her of Karen; she had the same leggy, loping gait, the wholesome good looks; her blonde hair bounced lightly around her head. Being so visibly reminded of Karen collapsed the last of Maggi's composure.

She had to make some connection with Karen, however tenuous. Then she remembered the tapes. Admittedly, it wasn't much, but was better than sitting around her apartment, cut off, waiting for the phone to ring. Before leaving, she tried Karen and Etta one more time then closed the door softly behind her and walked out across the park.

The day had been warm, but at dusk the temperature was quickly falling. Maggi hurried across the nearly deserted park, her wool muffler blowing out behind her.

She couldn't help thinking of how Karen had looked the day they met, how quickly her feelings for her had grown. Such powerful feelings of love had to be gifts, presents bestowed by a benevolent universe on the lucky few.

That the source of these gifts had always been women had never bothered her in the slightest. From the very first it had seemed the most natural thing in the world, and far from feeling guilty, she privately considered it her great good fortune. Not so with many, and certainly not for Karen, fleeing from her feelings only to find God knew what up the coast in Pelham Falls.

What was happening up there to Karen? Maggi quickened her steps. The only constant was the bright, warm love she carried, like a glowing beacon.

She unlocked the studio and waved to a couple of late working staff on her way to the viewing room. In the semi-darkness she inserted the most recent of the tapes and sat, chin cupped in hands, watching Karen's face materialize life-size onto the screen.

She had started with a full shot of Karen, then zoomed in for a close-up. As Karen talked, she had pulled back to a medium range shot, then held that range for almost the full length of the tape. As the zoom lens retracted, something caught Maggi's eye. There was a slight imperfection in the film, a flaw she must have overlooked during previous showings. She rewound the tape and watched again.

There was no mistaking it this time: a fuzzy shadow marred the film just to the left of Karen's shoulder. Once again Maggi pressed the rewind button and replayed in slow-motion. Again the blur appeared, this time more clearly. Maggi could note its tiny undulations and slight shifts in position. She felt a chill creep up her neck and down along her arms as she watched the formless bit of greyish cloud hovering over Karen's shoulder.

There had been moments during these last few days when she had wanted, even tried, to believe that Karen had been right, that perhaps she was making too much of the situation. Frightened by her powerlessness she had allowed her mind to retreat from the unknown, to rest itself in the comfort and security of the familiar. Had it not been for the prickly discomfort of her intuition. . . .

Staring numbly at the screen, Maggi knew beyond all reason that Etta's and her own sense of urgency had been valid. In all her experience she had never known a mere flaw to sway and undulate as did the strange blur above Karen's shoulder.

* * * * *

The hospital that served Pelham Falls was located in a larger town some fifteen miles distant. Etta had been tenderly placed into the back seat of Mr. Lyle's Buick and he and the stock boy had sped her to the little hospital.

Etta lay under the blinding glare of an overhead light, restrained, to her annoyance, by a covering of blankets. Several faces hovered over her, and as she fought to keep them in focus, she thought she recognized one or two. She tried to sit, both to get a better view of the faces and to ask to use the phone. Blinding pain as well as several pairs of hands restrained her. "Easy now, Miz Cavendish," one of the faces said, "We've given you something to make you sleepy."

Her tongue felt as thick and difficult to control as her thoughts. Yet she knew she hadn't time to dally. There must be someone who would place the call to Maggi.

"You don't understand," she tried to say, but it came out all wrong, like a small child talking with its mouth full. Again she tried to speak, but the sounds she made were as jumbled and indistinct as before.

Someone laid a hand on her shoulder. "Just try to relax. We'll have that arm set and your ribs taped, and in no time you'll be good as new. Lie still now."

Etta felt the sting of a needle in her arm, then little else. She quickly melted away into the soft blankets. Drowsiness oozed in around her. The voices were still talking but came from further and further away.

* * * * *

When she woke again she was lying in a room in a narrow bed, and there was no one standing over her. It was difficult to breathe, as if someone were sitting astride her chest. Tentatively she played the fingers of her right hand over her ribs and winced as she felt the wide strips of tape wound tightly around her. The cast on her arm felt like a sheathing of concrete; underneath, a dull ache radiated from her mended arm.

Memory returned slowly, first of her strange surroundings, then of the events that had led her here.

Etta moved her head gingerly on the hard pillow, taking in the room. Colorless liquid dripped into her arm from a bottle suspended on a metal stand. There was an empty bed next to hers and a door which she surmised led to a corridor. Beside her bed was a small table, and relief swept over Etta as she saw the phone next to a blue basin and a box of Kleenex. All she needed now was Maggi's number from her purse and someone to place the call for her. She pressed a buzzer attached to the mattress near her right hand.

A young woman, her arrival heralded by a starchy rustle, glided into the room. "How are you feeling?" she asked in a hushed tone.

"Please," Etta mumbled, her voice slurred, "Can you find my bag? There's something you must help me with." Etta tried to rise but found she hadn't the strength.

"Try to rest now, Miz Cavendish. There'll be time enough later for whatever it is. Just lie still and rest, okay? There's a good girl."

The nurse deftly smoothed the covers around Etta and moved to check the drip of the I.V. As she reached up toward the bottle, Etta grabbed the woman's arm, wrapping her fingers around the slim wrist in a vise. "No! There is something I must do. And it has to be done now."

Even through the blur of drugs, the nurse could see the urgency and determination in Etta's eyes. She tried to pry Etta's fingers from her wrist and spoke in a soothing tone. "Well, I'll try. What is it?"

"Find my bag, the woven one I came in with." Etta spoke with effort. "In it you'll find a number written on a scrap of paper, for a Maggi England. Please dial it then give me the phone."

"But Miz Cavendish," the nurse faltered, looking at the large watch on her arm. "It's after three in the morning. Are you sure you want to wake someone at this hour? Maybe we should wait till morning." The nurse's tone reflected her conclusion that Etta was speaking through a brain muddled with drugs. "I'll be happy to let someone on the morning shift know you need help with a phone call. Can't it wait?"

"No. It cannot."

Thus satisfied that Etta Cavendish didn't give a damn about the time, the nurse walked to a small closet and extracted Etta's bag, chatting in Etta's general direction as she did so. "We're in for a big one, the weather reports say. Lucky you're here tonight—the biggest storm of the year is headed this way." She held up a bit of paper. "Is this it?"

Etta nodded and the nurse stepped quickly around to the phone. Another eternity passed before Etta heard the nurse say into the receiver, "Is this Maggi England? Just a moment please." The nurse held the phone to Etta's ear.

* * * * *

Maggi heard the phone ringing, flung aside her comforter and ran across the icy room to answer. Outside large flakes of snow fell in swirling curtains. She crouched over slightly, shivering, and clasped herself with her free arm as she listened. The first rush of relief she had felt on hearing Etta's voice was quickly dispelled, replaced by a thick knot of fear. She listened as Etta recounted the story of her trip to the farm and what had happened there.

"I'm going to her Etta. I'll leave right now." Maggi broke in.

"No, you mustn't go there alone. Come here to the hospital. We'll go together."

Maggi got directions from the nurse and hung up. She switched on the radio, hoping for a weather report. It really did look nasty out there. She gulped hot coffee in mouth-stinging swigs as she dressed and poured the remainder of the pot into a thermos to take along. Dressed warmly in jeans and a heavy sweater, she pulled on her parka and thick gloves. Thermos and keys in hand, she bounded to her car in the basement garage. When had she last filled the gas tank? How far might she have to travel before finding a truck stop? She slid behind the wheel, saw that the tank was almost full, and slowly eased the car out onto the snowy, deserted streets.

Her tires crunched in the snow. There was absolutely no one about at this hour on such a night. The slow motion effect of the falling snow, the stillness, made her feel as if she had slipped silently into a preposterously enlarged Christmas card. With the holiday only a few weeks away, many of the dark houses she passed had already strung bright lights in trees or along roofs. But in the small hours before dawn the lights were all out, the people fast asleep in warm beds.

She felt monumentally alone, wrapped in the silent cocoon of her car, headed toward an unknown and frightening confrontation. She flipped the radio on, and after a burst of static, Paul Simon's voice rang clearly into the silence, 'Slip sliding away. . . .' Doubtless some late night D.J.'s idea of a joke. She rotated the dial to a station playing soft rock and tried singing along in an attempt to keep her alarm at bay. She passed the bedroom community of Lowell on Interstate 95 and the turnoff to Glouchester and Cape Ann. She would stay on this route until just north of Portland, then cut east toward the ocean and follow the coast up the twisting highway for another two hundred miles into Pelham Falls. Or, to be more exact, to the community hospital just to the south of town.

Snow bore onto the windshield in endless white sheets. No sooner had the wipers completed an arc than the windshield was again coated with a blanket of snow. Occasionally the car slid sideways as the tires lost purchase on a treacherous patch of ice. She inched along the road, mindful of the agonizing pace she was obliged to travel, cursing softly under her breath at the frustration. At this rate she should make Pelham Falls by noon. That is, if the storm didn't worsen. She clenched her hands harder around the wheel and mouthed a murmur of gratitude for the car's four-wheel drive, and that she had spent what seemed at the time too much money on expensive snow tires. She could make it—she had to.

Dawn arrived without fanfare somewhere along the road past the junction of the Interstate and Highway One. The thermos sat empty on the seat and her arms and legs ached from the effort of holding the car steady on the slippery road. Up ahead she could make out the glitter of lights through the blowing snow and in a few moments a truck stop materialized into her cocooned world, reminding her the ordinary world still existed. She needed a rest. An eerie phenomenon often occurred to her when driving headlong into driving snow; gravity became suspended and she felt as though she were moving through a white tunnel, as though at any moment she might fall through into another dimension.

The truck stop was all but deserted. A few diesel rigs stood to one side crusted with white, like so many overgrown sled dogs asleep in the snow. By the surprised looks on the faces of the few people in the brightly lit restaurant, she judged her entrance an event.

She sat at the counter and wearily lifted the thermos onto the formica top. A waitress approached, her eyebrows lifted. "Whatcha havin'?" Maggi ordered coffee and a fillup of her thermos. When the waitress returned with the scalding, bitter smelling coffee, she eyed Maggi. "Mighty bad night to be travelin'." She paused, providing Maggi an opportunity to volunteer the reasons behind her foolishness. Maggi smiled in agreement and stirred cream into her coffee. The waitress gave her a little smile, shook her head and returned to her conversation with the stranded truckers clustered around a booth.

Maggi stared down at the coffee and played a conversation with the waitress in the privacy of her imagination: Well, you see, it's this way. I'm out here tonight in this blizzard because a friend of mine may be in danger of being possessed by a ghost—and a violent one at that. I'm driving hell for leather to meet a seventy-year-old woman with a broken arm, and together we're going to do something about it. And what's more, I'm in love with the woman in question—the live one of course.

Now that ought to spice up this place for some time to come, she concluded. She rubbed a hand over her strained, red eyes.

Far from amusing, the inner ramble depressed her. There wasn't a word of it that wasn't true. Just what, for God's sake, were they going to do once she arrived? So far she had thought only of the storm, and of making it through to Pelham Falls and to Karen.

Gritting her teeth, she walked back to her car, paid for the gasoline and drove out again into the storm. She could no more see through the dense curtain of snow than she could see into the events which would take place once she finally reached her destination.

When at last she reached the turnoff to the hospital, Maggi was near tears from relief, at getting there at all, and from apprehension. She wouldn't even be able to see Karen right away. After picking up Etta at the hospital, they would drive home and make their plans there. If the situation was as bad as Etta had hinted, would Karen even recognize her? She hunched forward over the steering wheel, straining to see through a swirl of blowing snow.

She remembered being taken to church as a child by her parents. One hymn in particular had terrified her more than any other. Its stanzas reflected on the fate of those for whom it is too late—the hapless or stone-hearted, doomed to be cast aside from grace and from the light. Every time the last chords swelled around her and the congregation pronounced the closing words "Almost—But lost," Maggi's little heart would clench and her mind veer from the horror of such a fate. She would clasp her mother's hand more tightly and silently pray that such a terrible fate might never befall her.

Long ago she had discarded those beliefs and the intentional fear and guilt that went with them. But as she neared the hospital, she remembered the feelings of that hymn, and knew that fear again. Was she too late?

* * * * *

When Maggi walked into the room, Etta was sitting fully dressed, waiting, her left arm in a cast suspended by a sling hung from her neck. Despite Etta's obvious pain, Maggi could see that the woman sitting on the edge of the narrow hospital bed was very much the same person she had come to admire in such a short time.

So often, Maggi knew, when older people suffer a trauma

such as a broken bone or a bad fall, the deterioration is rapid and sometimes irreversible. Not so with Etta. That she was in pain showed clearly in the firm set of her mouth. The drugs she had been given smudged her otherwise keen eyes; other than that, she sat as a veritable bastion of strength, a woman at ease in the center of her own being.

They embraced, Maggi resting her arm gingerly around Etta. Even so, Etta winced at the slight pressure. "The cracked ribs are the most bothersome. I've been sitting here praying I don't have to cough or sneeze." Etta smiled up at Maggi and took her outstretched hand. She stood, only slightly unsteady. "Let's get out of here."

They checked Etta out at the desk to the protestations and soft tongue-clucking sounds of a clerk who urged Etta to stay—if not because of her condition, then certainly because of the terrible weather. Etta, paying no attention, hastily signed the forms placed before her. The tedious process at last ended, Etta rose from the chair, put her hand on Maggi's arm. "Let's go."

They drove slowly to Etta's farm, Maggi battling the storm and her temptation to pump Etta for information with equal energy. Etta, who could all but see the questions swirling around Maggi's dark head, tried to reassure her. "We'll talk just as soon as we reach my house. Just fix your mind on getting us there in one piece. We won't be any good to Karen if we end up in a wreck."

Maggi took Etta's good arm and helped her across the snow-covered ground. They settled comfortably in front of the reassuring warmth of the woodstove, Etta in her battered chair and Maggi in a rocker she had drawn up facing her. Maggi set the cup of tea Etta had provided on the linoleum and anxiously rubbed her hands along the tops of her thighs. Etta leaned back and closed her eyes for a moment and Maggi sensed she was thinking about how to begin.

Etta leaned forward and spoke in her direct, clear voice. "I've been turning it over in my mind about what's happening to Karen." She gestured toward the dark outlines of the McCartland house, barely visible through the thick snowfall.

"Things don't happen without a reason," she continued. "Not always a reason we can see clear, maybe, but somewhere there's a cause for every happening. In other words, what most folks assign to happenstance, or even just luck, isn't that at all."

Etta told Maggi about the journals that were started by her great grandmother and kept faithfully over the years.

"Blessing McCartland was an odd one in her life. Didn't mix well with people or even with her husband for that matter. Seemed to live in a world all to herself, mindful only of her paintings and some vision only she knew. That all changed with the arrival of Aimee. . . ."

Etta paused and placed her hand gently over her taped ribs. "Hand me my bag, won't you, Maggi? There's something I want to show you."

Maggi brought the bag over. Etta rummaged in its interior, at last pulling out the tiny gold locket. "I found this wedged between the floor boards under the kitchen." She handed the locket to Maggi.

Maggi turned the little trinket over in her hands and read the words engraved on the heartshaped surface: *My Heart Will Always Find You.*

"Open it," Etta said.

The face captured in the faded daguerreotype stared back at her, dim and waterlogged, yet still plainly the face of a once attractive young woman. Comprehension began to dawn. Maggi felt sure she knew what Etta was about to reveal.

"Blessing McCartland is earthbound because of her love for Aimee. In their time, of course, they could not love openly. But love they did, I believe. It's the only explanation that makes sense. Something in me just knows it to be truth."

Maggi walked to the window, still holding the locket, and stared at a light burning in the downstairs of Karen's house. The outlines of the house itself were obscured by dusk and blowing snow. Looking at that single patch of light, she felt vastly farther from Karen than the distance between the windows, as if the snow-covered ground had opened in a huge chasm. She turned back to Etta. "Then it's the resemblance between Karen and Aimee that Blessing sees. It's really Aimee she wants, or she thinks she has. Right?"

"That's what I think."

"But doesn't Blessing know it's Karen and not Aimee?" Maggi's voice rose. "I mean—can't she tell the difference?" She looked again at the lighted window, then at Etta. "We can just go over there and tell Karen. Tell her what's happening or take her away."

"I'm afraid it's a bit more troublesome than that," Etta replied. "You see, there has to be something in Karen that allowed this, some hidden part in her that accepted the spirit of Blessing. That's the part we have to know before we can try and help. As for Blessing, I figure she doesn't know the difference at all. She only knows her sadness, her longing. To her, Karen put an end to a lonely search that's taken almost a century. A search Blessing is only too happy to see ended."

Maggi sat heavily in the rocker. Arms on her knees, she looked down at the locket.

Sensing Maggi's apprehension, Etta remained silent for a moment then leaned forward over the protest of her cracked ribs and gently stroked Maggi's head.

"How bad can it get?" Maggi asked, her voice cracking. "What's going to happen if we can't get her out of there?

It's not as if we can just pick up the phone and call the psychiatric emergency team or the police. Lord, Etta."

"No, we can't do any of those things. Which leaves the two of us. She feels close to both of us and trusts us, I believe. But we must act now. Karen is in danger of losing her mind, her life—maybe both. You saw how frail she's become. She probably isn't in the real world anymore, at least not for very long at a time. The day might come when she simply can't find her way back. She isn't eating or sleeping, she's putting her body through more than it can bear."

Etta looked intently at Maggi. "Then, there's the less easy to explain. Maggi, you know how sometimes you meet someone and their very presence seems to drain your strength? You get so wrung out you just want to get away. Obsession by a spirit works much the same. We all operate on life force—energy—anything you want to name it. Ghosts have no such force of their own and must rely on the living. Karen's life is being sucked up by that spirit just as surely as a sponge soaks up water."

Maggi jumped to her feet. "Let's get over there! God, we've got to get her out!"

"Wait, Maggi. We need to know what to do once we get there. And there's still the missing piece of this puzzle. The part of Karen that's open to Blessing. Let's think about this a little more."

In the silence Maggi sifted through all that Etta had just said, stumbling again and again over the idea that something about Karen had invited Blessing to her. And that that unknown something held Blessing to her still.

Maggi checked off a mental list of Karen's personality traits and habits. Words like smart and determined floated immediately to head the list, followed by lively, interesting, witty. Soon the list became an inventory of Karen as viewed through Maggi's heart, and words such as wonderful, warm, sensual, began to replace the more objective descriptions.

Even before Maggi's search set her squarely in the midst of the answer to the puzzle, she felt her cheeks flush and her ears begin to ring to signal its impending arrival. She, Maggi, knew better than anyone what conflict Karen rained down on herself at the love Maggi offered. Karen's conflict, her battle with her own emotions, had been the weak link through which Blessing had poured herself.

The realization swept over Maggi with such force that she fell back to the rocker to wait for her breath. Just as she recovered herself, the second wave of the realization—that she must now tell Etta—swept over her. She would have to reveal the very thing Karen had fled to avoid.

Maggi looked at Etta sitting quietly in her chair and saw that the older woman was staring at her. Etta's eyes were soft and grey, yet they had the power to impale with only the strength of her gaze. Etta didn't speak, but merely rocked slowly in her lumpy chair. Her face said, Go on, Maggi. It's all right.

Maggi leaned forward in her chair, her hands clasped between her knees. "Etta," she began and paused to clear her throat. "There's something, something that will explain what you want to know." Maggi shifted, curled one of her long legs under her and rocked herself slowly with the toe of the other. Her eyes searched the room a moment before she went on. "Karen is very concerned that anyone should know what I'm about to tell you. But under the circumstances I really haven't a choice. You see, Etta, I'm more than just a friend of Karen's. We're lovers. I mean—I'm in love with her. And I believe she loves me, too."

Maggi stopped to breathe and gauge Etta's response. Etta nodded and smiled, encouraging Maggi to continue.

"She's very afraid of her feelings. Shortly after we

became lovers, she began to pull away—one day she leased this house and was gone. It was her way of escaping, a way of running away from herself. She feels very threatened by all this, Etta. She's worried she could be involving herself in something potentially harmful to all her career plans."

Watching Etta's face was to watch an epiphany in progress. Lines of doubt and spots of pinched confusion fell away, replaced by smooth understanding.

"Poor thing," Etta offered and touched Maggi's knee.

Encouraged, Maggi continued, "I hope this doesn't sound corny, but there is something very special between Karen and me. I knew it from the start. Whatever she decides about her life and her feelings I'll have to accept. But I love her more than anyone or anything. There's nothing I wouldn't do for her, Etta. Nothing." Maggi looked down at her hands and bit hard on her lip, then met Etta's eyes.

Etta fixed her eyes on Maggi with a look that spoke great admiration. "So. Now we know," she said, her voice as straightforward as ever. "Finally the last piece falls into place. I feel terrible for Karen, so sorry she feels as she does. But I'm thankful you told me. You did the right thing, Maggi. Now we must get Karen out of harm's way."

With a long sigh of relief, Maggi asked if Etta would like more tea. A few minutes later she handed Etta a cup of camomile and sat again beside her.

"If it had been up to me," Etta said, "I'd have made the rules a heap different. Seems like we should celebrate love and worry less about who we choose to celebrate with. I do understand about strict rules and those who choose a different way. I've taken my own different way."

Etta shook her head, almost sadly, then looked up at Maggi. "I was an odd one because I chose not to marry, but to work the farm instead and spend a fair amount of time by myself. I came to understand the gifts I'd been given and to use them, but many branded me a crazy woman who went around talking to animals, treating illness with herbs, even laying hands on." Etta laughed lightly and flicked a hand as if swatting away a gnat. "But I just went right on anyway, living near to nature, staying close with myself, doing what I knew to be right for me. All in all, I feel very blessed to have lived the life I have."

Etta looked away from Maggi, toward the window and beyond. "The thing is, there was really no other choice. Otherwise I'd have lived separated from myself. I can't imagine a worse existence."

"No. Nor I," Maggi said softly. It was this realization she hoped in her soul that Karen would come to. She walked over to Etta and put her arms around the sturdy woman, not pressing too tightly for fear of jarring the cracked bones. In that moment she felt closer to Etta than she had to anyone in a long time. Understanding and respect had passed between them.

Favoring her left side, Etta moved across the worn linoleum to turn on a lamp by the piano. From there, she moved to the window and looked out across the expanse of blowing snow. "What time is it?" she asked softly. "I haven't worn my watch since they rigged me up in this thing."

"Almost six," Maggi replied and walked over to stand next to Etta at the window.

The distant house was only darkly visible, its lone lighted window taunting them over the frozen night. Etta thought the wind, bending around the house, made a sound similar to one her nerves might make were they capable of sound. Nothing she could think of in her past had fully prepared her for the battle that lay ahead. In the young woman standing beside her, she sensed strength and endurance. Maggi was a woman not easily given to fear or helplessness. And the same was true of her. Yet, as she looked over at the dark outlines of the house, it seemed that much more would be required of her than ever before. Sitting with sick animals, having second sight—all of that was one thing—but confrontation with a ghost was something much worse.

Etta turned further into herself, quelling her uneasiness by sheer effort of will. Her mind, freed from its trembling and doubt, began assessing the possibilities. As she ticked off the facts as she knew them, a plan formed—a plan which left no doubt as to its difficulty. Etta shivered a little and Maggi moved closer to her, placing her arm over Etta's shoulders.

Never taking her eyes from the house across the way, Etta said, "When we get there, we will have to call up the spirit of Blessing McCartland. We will have to bring her into our midst. . . ."

"Why can't we just go over there and take Karen out?" Maggi asked, her eyes wide and questioning.

"What about the fact that it's a mutual thing? Have you ever been carted away from someone? I haven't, but I imagine it only serves to make the bonds stronger. We can't just take her—we must make her go on her own. And we must make Blessing let Karen go as well. Otherwise, we've only placed a bandage on a wound when we must somehow stop the flow of it."

"Okay. But *how* is the big question. Just how do we call up a ghost, and what do we say to her?"

"Well," Etta said, "I think I'm just going to call for her. Conjure her up, you see, and then somehow convince her to go on to the world where she belongs. It can't be peaceful for her here even if she thinks she's with Aimee again."

"But what about Karen? What about getting her to let go?" There was a tremor in Maggi's voice.

"We must convince Karen to release Blessing so that Blessing is free to go on and Karen herself is free to live in the here and now. They must do this for each other . . . release each other. Otherwise. . . ."

Etta paused. Maggi found the courage to ask the question

she had feared more than any other. "Is there such a thing as too late?"

"Everything has its point of no return. Let's be strong and as positive as we can. Our own lives and Karen's may well hinge on it. I was pushed down on the ice by a foul smelling wind that I know was Blessing. Anything could happen over there, Maggi. Blessing is very powerful. Sure you're up to this? It isn't going to be easy."

Without hesitation, Maggi answered. "Yes."

"Give me a few minutes alone then we'll go." With that, Etta turned and walked into the kitchen leaving Maggi alone to stare at the storm.

* * * * *

Something was wrong. Karen knew it. They had loved hard and long for an eternity, as far back as Karen could remember. Yet, the dark lover sat stonily before the fire, her back turned in an unbearable, articulate silence. She showed her displeasure in the stiff turn of her shoulder, the hard set of her cold, full mouth. Karen had been explaining the papers on her desk, trying to make the woman see what she knew how to do. She had asked for time, between loving and the routine of their lives, to work at her desk. The woman had turned silent, frosting Karen's cheeks with her ice stream of words. *There will be nothing else but us.*

Karen had turned toward the desk anyway, groping for it as though struggling for breath. She sat resolutely, stiffening her own back to match the one turned to her at the fire. Everything they did together seemd so hazy, as if it weren't really happening at all, except for their lovemaking. But other things like making meals, churning butter, or taking walks—all had a filmy, unreal quality.

She took her pen and began to write furiously. Perhaps if she pressed hard enough and wrote fast enough, the very activity of it would cause the woman to turn around and talk to her. She wrote until she could write no more and, exhausted, lay her head on the desk to rest. Her body trembled, her limbs gone weak from the exertion. But still the woman sat facing the fire, neither moving nor speaking.

Karen felt her head spin and a wave of nausea seize her. Something else was wrong, something besides the controlling silence. She felt herself falling and grew terrified she would never stop, that for all eternity she would spiral in slow circles downward.

Dizzy from the slow downward spirals and unable to bear it any longer, she felt the icy touch of the woman's hand on her shoulder. *Come,* she said, *let's not have this quibbling. Why don't we take a long walk before supper?* Blessing had relaxed her manner and become loving again.

Karen took her hand and walked with her out to the beach. It was very cold and dark, and Karen fell often, collapsing in the deep snow. Each time she fell the woman reached down to help her up and then, smiling, led her further down the snow-covered beach.

When they at last returned to the house, Karen sat swaddled in a blanket in front of the fire she had built, but she didn't feel warm. She shook terribly, and felt as if her shrunken frame might simply evaporate into the dust hanging thickly in the air.

She turned to the woman and saw that she sat quietly, neither trembling nor cold, but smiling that inward, satisfied smile Karen had seen so often.

CHAPTER 10

Maggi slid behind the wheel of the jeep. Both women zipped their side curtains and sat waiting in a cloud of vapor for the motor to warm. Maggi rubbed her gloved hands together and peered across at Etta's lantern-jawed profile, cast in a greenish glow from the dash instruments: "Do you mind if I ask what you were doing in the kitchen before we left?"

"I was saying some prayers, trying to gather up protection for us."

"I hope they work," Maggi said grimly.

"They have in the past, but mostly for animals. Hasn't been a deer killed on my property for many a year. I figured it couldn't hurt us none neither." Etta turned to face Maggi and gave her a thumbs-up sign. "Let's go."

Maggi inched the jeep along Etta's drive and made a right turn at the road. Less than an eighth of a mile further, she made a hard left into the lane that led to Karen, to a house which she couldn't see through the thick wall of snow, and to a meeting which promised to be like no other.

She gripped the wheel and stared ahead through the yellow swath cut by the headlights, driving very slowly for fear of missing the lane, obscured as it was by all the snow. She spotted the familiar line of trees and made a cautious turn onto a lane that had not been plowed nor driven over.

She remembered the other time she had driven along this road. A smiling Karen had bounded out in stocking feet to greet her, and Maggi's heart had leapt to her throat. As the jeep's heavy tires crunched on the fresh snow and the wipers made a rhythmic thwacking noise, Maggi's heart was again in her throat.

The house, viewed down the long procession of skeletal maples, appeared empty and unused. There was the look about it of a house boarded up, a place not accustomed to hosting life's activities. Not unusual for a dark house in the middle of winter—except this house wasn't dark. Muted light spilled out onto the snow in a puddle from the parlor and a thin wisp of smoke curled upward from the chimney. The sea, glimpsed through the swirling snow, rolled thick and heavy onto the frozen shore. Everything, the house, the snow-covered fields, even the sea, seemed immutable, stiff and unyielding. Karen's car, still parked by the front door, was almost completely covered with snow, frozen too in the death-still scene. It was a place not fit for human trespass, a twisted caricature of what once had been.

At first Maggi thought the wheels had lost traction. The jeep suddenly seemed to float just off the ground and lose forward movement. They were in the middle of the road, about two hundred yards from the house when the engine stalled and finally died.

"Crank it again," Etta said, and Maggi turned the key. A futile grinding spat back at them. Maggi pumped the gas pedal and tried again. Nothing. Even the grinding noise drifted away to a sickening click. The wind whipped down through the trees with unusual force, rocking the jeep angrily from side to side.

"We'll have to walk in," Etta announced, her jaw so tightly clamped a small bulge appeared on her cheek. "Here, wrap this around your face and head." Etta handed Maggi a knitted shawl and wrapped another around her own head. The wind slammed into them as they emerged from the safety of the jeep; Etta struggled for footing in the slippery snow.

Heads bent to protect them from the furious gusts, they crept slowly forward on each side of the useless vehicle until they stood together in front of the grille. "What now?" Maggi yelled above the howl of the storm.

"Start walking toward the house. Be careful of your footing and hold onto me."

Pressed closely together, using each other for balance, they bent forward into the blowing snow. The bare trees shook in a frenzy, twisting limbs and branches in a groaning counterpoint to the wind.

The closer they got to the house, the more Maggi sensed its foreboding presence. It seemed to brood, daring them to come closer. Etta sensed death—the pervading aura of it swam out to greet her from the snow-draped structure just ahead. She thought she could smell it, too, way out here in the snow-filled air.

With each step, the wind seemed to grow in velocity. Etta's shawl had blown away from her head and her grey hair was coated with a layer of snow. Snow clung to her eyebrows and lay in a thin dusting on her cheeks. Maggi had been able to keep her head covered with her free hand, a luxury not available to Etta who, undaunted, stepped with iron determination through the maelstrom. Maggi looked back at the jeep, its bright red finish already disappearing under a coating of white. Each woman held identically fervent thoughts. Are we in time? Is she still alive?

At last they reached the kitchen steps. Maggi placed her booted foot on the top stair, then extended her gloved hand to Etta. Wincing slightly, Etta pulled herself up onto the step. Holding onto one another against the buffeting wind, Maggi knocked loudly on the makeshift covering over the window, Etta anchoring them with her free arm around the door post. As expected, the knock went unanswered.

Maggi didn't hesitate to slam her fist into the thin plywood. She heard the squeaking sound of nails pulling loose from moorings and a slight splintering as a little of the plywood gave way. "Karen," she yelled, "Karen, can you hear me?"

Only silence. Her throat felt raspy from the force of her bellow and her nostrils ached from the rank smell in the air. She directed her fist savagely into the wood, this time releasing a small corner of it from the door.

Etta, wishing she hadn't done such a good nailing job, removed her hand from the door post and slammed it in rhythm with Maggi. Suddenly the wood gave, falling with a thud to the floor inside. Etta reached down and undid the latch, moving into the darkened room behind Maggi.

The utter stillness was punctuated by a sharp intake of breath as both women stared at the mess Karen's cheery kitchen had become. Dirty dishes were strewn on the table, bits of half-eaten meals lay over the counter and floor. By the fridge, a cardboard carton of milk lay spilled in a congealed pool. The smell was overwhelming, a smell of perspiration, sickness, unwashed bodies and the nauseating redolence of mildew, and over it all the cloying smell of lilac sachet.

There was a loud crash from the parlor. Maggi's heart pounded so loudly she wasn't sure if she heard Etta speak to her. She felt caught in that terrible moment when fear of what lies around the corner and the certainty that one must know, bear in with an equal force. She crossed the kitchen with Etta, half running toward the doorway and the parlor.

The tableau before her turned Maggi's knees to liquid.

"Ohmygod," she groaned. Etta mumbled something which Maggi didn't hear. They stood frozen in the doorway, looking into the semi-darkness of a room lit only by a dwindling fire in the hearth.

Karen sat huddled in a blanket, her eyes unfocused. Maggi could not be sure she had seen them. Karen raised her head once, then dropped it back as if its very weight were too much to bear. Her skin was sallow and waxen, except for the unhealthy red of a high fever. Had she not moved, her features could have been mistaken for those of a corpse. In the middle of the floor, well away from the tables and bookcases along the walls, lay the remains of a black amethyst vase, a vase Maggi knew Karen treasured. It lay broken into hundreds of pieces as if hurled by someone in possession of enormous strength and great anger. The collapsed woman sitting huddled in the chair could scarcely have mustered either such strength or such violent emotion.

As if on cue, Etta and Maggi raced across the room toward her.

They were stopped in mid-stride by disjointed banging sounds from everywhere in the room at once. Papers on the desk ruffled into the air and littered downwards as though the wind outside had somehow reached in to them. Maggi and Etta whirled around as books from the cases behind them thudded to the floor. The window panes rattled in a gust of wind, a gust that blew from inside the house. The stench of mildew was everywhere. The fire which had been burning low flared up and sent puffs of dense acrid smoke into the room.

Maggi clutched Etta's hand and stared at the destruction

around them.

The careening anger in the room was not selective. More books and papers, pictures from the walls, a small pink shell from the mantle, came crashing to the floor. At length there was little left in the room to hurl.

The tirade ceased. A couple of lone books stood in the cases and one *Mola* teetered askew on the wall. Everything else lay in a mass of broken and torn pieces on the floor. Karen's desk top had been swept clean.

"And so," Etta breathed in the silence. "Wraith who walks by the sea, at last we meet."

She girded herself, no longer mindful of the ache in her ribs and arm. Such anger, she thought, such unearthly anger. Despite the violence around her, Etta felt a moment of sadness. Sadness for the unhappy soul of Blessing McCartland. "I am sorry for you," she whispered.

Maggi had moved across the room. Wide-eyed and trembling herself, she put her arms around a weak and trembling Karen.

Etta remained poised in the center of the room, every sense sifting the fetid air. "She's here," Etta mouthed softly to Maggi. "She's with us."

Maggi nodded and pressed Karen close to her.

Satisfied that Karen was for the moment all right, Etta held her ground in the middle of the room. She cocked her head in the direction of the fireplace. There, she thought. Over there by the fireplace is where she stands.

She took in a deep breath and slowly expelled it, repeating the exercise three more times. Then, she whirled to face the fireplace, the flickering shadows. She raised her good arm and pointed a finger toward the hearth. Her voice boomed through the room. "Blessing McCartland."

Maggi looked up, startled by Etta's loud voice and by the words she so firmly intoned. Karen, too, stirred in her arms, roused by the booming voice and the name it called out.

"Blessing McCartland!" Etta boomed, her voice a ribbon of steel. "You have nothing to fear. Let yourself be seen."

Maggi got to her feet and stared, incredulously, as a filmy haze began to take shape in front of the fireplace. It wasn't distinguishable as any particular thing as yet, but undulated and drifted, a mass of cloudy matter. A heavy groaning sound filled the room, like earth giving way before an avalanche. The wispy matter began to take form, indistinctly at first, then growing more clearly outlined. Where only a few moments before had been only a swirling grey mist, there slowly appeared a tall, dark figure, her hair unfurling from her head in thick black coils. Her eyes burned. Her face was frozen in a white mask of fury.

She pointed her finger at Etta, and spoke, her words drifting around the room in a steamy whisper. *Get out.*

Karen stirred at the sound and looked as if she wanted to move forward. She glanced first at Maggi, then Etta, as if amazed by their presence. "What are you doing here?" she mumbled. Maggi reached out to her, pulling her deep into the chair.

This is my house, Blessing raged. *Get out!*

"No! This is not your house." Etta's voice more than matched Blessing's in force and determination. "It is you who must leave."

No! Blessing screamed, her voice cold as the wind at the corners of the house. *Get out and leave us alone!*

"I will not," Etta boomed. "This," she pointed to the slumped figure in the chair, "this is not who you think."

Blessing turned to face Karen, boring into her with cold eyes, *Aimee?*

"This is not Aimee!"

Blessing stared, sneering, never relaxing the pure hatred that spewed from her. *Aimee,* she said loudly, blistering Etta with a look of disdain.

"Blessing, the Aimee you love is dead. She is not here."

Blessing spat a thin line of bluish crystals on the floor at Etta's feet.

"Blessing, listen to me. Love should never destroy. Karen isn't Aimee. Your love is hurting her."

Sweat poured from Etta's brow, but her voice lost none of its firmness. "Karen is a mortal and you must release her. She is alive now, but soon she'll be dead too. You'll be left alone again. Do you want that? More of your sorrowing? More empty searching?" On the last sentence, Etta's voice rose, echoing through the still dark house.

Karen looked at Etta, and at Blessing, confusion showing in the deep shadows and hollows of her face. The commotion and loud voices had startled and unsettled her.

What was everybody talking about? She tried to speak. She felt a sinking in her chest and leaned against Maggi for support. The dark woman was talking about Aimee—and calling her by that name.

Karen's ears rang. She felt sick and dizzy. Though she strained to make sense of the things happening around her, her mind registered only confusion. Why was the dark woman calling her Aimee? Why were Maggi and Etta here? She tried to say something, to ask someone to explain. But she was hanging somewhere, weightless and drifting.

At that moment Blessing looked at her and said through barely parted lips, *Aimee, you must not leave me again. Remember what the locket says. It will always be true. Promise me.*

Etta's voice sliced the air. "No, Blessing, it won't. It's not even true now. Your heart has not found Aimee. Look hard at her, Blessing. She is not the one you seek."

Blessing hissed and pointed to Karen.

Karen tried to speak, but Etta stopped her with a palm-forward thrust of her hand. "Don't respond, Karen." Etta's words were harsh and angry, but she knew she had to make Karen hear. She was, after all, a sensate being, still capable of rational thought. "She's dead, Karen. She's a ghost," Etta said, again relying on sheer volume to pierce the muddled look on Karen's face. "Look closely," she commanded. "She has no reflection in the mirror!"

Karen leaned forward, her mouth open, yet no sound escaped her lips. Eyes wide, she appeared to teeter on the brink of consciousness.

She could not see Blessing's reflection in the mirror over the mantle. She shrank back into the chair.

"Don't be afraid," Maggi said and pulled her arms tightly around her. "Concentrate. Hear what Etta is saying. Tell her to leave. Do it, Karen."

Maggi's voice, soft and even, brought a searing look from Blessing. The ghostly face curled into a sneer and, as if noticing her for the first time, turned her cold anger in Maggi's direction.

Blessing's words flew from her mouth in a stream. *Take your hands from her.*

Karen felt Maggi tense and increase the pressure on her arms. It all felt so strange. Her head swam and her eyes blinked rapidly, as though she were trying to clean away a film that had settled over them. Maggi and Etta looked so different here, like strangers, people she had known a long time ago and in a different place. Yet there was something undeniably concrete about them. They parted the space where they stood much more distinctly than did the woman glowering and swaying before the fire. Dead? Dead? Did Etta say dead? Karen recoiled at the word and pulled the scratchy blanket closer.

Take your hands from her, Blessing spat through clenched teeth. *Let Aimee come to me.*

Maggi held Karen closer. Masking any hint of fear, she said, "Karen, look at her. She's a *ghost,* Karen. She's not real."

Karen looked at Blessing and, for the first time, saw how

pale and grey she appeared, compared to the healthful pinkish tones of Etta standing next to her. Karen felt queasy beginnings of fear and looked quickly from Blessing to Etta. Everyone seemed so intent on having her understand something. She could sense a current of fear in their voices, a brittleness lying just under the firm commands and warnings. If they were afraid, then perhaps she should be as well. Maybe there was something wrong here.

The more the damp wool of her trance uncurled, the more she sensed the chilling approach of certainty. She felt like a swimmer pushing upward from the bottom of a muddy lake, straining to break surface and find air. The sensation was so real that she held her breath in her throat and mentally flailed against the suffocation.

There was something terribly wrong. She could see Etta standing beside the swaying form but Etta was staring intently at her, willing her to see.

And see she did. But what she saw made her recoil in horror.

There in front of the hearth, the lover from her dreams was changing, swaying and changing into something else, there was a hollow, sunken countenance about her Karen had never seen and her bluish grey skin looked cold and dead. And the smell—a horrible stench, nothing like the seductive scent of musty lilac she had known before. . . .

She felt stinging needles of panic and knew she had to move away, away from the undulating presence. She grasped Maggi's hand, surprised at the warmth there, and prayed that the touch might help her pull up from her own weightless swaying.

Blessing spat and lunged for the chair.

Etta moved quickly to intervene, but Blessing passed through her as easily as if she hadn't been there. The chair toppled over, spilling Karen and Maggi in a heap at Blessing's feet. Karen felt the chill of Blessing's presence and let out a scream.

Aimee! the dark shadow shrieked. Blessing lunged for Maggi, intent on dislodging her from Karen's side.

Karen saw the blue line of marks Blessing's hand imprinted on Maggi's arm and saw, too, how easily the hand had passed through Etta's body and the chair. Karen let out another scream and raised her hands to her face.

Etta, knowing this moment was destined, raced across the room in three long strides and placed herself between the two women on the floor and the towering form of Blessing McCartland. All that she knew or ever had known about this woman and the inevitability of their encounter flashed in her mind. She knew she must reach deeply into her store of knowledge. If deer could be protected from the bullets of hunters, then the same knowledge must be capable of protecting Karen and Maggi from the ghost now towering over them.

I am an old woman, she thought, an old woman who has always known too much. May all in heaven and all beneath it help me to know now.

With one hand securely around the locket in the pocket of her coat, Etta took long deep breaths and prayed earnestly for the powers she knew to exist to shield them from harm. She imagined a webbing of light between the ghost and the two women on the floor and, while she knew it could never be seen by ordinary eyes, she forced every ounce of her being into the visualizing.

Etta reached into her pocket and extracted the locket, holding it between thumb and forefinger, swinging it lightly back and forth near Blessing's face. She opened the clasp so that the faded picture inside could be seen. "Stop, Blessing," she said. "Look. This is Aimee. This is the one you seek."

Blessing lifted her eyes and focused them on the slowly

swinging locket. Cold ire was replaced for an instant by a look of tenderness. *Mine!* she hissed and lunged for the locket.

Etta pulled it back, "Look, Blessing. Look at Aimee."

Transfixed, Blessing followed the locket with her eyes and again reached for it as Etta slowly swung it before her face. Again Etta drew it back.

"Aimee gave you this a long time ago, I'm sure she wants you to have it again. Look at the picture."

When at last Blessing appeared calmer, transfixed as she was by the locket, Etta said, "Here, you may have it," and extended the locket toward her, returning it to the hands that had so long ago received it.

Blessing reached her long, icy hand forward to grasp the precious object. The locket slipped through the wispy shadow of Blessing's hand and fell with a tinkling sound to the floor at their feet. Through the power of her anger and her obsession she could cause fires to start and send objects flying, but the ghost could not hold to material form. Blessing knelt on the floor and Etta could hear her whispered murmurings.

Karen started away from Blessing, away from the noise and confusion, crawling on her hands and knees. She moved through the debris of Blessing's rage, scattering broken glass and paper, clutching pages of her notes at random. Her hand slipped on a piece of paper and she fell but continued crawling, using the little strength in her hands and arms.

Deep inside something flickered, weak and uneven, like a candle set in a draft. Any second now the tiny flame might waver and die, leaving only a thin trail of smoke, an echo of something once bright and beautiful.

Everything but the image of the flickering candle blurred; the lines separating floor from chairs, Maggi from the windows at her back, even the lines of her mind no longer seemed to distinguish one thing from another. What should be—wasn't. Or was it?

Maggi raced to Karen's side. She knelt and taking Karen's face gently between her hands said, "Sshhh, it's all right. I'm here. Look at me, Karen. Wake up. Oh please. Try."

Raising her eyes slowly Karen looked into Maggi's face and, seeing warmth and safety in her soft brown eyes, the sweet line of her lips, let herself fall against her.

Maggi sat as a wall of protection between Karen and the figure at the hearth, her body a shield between Karen and the horrible sound of dream shattering to nightmare.

She was clearing the surface, breaking free of a suffocating dark. She pressed more tightly against Maggi's body, against the powerful surge of life in her pulse. Blinking back tears, she took Maggi's hands in hers and caressed the substance of warm skin.

An image, brief but vivid, flashed across her mind. In it, she ran toward Maggi across a mountain field. Everything in the image, the tree tops, the waving grasses, even the ribbons that streamed from her hair, all glowed with the pale pink and yellow of sunrise. In the center of the field a brook curled and eddied its way through golden dandelions. Without so much as a pause at the bank, Karen leapt, soaring high in the air, crossing the swirling water in a joyous leap. Maggi's outstretched arms enfolded her.

The image faded quickly but the feel of the colors remained to warm and strengthen her.

Karen let her head fall onto Maggi's shoulder. She was waking—there was nothing to fear. "Hold me," she said. "Hold me Maggi."

Blessing, still trying to grasp the locket, looked up as Karen's words sounded. Her eyes were cold yet filmed with the opaque fear of betrayal. *Aimee,* she hissed. *Remember—*

Etta strode to Karen's side and knelt beside her. "Now

you can choose, Karen," she said firmly and grasped Karen by the shoulders. She looked deeply into Karen's face, a smile of recognition already spreading as Maggi said, "She has, Etta. She has."

Blinking back tears, Karen nodded.

A hissing moan from the hearth sounded, Blessing stretched her icy hand toward Karen. Karen stared at her, at this shadow with whom she had dreamed such pleasure, had danced to worlds she never knew existed. And none of it had been real—her life offered in exchange for passion no more real than thought never formed.

"No," Karen rasped. She moistened her lips and mouthed the word again then, repeating it louder. *"No!"*

Blessing cried out and began spinning, slowly at first then more quickly, like a column of dark smoke until at last she slowed and stopped, like a phonograph shut off in mid-song.

Etta, knowing the circle was still unbroken, the healing yet incomplete, walked slowly across the floor to the crumpled shadow of Blessing McCartland. "Come," she said and extended her hand. "Come with me, Blessing."

Hesitatingly at first Blessing floated toward Etta, then followed as Etta led her toward the door.

With Blessing hovering beside her, Etta pulled her coat tightly around her before heading out into the storm-filled night. On the steps she raised her hand as a visor and sighted down the dark lane of maples. She motioned Blessing to follow and stepped out into the snow.

"Watch the lane ahead," she yelled above the howl of the storm.

Etta's feet crunched deep into banks of snow but she did not feel the cold, so intent was she on the picture she held. What the mind can picture, the soul already knows as truth, and Nature can make real. Etta forced all her power into the image in her mind and stared at the row of maples.

There were, she knew, shadows of every event, imprints left in the warp of time, each fragment endlessly echoing its moment in reality. Find the fragment, she prayed, find it and shape it once more in this plane.

She couldn't be sure, at first, she had actually seen it, the night and blowing snow were so deep. She strained harder, concentrating her attention on the head of the lane. Etta quickened her pace and motioned Blessing to follow.

She looked again and in that instant was sure. Where only the blink of an eye before there had been a gap in the line of trees, there now was none. Etta's heart thudded against her chest.

Slowly, shimmering and incandescent, a wagon drawn by two horses pulled onto the lane. A lone occupant rode in the seat.

Standing in a world such as this, a world without time, Etta knew peace, and exaltation. A thousand bells rang in her ears. Though the wind screamed, it was as if the very molecules of air had ceased circling their eternal path.

Holding tightly to herself to remain fixed on the earth, Etta watched the wagon draw nearer. The night was pushed back from it in a pale circle of golden light. In the circle of light a fair young woman smiled, on her face a look of radiant anticipation.

"Now," Etta said. "Now, Blessing. Go to her."

Blessing glided toward the light, her dark aura melting away.

A tear coursed along Etta's face as she thought of the words promised so long ago: *My Heart Will Always Find You.* Words made truth by the passion of belief. "There is no difference in mortality and immortality," she breathed softly, "for we are both, and at once."

Aimee reached down from the wagon as Blessing stepped into the light, her mouth full with the name—*Blessing.*

There was a groaning sound, and the tearing of wood.

A bright explosion split open the night.

Etta shut her eyes against the glare and fell back in the snow, rocked by the collision between time and eternity.

When she roused again and looked down the lane it stood empty. Snow lay in a pristine, undisturbed blanket, there was again a gap in the line of maples. Etta turned back to the house. It sat silent and composed, its austere face to the sea.

A few of the publications of
THE NAIAD PRESS, INC.
P.O. Box 10543 • Tallahassee, Florida 32302
Mail orders welcome. Please include 15% postage.

THE LOVE OF GOOD WOMEN by Isabel Miller. 224 pp. Long-awaited new novel by the author of the beloved *Patience and Sarah.* ISBN 0-930044-81-9 $8.95

THE HOUSE AT PELHAM FALLS by Brenda Weathers. 240 pp. Suspenseful Lesbian ghost story. ISBN 0-930044-79-7 7.95

HOME IN YOUR HANDS by Lee Lynch. 240 pp. More stories from the author of *Old Dyke Tales.* ISBN 0-930044-80-0 7.95

EACH HAND A MAP by Anita Skeen. 112 pp. Real-life poems that touch us all. ISBN 0-930044-82-7 6.95

SURPLUS by Sylvia Stevenson. 342 pp. A classic early Lesbian novel. ISBN 0-930044-78-9 7.95

PEMBROKE PARK by Michelle Martin. 256 pp. Derring-do and daring romance in Regency England. ISBN 0-930044-77-0 7.95

THE LONG TRAIL by Penny Hayes. 248 pp. Vivid adventures of two women in love in the old west. ISBN 0-930044-76-2 8.95

HORIZON OF THE HEART by Shelley Smith. 192 pp. Sizzling romance in summertime New England. ISBN 0-930044-75-4 7.95

AN EMERGENCE OF GREEN by Katherine V. Forrest. 288 pp. Powerful novel of sexual discovery. ISBN 0-930044-69-X 8.95

THE LESBIAN PERIODICALS INDEX edited by Claire Potter. 432 pp. Author and subject index. ISBN 0-930044-74-6 29.95

DESERT OF THE HEART by Jane Rule. 224 pp. A classic; basis for the movie *Desert Hearts.* ISBN 0-930044-73-8 7.95

SPRING FORWARD/FALL BACK by Sheila Ortiz Taylor. 288 pp. Literary novel of timeless love. ISBN 0-930044-70-3 7.95

FOR KEEPS by Elisabeth Nonas. 144 pp. Contemporary novel about losing and finding love. ISBN 0-930044-71-1 7.95

TORCHLIGHT TO VALHALLA by Gale Wilhelm. 128 pp. Classic novel by a great Lesbian writer. ISBN 0-930044-68-1 7.95

LESBIAN NUNS: BREAKING SILENCE edited by Rosemary Curb and Nancy Manahan. 432 pp. Unprecedented autobiographies of religious life. ISBN 0-930044-62-2 9.95

THE SWASHBUCKLER by Lee Lynch. 288 pp. Colorful novel set in Greenwich Village in the sixties. ISBN 0-930044-66-5 7.95

MISFORTUNE'S FRIEND by Sarah Aldridge. 320 pp. Historical Lesbian novel set on two continents. ISBN 0-930044-67-3 7.95

A STUDIO OF ONE'S OWN by Anne Stokes. Edited by Dolores Klaich. 128 pp. Autobiography. ISBN 0-930044-64-9 7.95

SEX VARIANT WOMEN IN LITERATURE by Jeannette Howard Foster. 448 pp. Literary history. ISBN 0-930044-65-7 8.95

A HOT-EYED MODERATE by Jane Rule. 252 pp. Hard-hitting essays on gay life; writing; art. ISBN 0-930044-57-6 7.95

INLAND PASSAGE AND OTHER STORIES by Jane Rule. 288 pp. Wide-ranging new collection. ISBN 0-930044-56-8 7.95

WE TOO ARE DRIFTING by Gale Wilhelm. 128 pp. Timeless Lesbian novel, a masterpiece. ISBN 0-930044-61-4 6.95

AMATEUR CITY by Katherine V. Forrest. 224 pp. A Kate Delafield mystery. First in a series. ISBN 0-930044-55-X 7.95

THE SOPHIE HOROWITZ STORY by Sarah Schulman. 176 pp. Engaging novel of madcap intrigue. ISBN 0-930044-54-1 7.95

THE BURNTON WIDOWS by Vicki P. McConnell. 272 pp. A Nyla Wade mystery, second in the series. ISBN 0-930044-52-5 7.95

OLD DYKE TALES by Lee Lynch. 224 pp. Extraordinary stories of our diverse Lesbian lives. ISBN 0-930044-51-7 7.95

DAUGHTERS OF A CORAL DAWN by Katherine V. Forrest. 240 pp. Novel set in a Lesbian new world. ISBN 0-930044-50-9 7.95

THE PRICE OF SALT by Claire Morgan. 288 pp. A milestone novel, a beloved classic. ISBN 0-930044-49-5 8.95

AGAINST THE SEASON by Jane Rule. 224 pp. Luminous, complex novel of interrelationships. ISBN 0-930044-48-7 7.95

LOVERS IN THE PRESENT AFTERNOON by Kathleen Fleming. 288 pp. A novel about recovery and growth. ISBN 0-930044-46-0 8.50

TOOTHPICK HOUSE by Lee Lynch. 264 pp. Love between two Lesbians of different classes. ISBN 0-930044-45-2 7.95

MADAME AURORA by Sarah Aldridge. 256 pp. Historical novel featuring a charismatic "seer." ISBN 0-930044-44-4 7.95

CURIOUS WINE by Katherine V. Forrest. 176 pp. Passionate Lesbian love story, a best-seller. ISBN 0-930044-43-6 7.95

BLACK LESBIAN IN WHITE AMERICA by Anita Cornwell. 141 pp. Stories, essays, autobiography. ISBN 0-930044-41-X 7.50

CONTRACT WITH THE WORLD by Jane Rule. 340 pp. Powerful, panoramic novel of gay life. ISBN 0-930044-28-2 7.95

YANTRAS OF WOMANLOVE by Tee A. Corinne. 64 pp. Photographs by the noted Lesbian photographer. ISBN 0-930044-30-4 6.95

MRS. PORTER'S LETTER by Vicki P. McConnell. 224 pp. The first Nyla Wade mystery. ISBN 0-930044-29-0 7.95

TO THE CLEVELAND STATION by Carol Anne Douglas. 192 pp. Interracial Lesbian love story. ISBN 0-930044-27-4 7.95

THE NESTING PLACE by Sarah Aldridge. 224 pp. Historical novel, a three-woman triangle. ISBN 0-930044-26-6 7.95

THIS IS NOT FOR YOU by Jane Rule. 284 pp. A letter to a beloved is also an intricate novel. ISBN 0-930044-25-8 7.95

FAULTLINE by Sheila Ortiz Taylor. 140 pp. Warm, funny, literate story of a startling family. ISBN 0-930044-24-X 6.95

THE LESBIAN IN LITERATURE by Barbara Grier. 3d ed. Foreword by Maida Tilchen. 240 pp. A comprehensive bibliography. Literary ratings; rare photographs. ISBN 0-930044-23-1 7.95

ANNA'S COUNTRY by Elizabeth Lang. 208 pp. A woman finds her Lesbian identity. ISBN 0-930044-19-3 6.95

PRISM by Valerie Taylor. 158 pp. A love affair between two women in their sixties. ISBN 0-930044-18-5 6.95

BLACK LESBIANS: AN ANNOTATED BIBLIOGRAPHY compiled by J.R. Roberts. Foreword by Barbara Smith. 112 pp. Award winning bibliography. ISBN 0-930044-21-5 5.95

THE MARQUISE AND THE NOVICE by Victoria Ramstetter. 108 pp. A Lesbian Gothic novel. ISBN 0-930044-16-9 4.95

LABIAFLOWERS by Tee A. Corinne. 40 pp. Drawings by the noted artist/photographer. ISBN 0-930044-20-7 3.95

OUTLANDER by Jane Rule. 207 pp. Short stories and essays by one of our finest writers. ISBN 0-930044-17-7 6.95

SAPPHISTRY: THE BOOK OF LESBIAN SEXUALITY by Pat Califia. 2d edition, revised. 195 pp. ISBN 0-930044-47-9 7.95

ALL TRUE LOVERS by Sarah Aldridge. 292 pp. Romantic novel set in the 1930s and 1940s. ISBN 0-930044-10-X 7.95

A WOMAN APPEARED TO ME by Renee Vivien. 65 pp. A classic; translation by Jeannette H. Foster. ISBN 0-930044-06-1 5.00

CYTHEREA'S BREATH by Sarah Aldridge. 240 pp. Women first entering medicine and the law: a novel. ISBN 0-930044-02-9 6.95

TOTTIE by Sarah Aldridge. 181 pp. Lesbian romance in the turmoil of the sixties. ISBN 0-930044-01-0 6.95

THE LATECOMER by Sarah Aldridge. 107 pp. A delicate love story set in days gone by. ISBN 0-930044-00-2 5.00

ODD GIRL OUT by Ann Bannon ISBN 0-930044-83-5 5.95

I AM A WOMAN by Ann Bannon. ISBN 0-930044-84-3 5.95

WOMEN IN THE SHADOWS by Ann Bannon. ISBN 0-930044-85-1 5.95

JOURNEY TO A WOMAN by Ann Bannon. ISBN 0-930044-86-X 5.95

BEEBO BRINKER by Ann Bannon ISBN 0-930044-87-8 5.95

Legendary novels written in the fifties and sixties, set in the gay mecca of Greenwich Village.